The Look of a King

Pillars of Peace: Book I

By Tom Dumbrell

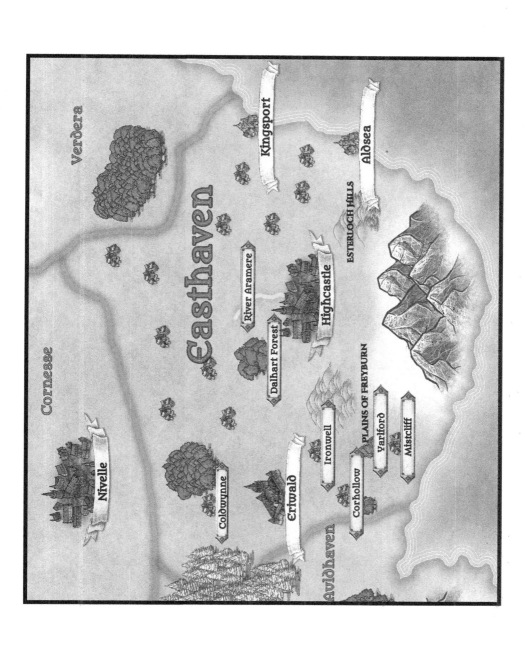

CHAPTER
I

Augustus spat blood into the sand, sweat-drenched golden hair falling to cover his eyes. It had been the same all afternoon—a petulant display with as much respect for his opponent as for Thaddeus's teachings. Only now his father was watching. And his father was the king.

"How can this boy be expected to rule Easthaven?" King Anselm asked his chosen shield, Garrett, while glaring at his son. "He's yet to master his own emotions, let alone his vanity."

Garrett, who had known similar failings in Anselm when they were younger men, attempted to lighten the mood as training ended and Augustus's opponent made inconspicuously for the exit. "It's a difficult age," he commented, scratching at his dark stubble. "He's strong and brave, he has potential—"

Garrett was cut short by a snigger from Thaddeus. "Ever the optimist, aren't you, Garrett?" Thaddeus ventured. "Augustus is a difficult child without the maturity to realise his potential."

1

This left Garrett silent, accepting the truth in Thaddeus's words.

"What happened?" asked Anselm, and Garrett replayed the events in his mind as Thaddeus explained them to the king: it had seemed like an evenly matched contest, two young warriors on the cusp of manhood. Both wore loose linen shirts and dark cotton trousers and wielded wooden training blades as weapons. Augustus was the taller of the two, with piercing blue eyes and a smooth complexion that accentuated his angular cheekbones. His opponent, meanwhile, had darker features, and where Augustus was lean and rangy, he was broad with sinewy legs that added strength to his attacks.

As evenly matched as they seemed to be, however, the contest had been embarrassingly one-sided. For all of Thaddeus's efforts as mentor to the prince, the old man cut a frustrated figure, pulling strands of grey hair away from his face before slumping a bearded chin into his hands. The sparring between the two young men had started with the normal flurry of early exchanges, but with technique and discipline so lacking in Augustus, Thaddeus urged him to regain his composure with the aim of forcing his opponent onto the back foot. The other boy was not without skill, but it was obvious to anyone with an eye for these things that his flank was often exposed, his counterattacks delayed and predictable. The opportunities were there for Augustus, but Thaddeus found himself with little faith in his most challenging pupil, and for good reason.

"You both know how it is, having me as a mentor," boomed Thaddeus, breaking through the daze that Garrett had fallen into. "I only ask for three things."

"Yes, we remember," said Anselm, rolling his eyes. "Trust, commitment, and honour."

"Exactly," answered Thaddeus, persisting in spite of Anselm's obvious mockery. "I have worked with Augustus in sun and rain, by sunrise and sunset, but the boy has grown into a stubborn adolescent with the resolve of a king and the pampered privilege of a prince!"

Garrett understood Thaddeus's frustration. Augustus was at an age where instruction only seemed to bring about the very opposite of the desired effect. His attacks were distinctly off-balance during the contest, and no matter how many times he mocked or cursed his opponent, it was always the same result: an easy parry and a drop of the shoulder before the dark-haired boy was safely out of range. At one point, Augustus's frustration and impatience had manifested in an attack so ill-judged that his opponent had been able to deflect the weapon nimbly from his hands and send it skidding across the floor. Naturally, this had left Augustus embarrassed and angry, a fairly common blend in boys of that age, and when his rage had boiled over, he had cast a handful of sand into his opponent's eyes before unleashing a vicious assault. Staggered at first, the other boy had been able to fight on impulse alone, but as his vision returned, a nod of approval from Thaddeus consented him to finish the contest. In the end, it had only taken a routine drop of the knee to swipe the prince's leg before a rising blow had left him sprawled in the sand with a mouthful of blood.

It was then that the king had arrived.

"I pray that you have a few years left in you yet," said Thaddeus, shaking his head as he finished his story. "The boy never listens, and he never learns."

3

A man of great stature, Anselm was as tall as Augustus but larger across the chest, with a mass of dark hair and a grey beard that obscured his features. He was known for a light-hearted, jovial demeanour, yet his expression had soured during Thaddeus's summary of events. "Your aversion to regicide is some consolation," he said, "if somewhat overshadowed by the lack of progress that Gus seems to be making."

Thaddeus was still and silent, and Garrett noticed the old man's forehead glistening with a developing sweat.

"My most valued mentor and my chosen shield," Anselm continued, addressing Thaddeus and Garrett respectively. "Who better to aid me in teaching my son the skills necessary to rule?" He placed a hand on each of their shoulders. "Every day is a different challenge, a new threat, and though it is rare for a king to take up arms against a single man, he is ever expected to find solutions to difficult problems." He removed his hand from Garrett's shoulder to instead rest it on the pommel of his sword. "More than ever, I am called upon for the subtle arts of craft and cunning, but in any case, a king's actions must always demonstrate dignity and distinction."

Anselm looked in the direction of his son, who was still inspecting a bloodied mouth for missing teeth as he walked over to join them. Assuming Gus had been listening in on their conversation, Anselm asked, "Do I assume that after five years, we are yet to learn this most basic of lessons?"

Gus's mouth had settled into a hard line as he listened to his father speak, and he made no move to answer him. Thaddeus, on the other hand, opened his mouth to say something, but Anselm continued, cutting the man off, "Today marks the celebration of my fiftieth year, and I'm glad to hear that I am not alone in hoping for many more." He flashed a smile at Thaddeus, who smiled back as his shoulders visibly relaxed. "I am no longer a young man, and I feel my vigour passing with each day. Your time will come, Gus, and when it does, I hope you are ready." He turned to Augustus, pausing to ensure that he was being heard. "Strength and aggression will only take you so far, son. You were taught a hard lesson today, and I can only hope that you will learn from it."

This exhausted the very last of Augustus's patience. Red-faced and with teeth bared, he was about to deliver his rebuttal when Anselm turned to summon Marcia, an unassuming house maid who had been waiting in his shadow. Her skin was fair, and her auburn hair matched the freckles dotting her cheeks.

"Marcia, my son has had a rather rough education this afternoon. Please bring a towel so that he might wipe his face. We've a banquet to attend, and his appearance is rather affecting my appetite."

Despite their best efforts, Garrett and Thaddeus couldn't resist laughing, albeit as stifled as possible, as the king exited, leaving Marcia to approach the bloodied prince.

"Thanks," snapped Augustus, rolling his eyes as he snatched the towel, and Garrett thought his pride was probably suffering more than his appearance. "You know…" Gus continued, appraising Marcia as he climbed to his feet, "You could probably be quite beautiful, if you wanted to. A bit of attention to the hair, some colour in your face, a change of clothes, and we could soon clean that lowborn stench from you." He brought strands of her wavy hair to his face to judge the scent. "Yes, a little project. A plaything for the future king, and from such humble beginnings. Aren't you going to thank me?"

A momentary silence fell upon the group as Marcia looked at her feet, the corner of her mouth trembling before she eventually mustered a gracious curtsy and began to move away.

"That's enough," Thaddeus intervened, stepping beyond the housemaid to face Augustus.

Garrett moved to stand at Thaddeus's side and added, "Your father is a great king, loved by his people. Is this the man you are destined to be?"

He left the question hanging in the air. With no sign of an intelligible response, he hefted a comforting arm around Marcia and began walking her towards the exit, the prince's quiet curses unheard by the others as they went.

How dare they? thought Augustus, wiping blood from his face. With his outburst to Marcia, there was an element of her having been in the wrong place at the wrong time. In her defence, she was just an ignorant lowborn, and he felt some regret at lashing out at her, even if she did need to learn to show respect. He meant it when he said that she had blossomed of late, and she really was rather attractive for a commoner, but her reaction when he looked at her was unacceptable: cold and unwilling to meet his gaze. She should be thankful for the attention of her betters, and today, he concluded, was a much-needed lesson for her.

Thaddeus and Garrett on the other hand…well, that was a different matter. A couple of loathsome old men, questioning royalty without any fear of consequence from his father. They were a troubling example of how weak the king had grown, softened by the sweet words of his sycophantic aides. Things would change when Augustus's time came, and it couldn't come soon enough!

He paused at this thought, internally grimacing with the guilt of what this would mean for his father. He wasn't much of a king, but Augustus supposed that Anselm had tried his best as a parent, and it was the contest—not his father—that had sparked his frustration after all.

He sighed, and then his mind took a different tack. Thaddeus had clearly attempted to humiliate him by giving his opponent special insight into the slightest imperfections in his technique. Come to think of it, the old man had even allowed his opponent first choice of sword from the castle armoury. A boy of no consequence given priority over a prince! It was a privilege in itself to share the training circle with royalty, but to have the audacity to think he could actually win…

Augustus stewed on the injustice of it all until the sight of the wooden sword graced him with a realization. Yes, that was it, the sword had seemed heavy from the moment he had selected it. In the right light, the colour was clearly darker than usual; it couldn't possibly be hickory from Dalhart Forest, the very standard for training weapons. He shook his head, laughing to himself. That's how they had done it, by conspiring against him to slow his attacks. It was obvious now that he had been deceived, but he was not like his father, and he promised himself that these slights would not be forgotten. Anselm had asked for craft and cunning, but none of them had any idea what he was capable of.

Augustus threw his blade at the wall, where it cracked on impact, showering a short, stout man with splinters of wood as he came through the door, his hands covering his head instinctively.

"So strong, my prince," Wendell said breathlessly, elevating his red cheeks with a smile while glints of light caught the angles of his bald head. "Only peasants fight with wood," he added, gliding towards the centre of the room with long red robes dragging in the sand. "Your opponents are lucky that Thaddeus continues to protect them. Put steel in your hand, and I fear that heads will roll!" Still smiling, Wendell took the towel from Augustus's grasp and proceeded to dab any evidence of defeat from his face.

"I was tricked," said Augustus, pushing Wendell away in frustration.

The older man was not discouraged and chose to continue as he had started. "Of course, my prince, but there are many who seek to belittle you." He returned to Augustus's side, lowering his voice to a whisper. "The people love your father, but they take advantage of his good will. You will reign with strength, and they will respect you, even fear you." The prince narrowed his eyes as Wendell continued. "I believe that your actions will alter history, and I will stand proudly by your side," he paused for effect before adding gently, "my king."

Pride swelled in Augustus's chest briefly at Wendell's words, but then he thought of his father, cold and dead as he, Augustus, placed the crown on his head, and his stomach turned over. "Your words are tantamount to treason, old man. Is today not my father's birthday? A celebration of his fiftieth year and the love of his people?" The young prince suddenly loomed above his inferior, who was forced low in subservience.

8

Wendell lowered his eyes, and his tone turned pleading. "Of course not, please do not mistake my intentions," he added in deference. "It simply pains me to see you treated this way. I know a warrior when I see one."

"What do you know of warriors, cripple?" Augustus snapped. "You are the master of coin, a scholar, but one known to overstep your position," he finished pointedly as Wendell's cheeks deepened in their red hue. Augustus strode towards the older man, forcing him back with forefinger pressed into his chest. "There is much truth in the words that you speak, but you would do well to stick to what you know. I'd hate for you to learn what kind of warrior I really am."

At this, Wendell seemed to accept defeat, raising both hands to halt their progress. Small stumps of scarred tissue stood in memory of the middle and index fingers on his right hand, and Augustus made no effort to hide his disgust before Wendell adjusted the long sleeves of his robes to cover his shame.

"Your wish is my pleasure, young prince," he said, with an obsequious bow, "but remember, as master of coin it is my job to recognise a good investment. I trust you will do the same." With this he stalked away, leaving Augustus with his brow furrowed and his head full of conflicting thoughts.

The blood-orange late afternoon sun hung low in the sky, and candles caused shadows to dance on the castle walls as Thaddeus and Garrett passed through labyrinthine corridors and into the throne room of Eldred's Keep. The room itself was cavernous, with royal banners of epic scale adorning the four walls. Each piece was mounted beside smaller crests representing twelve noble families most loyal to the crown. Weapons of great deeds provided further decoration, along with ostentatious portraits depicting the celebrated kings of old.

Garrett considered the collection of steely eyes and hard-set jaws before he eventually broke the silence. "He's not his father, you know?" His words echoed about the room and caused him to lower his voice as he continued, "We both knew Anselm as a young man. Need I remind you that he wasn't always so likeable?"

Thaddeus nodded, and the two of them considered the statement for a moment as they continued lost in thought towards the foot of Isidore's chair, a commanding construction of intricate craft, wrought with black iron and towering ominously from the height of a great dais.

"Of course, you're right," Thaddeus responded with a deep sigh. "King Anselm is a leader who will be remembered among the very best. How many years have we known peace?" he asked, pausing only briefly, as though he did not expect an answer. "Time flies, Garrett, but it has been eight years since Anselm signed the Treaty of Eriwald. Yes, eight years," he reiterated as his friend's eyebrows raised in disbelief. "It may have escaped your notice, but we are not young men anymore, and the world is changing around us. In the North, King Maxim passed with no male heir, and his daughter Mathilde now sits upon the Throne of Cornesse. Our neighbours to the East remain predictably unpredictable under King Ferdinand and his murderous sons. Meanwhile, Simeon speaks of trade and free movement from the West, but of course Auldhaven will always harbour ambitions towards our borders." Thaddeus paused for a moment, surveying the great hall to ensure they remained alone. "Anselm is a great man, on that we agree, but he no longer commands the reverence he once did. Look beyond our king, and Prince Augustus has already established the well-earned reputation of petulant man-child."

Garrett, whose only response was a quiet sigh, was briefly aware of how much Thaddeus had aged, his silver hair starting to thin and deep lines framing his eyes.

"Our enemies can smell weakness, old friend," Thaddeus continued. "Each day uncovers rumours of new threats to the Low Country." A nearby noise suddenly caused him to stop in fear that they might no longer be alone. "Peace can only last so long," he whispered, making hastily in the direction of the door. "Pray that we are not too late."

C yrus knelt perfectly still, silent but for his breathing and rhythmic, pounding heartbeat. He was too focused to notice how the temperature had fallen; his breath was visible in the cool evening air. The light was beginning to fail him as the fading sun retracted behind the tree line, and it suddenly occurred to him that his pursuit had lasted almost an entire day. With the hopes of an entire village resting on his shoulders, Cyrus scratched an itch in his short blond hair before slowly training his bow on the elusive quarry. It had been worth the wait. Strong and tall, she was a perfect specimen, and with Cyrus hidden within the dense brush, the deer was oblivious to his presence or intent as daylight continued to fade. This was his moment, a chance to give something back to those who had taken him in. A chance for the villagers to eat well after another lean winter. His chance to be a hero.

Cyrus knew he would only get one shot, and failure to kill would see the beast long gone. Esterloch deer were, after all, renowned for their remarkable speed and athleticism, and Cyrus knew this perfect beast would be no exception. He adjusted his aim menacingly, determined that this particular pursuit would soon end in triumph.

At that moment came movement nearby, a gentle rustling that seized the attention of his prey. Alerted to danger, the deer eluded Cyrus's sightline momentarily, considering the disturbance in the thicket. It was imperative that Cyrus remain perfectly silent, and with damp soil at his knees, he was able to rotate slowly and align his bow with the hind legs of his prey. This was the last shot that he would have chosen, but it did present a chance to slow the deer and from there, well, he would have to improvise. He internally winced at the knowledge that this wouldn't be a quick, clean kill, but he quickly set such thoughts aside. He sensed it was now or never, and the bow string provided resistance as he primed the weapon to deliver its judgment, a light fuzz of beard tickling the back of his hand. Notched and ready, he steadied himself and began counting down towards the creature's demise.

"Three," he started in a whisper as the target remained still and ignorant to his plight.

"Two," he continued with nervous energy building, heart fit to burst from his chest.

"One," he finished under his breath, simultaneously releasing and awaiting the inevitable. But to his surprise, the deer remained unharmed and entirely calm. Cyrus looked to his bow and was shamed to see the arrow still nocked; his release had obviously been a false one. He had faltered under pressure again, and while there was some comfort in seeing an ungainly fawn emerge to join its mother, Cyrus accepted that this would not be his day. He chose that moment to fall away quietly and begin his return to the village, his head hung to watch his feet as he walked.

Heart stinging with shame, Cyrus was mortified to find his father, Osbert waiting at the village gates. The tall man was scratching at the roots of his dark hair, and Cyrus noticed a frown upon his face as Cyrus approached empty-handed.

"The wanderer returns," Osbert cried out, raising his arms in flamboyant welcome and quickly turning his frown into a forced-looking smile. "Your sister and I were beginning to worry about you. Where have you been?"

Cyrus momentarily thought to reach for a story—he'd had long enough to plan his excuses—but in that particular moment found himself uncharacteristically short of words. "The hunt," he grunted, brushing past his father, his mouth hard-set and his eyebrows slanted.

"It's okay," Osbert called after him, chasing to catch up to Cyrus, who was now moving through the village. "We have plenty of small game, grain, and other foods sent from the capital."

"Not to mention ale. We've got plenty of that!" added Bertram, the plump barkeep, rolling a huge cask across their tracks.

"And ale," reiterated Osbert light-heartedly as they continued on their walk. Cyrus held clenched fists at his side, bracing himself for the lecture he knew was coming. "Look Cy," continued Osbert, and Cyrus had to stop himself from groaning, "we can't, everyone, be good at everything." He gestured around the village suggestively, adding emotion to his tone. "We all love you, Cyrus, however hard you can make it sometimes. Do you think your sister cares if you caught anything? No," he answered before his son had chance to reply. "Now, your Aunt Aggie needs help preparing vegetables for the feast. You know she's fond of you. Why don't you drop the sulking and help her out, and then we can all start enjoying ourselves, okay?"

Cyrus felt anything but *okay*, but he settled for an insolent amble away from his father that was effective if a little cliché, something he was aware of but chose to ignore.

All around him, Corhollow was bustling with activity in anticipation of the spring festival. The market square sat at its heart and was decorated with colourful woollen flags and bunting that hung in contrast to the earthy tones that otherwise characterized the village. It was only a small settlement of single-storey wooden structures with thatched roofing and occasional brickwork from which smoke billowed into the sky. Despite the best efforts of his fellow villagers, Cyrus still concluded that it was about as boring a place as he could imagine. He certainly couldn't see cause to celebrate, so as soon as Osbert was out of sight, he upped his pace and headed for home.

Home, he thought, as he passed by Bertram's Tavern and a row of small shops and houses lining the dusty path that served as a road. It had been eight years since he and his sister had arrived here, and boring as it was, Cyrus had to admit that life wasn't so bad. Osbert had his moments, but he had good intentions. He had taken in Cyrus and Francine when they needed him, raising them unquestionably as his own and allowing Fran to flourish. It seemed to Cyrus that she was taller and smarter with every passing day, just twelve years old but already a useful hand in the kitchen under

Aggie's tutelage. He supposed they were all his family, really, or the closest he could hope for.

As Cyrus approached, Fran came running from Aggie's house towards the market square, her corkscrew brown hair bouncing as she collided with Cyrus in her haste to get past him. "Edgar!" she shouted excitedly, and Cyrus had to stop himself from rolling his eyes as he watched his sister run to their older adoptive brother, Osbert's son.

Cyrus remembered a time when Fran had looked at him like he was her entire world. He had taken her into his care as the two of them escaped their old lives together and developed what felt like unconquerable closeness despite the fact that they were not siblings from birth. But with every inch taller and every lesson smarter she grew, they only seemed to grow apart. On this occasion, she had barely even noticed him and instead continued unswervingly to Edgar, who lifted her effortlessly into the air as a group began to form in his presence.

Curious to the commotion, Cyrus started for Fran and their brother with the notion that his day couldn't possibly worsen. But with a backdrop of applause and appreciation, he realised he'd been wrong again, for at Edgar's feet lay the most perfect prize that he had ever seen, legs bound and with an arrow protruding from its neck.

Well-built and middle aged, Aunt Aggie was a woman who was always busy but still managed to approach life with an unfalteringly cheerful disposition. Like any other day, her grey hair was neatly concealed in a headscarf, and her kitchen echoed with bouts of singing that were devoid of lyric or melody.

"Add salt to the pan of water and bring it to boil," she called abruptly, breaking her song to call across at Cyrus.

"Yes, ma'am," he responded sarcastically under his breath before repeating his answer in a much louder, more earnest tone so that Aggie could be sure she'd been heard. Set to task, Cyrus felt it was easier to simply do as he was told, but Aggie was known to be meddlesome, and he could feel her gaze upon him, waiting for her moment.

"Something's wrong," she ventured finally, appearing soundlessly by his side. He knew she wouldn't be easily dissuaded, but Cyrus decided it was best to focus on the task at hand and hope she'd lose interest. "It's to do with Edgar, isn't it?" she persisted, probing with no indication of letting up.

"Won't they be needing this food soon?" Cyrus responded, rolling his eyes in an effort to move the conversation along. But when Aggie raised her eyebrows in response, he realised that there were limits to his patience. "Yes, Aggie," he snapped. "Is that what you want me to say? It's all about Edgar. Isn't everything?"

He loved his brother and had idolized him while growing up despite their closeness in age. Edgar was tall and handsome, with a muscular physique and dark, flowing hair, all of which left Cyrus struggling to compete for attention or to find an identity of his own. He hated himself for feeling this way about his brother, but sometimes perfect was just too…perfect.

"It's just all so easy for him, isn't it?" Cyrus added as Aggie gave a gratified smile to suggest that the conversation had gone exactly as intended.

"I understand," she said softly. "It's true that your brother has grown strong. He will one day be warden of Corhollow, and people already love him." Cyrus narrowed his eyes to prompt a change of tact. "What I mean is, yes, your brother has his strengths, but this world isn't built on brawn alone, and his strengths do not take away from your own. You are smart—god knows you think too much most of the time. But you know what? I spend plenty of time with that sister of yours, and all I ever hear is what a great brother you are, how you are always there when she needs you, and your stories—"

"Stories, Aggie," Cyrus interjected abruptly, throwing vegetables into the pan in frustration. "That's all they are. Kings and queens, pirates, bandits, heroes of war. People never tire of adventures, but I can't recall any of them starting with a damn storyteller in Corhollow." He spat the last few words before resting his hands on the kitchen worktop and letting his head drop for the second time that day. With a sigh, he added, "When will I have my own adventures instead of simply telling everyone else's?"

"All right," acknowledged Aggie sympathetically, fetching a clay jug from a nearby shelf, "but not all heroes are killers, Cyrus, and not all adventurers set out looking for adventure. Sometimes, it just finds you. If you think yourself any less heroic for brushing the curls out of Fran's hair every morning or helping her to sleep at night, then maybe you don't really understand the stories at all." Her expression changed as she poured a dark, frothy ale into two giant tankards. "Now, be a hero and help me finish this."

Cyrus managed a wry smile as they clinked mugs before consuming their drinks in one.

By early evening, Corhollow throbbed with palpable energy and anticipation. Candlelight flickered in the windows of every ramshackle lodging, but nobody was home. The entire populace was gathered in the heart of the village with music playing and cheerful dance already underway.

It was a mild spring evening even as the sun faded, and Cyrus felt that his day had improved immeasurably. The improvements had started in Aggie's kitchen and continued with a number of drinks since. He was a little unsteady on his feet, but his head was fuzzy, and he felt it would take a great deal to spoil his mood.

Not one for dancing, Cyrus slipped furtively through the throng to escape any unwanted attention and procure more of Bertram's signature brew. He started quickly and with purpose, but in the midst of the celebrations, a misplaced step took him from his feet, dragging the nearest person with him as he attempted to remain upright.

"Watch it!" cried a female voice, and as Cyrus hurried to his feet in apology, he realised just how shaky his legs had become.

"I'm so sorry," came his instinctive yet feeble response. By now, the girl he'd toppled over had returned to her feet and was already pulling long, russet hair away from her face to reveal light skin and dark, piercing eyes that instantly captivated him.

His unwitting company was Alana, who worked with Tabitha as an assistant weaver. She had delicate white flowers braided into her hair and an infectious smile that was framed by inviting red lips. He had spoken to her in passing but found that her presence made him hot and nervous, with a shortness of breath that made words hard to find. Today was no different.

"I'm so, so sorry," he said again, brushing dirt from the arm of her dress before Alana stopped his hand with hers. He realised he was repeating himself.

"Great party, isn't it?" he ventured, cringing as her eyes looked beyond him with disinterest, the question hanging awkwardly between them. "Perhaps I can replace your—"

"Thanks, but I have to go," she responded impatiently. "See you around, Cyrus." With that she left, and Cyrus went, red-cheeked, in search of a drink of his own.

It took a sturdy nudge to gain his attention.

"She knows my name," he said to no one in particular, before turning to see Fran and her friends sitting cross-legged around a small fire, looking on with wide-eyed expectancy. Buoyed by the upturn in his evening, Cyrus agreed to entertain them and bade silence from the group before proceeding to tell his tale.

"Our story is one of legend," he began, before pausing both to ascertain he had their absolute attention and to make sure he wasn't slurring his speech. "Our hero, Isidore, first king of Easthaven and liberator of the Eastern peoples. The very man who freed us from the shackles of western oppression."

"You mean Auldhaven?" asked one of Fran's friends, but Cyrus was intent on proceeding without interruption.

"After months of uprising and lethal raids against the king of Auldhaven," Cyrus persisted, emphasizing the last word with a glare at the child who had asked the question, "the tyrant king, Edmund, agreed to meet Isidore in open battle, upon the plains of Freyburn in the Lowland steppe." Cyrus took a swig of his drink, savouring the captivated silence of another satisfied audience. "Battle was to take place at the height of summer, on the longest day of the year," he went on, wiping ale from wispy hairs that lined his upper lip, "but when Edmund arrived, his armies stood alone, without opposition." A chorus of curiosity broke out among the girls, breaking the silence, and Cyrus was relieved to see a look of admiration back on Fran's face. "Dehydrated and restless under the glare of the burning sun," he began once more, "Edmund waited as long as his patience would hold before announcing victory and proclaiming a coward of his rival. But Isidore would not be so easily removed…"

He took a deep breath in anticipation of the thrilling finale and smirked, looking around at his audience. This tale was a personal favourite, and Cyrus knew he was delivering it with precision despite his previous unsteadiness. "Incapable of facing Edmund's far greater resources head-on, Isidore and his devoted followers concealed themselves on the blindside of a nearby ridge. Their plan was to frustrate the enemy and emerge under the glory of a setting sun."

Fran was on her feet by now, her wide eyes urging Cyrus on as though she herself was trying to climb into the story and fight alongside Isidore's rebel hoard. Cyrus continued undeterred and with a small smile to his sister, "True to his calculation and with surprise on their side, Isidore's army washed over their opponents, who were unsighted by the glare of a dying light." At this, Cyrus reached into his pocket and threw a small pouch of flour onto the fire, sparking new life into the flames and illuminating the awestruck

21

faces of his audience, just as he had hoped it would when he had spirited the flour from Aunt Aggie's kitchen earlier that day. "Celebrations had been premature, and Edmund was forced to accept a humiliating defeat before negotiating terms with Isidore, a man whose compassion remains an example to us all."

"What did they negotiate?" came the abrupt voice of the same inquisitive girl, interrupting an inevitable applause. Cyrus wasn't sure what was more frustrating, the incessant questioning or the fact that he had overlooked this detail in the first place, but he felt it only fair to answer.

"There were three terms," he began, raising his index finger to introduce the first. "The country we now know as Easthaven would never cross the borders of Auldhaven in malice." He stopped to add the middle finger. "An annual tax of food crops would be compensated to Auldhaven in lieu of arable lands lost to the newly formed Easthaven." Cyrus paused before raising a third finger and asking, "Does anyone know the third?"

Blank faces stared back at him, and Cyrus wasn't sure if it was the lack of an answer or a loss for words following his gripping account. He hoped it was the latter. "The third and final term," he said emphatically, "was that the second prince born unto any king of Easthaven must be pledged into the adoptive care of the king of Auldhaven. The plan was to see the prince grow and become an envoy for continued peace, though history recalls no such example."

It was not the way he had wanted to end the story, but he knew he had done it justice with enthralling inflection that brought the action to life. Cyrus stood with a wide smile, anticipating the group's appreciation, when Osbert called for attention, bringing a halt to proceedings in order to address the gathering crowd.

"People of Corhollow," he began assertively, stepping onto a log-stool to gain attention. "Friends, family, and those passing through—I trust that you are enjoying the merriment. Perhaps too much in some cases!" He earned himself a round of laughter by frowning at Bertram, who was resting against a tree to keep himself upright. He continued, "Today is a day for thanks. Thanks to the great King Anselm, who celebrates the anniversary of his birth, and to whom we are grateful that we shall never go hungry." The audience responded with a warm round of "hear, hears" and cries for the King's continued good health. "We also mark the start of a new hunting season, and I take great pride in announcing that my son Edgar has come of age to deliver the meat on which we will dine tonight."

Applause broke out as Osbert gestured the celebrated hunter to his side, and Cyrus attempted to quell his envy with the aid of yet another drink. "In this young man, I know that my legacy will prevail and that our village of Corhollow is in safe hands. I see now that it is time to plan for the future and that I must prepare him for the demands of responsibility." He gave his son a look of pride, Edgar embracing the moment with appropriate enthusiasm. "But that is all for another day." Osbert shifted to a light-hearted tone, placing a hand upon Edgar's shoulder from above and continued, "Tradition dictates that the festivities culminate with sport. You've seen me play my part for many a year, but this year I would seek to usher in a new era." He stepped down to draw eye-level with his son. "Edgar, I ask that you take my sword and stand for our name." Cyrus watched on with a scowl as Edgar accepted without hesitation, taking the sword and his place in the centre of a newly formed circle. Osbert applauded his son before continuing. "But great men are forged by great victories, and I now ask if there are any among you with the courage to stand against him?"

He searched the crowd with his eyes, as some of the younger men encouraged each other with nudges, smirks, and guffaws; others simply avoided eye contact. Cyrus snarled at the cowardice of the group. He'd watched Edgar fight countless times, and he was good, but not without weakness or vulnerability. If anything, Cyrus suspected that his brother's elevated status was likely to make him careless and prone to defeat. He narrowed his eyes, searching for someone to humble Osbert and take the smirk from his face.

"Surely there must be one?" added Osbert, as Cyrus took another large swig and peered at Alana across the circle. "I'll do it," came a voice and to Cyrus's surprise, he found it was his own.

An expectant energy surrounded the combatants as Cyrus walked slowly to take his position.

"What were you thinking?" asked Osbert extending an arm around Cyrus's shoulders to draw him in. He sensed his father's concern, but the permeating lack of belief only served to encourage Cyrus in his actions.

Cyrus turned away from his father and looked for Alana again, slicing his blade through the air in preparation while searching among the faceless crowd. Perhaps this was his moment. Perhaps this was when people would really start noticing him. Maybe even Alana…

Edgar left Cyrus no time to ponder these questions and came at him without warning. Though he fought desperately against the shapeless blur that was his brother, Cyrus soon realised just how slow and heavy his limbs had become after so many tankards of ale. He was sluggish even by his own standards, and it was all the more infuriating to see Edgar playing to the crowd.

A moment of brief respite allowed him to take breath as Edgar stood flourishing his sword ominously. It occurred to Cyrus that this had in fact been a bad idea and one that might have been influenced by his consumption throughout the evening. As self-belief faded, it made way for the harsh truth that Edgar was stronger and faster with enough skill to end the contest at any moment.

Cyrus looked to his brother for any kind of mercy, but Edgar continued to prance around the circle, arms raised as though the outcome was certain. The only solution was to fight, but if he couldn't compete on strength or speed, then maybe he'd have to fight smarter. His eyes fell on Edgar's left flank, so often exposed when his brother attacked with his stronger right side. He would never expect it; Edgar had clearly underestimated him. Cyrus's face lifted into a spiteful grin, and he mustered all his remaining vigour, launching to attack.

His strikes were clumsy, but the element of surprise and the strength of his convictions forced Edgar back towards their ever-enclosing audience. Over and over, Cyrus hacked at his brother until he noticed a subtle shift in Edgar's body, in preparation for an assault of his own. The crowd shouted relentlessly, perhaps sensing an upset, and when the opportunity presented, Cyrus pivoted to drive a solid shoulder into Edgar's unguarded flank. The plan had been perfect, his execution flawless; the only problem was that he'd been baited into doing it.

Cyrus wondered if it had been obvious to those watching. Edgar's subtle feint left him clutching at air as the crowd parted, allowing him to fall from their makeshift arena.

Helped to his feet, Cyrus flushed with embarrassment as his brother drove his sword into the ground. A looping fist in Edgar's direction was a poor attempt to restore pride, the wishful effort sidestepped routinely by Edgar and rewarded with a thudding blow to Cyrus's skull, which earned gasps from those watching. Dazed by the impact, Cyrus lashed out aimlessly, but Edgar stooped on instinct before slamming full force into his midriff, folding Cyrus in half and gaining the applause that he had been seeking all evening. This wasn't exactly how Cyrus had imagined causing such uproarious noise from the crowd. His stomach was twisted, but he wasn't sure where the shame ended and the pain began as Edgar stood over him basking in the moment, looking not at Cyrus but at the chanting crowd.

"My sons," proclaimed Osbert proudly as he helped Cyrus to his feet and held an arm aloft from each of the boys. Cyrus could hardly bring himself to look up as dizziness swept through his sagging head. All around him, people were celebrating, whooping, dancing, and congratulating. He felt as though they were getting closer and reaching for him, trying to draw him in, that they were spinning and spinning in an inaudible cacophony of sound. Cyrus noticed that his clothes were soaked with sweat, and his stomach was bubbling while his chest and throat burned. He needed space, he needed to be elsewhere, he just needed room to breathe, but he realised all of this too late.

He fell to his knees as he was sick on the ground in front of him, just when he thought the shame of losing could burn no brighter.

"Come on," said Fran, grabbing his arm as laughter broke out all around them. "Let's get you home."

The walk back was sobering in every sense, and as they passed through the streets of Corhollow, Cyrus felt his mood darken with their surroundings as families reluctantly brought the night to a close. Steeped in shadow, there was little solace in their arrival, but Fran soon had a fire burning, and the house was enriched with warmth and light.

"Tell me another story, Cy," said Fran, bounding onto her bed and crawling beneath the covers.

It was either an attempt to provide distraction or delay sleep, but Cyrus was so overcome by the day's events that he relented and perched on her bed to begin. "Which story?" he asked warily.

"Tell me the story of how we came to live in Corhollow," she commanded, looking up at him as her head rested on her pillow.

It was another story that Cyrus had told many times but clearly one that Fran enjoyed, and he'd had enough of fighting for one day.

"Well, if we must," he began, with decidedly less energy than his last offering. "Our story begins almost eight years ago to the day. With two children—a boy and a girl—in the woods outside of a small village called Coldwynne." Fran nodded in encouragement as her eyelids began to sag, and he continued, "The two heroes were still strangers at this point. The handsome male protagonist, Cyrus—" this drew a bout of drowsy laughter from Fran before he continued, "As I was saying, Cyrus was out walking in the woods, while a young girl known as Francine had been doing the same with her parents." He paused and bit his lip, considering the right words. "Her first parents, that is." A yawn escaped Fran, but she was still listening intently. "It was a bright day, and Cyrus was enjoying his adventure when he saw a group of odious thugs heading towards the village."

"What does odious mean?" asked Fran quietly, her head sinking deeper into the pillow.

"Sorry," said Cyrus. "it means nasty or horrible, but Cyrus wasn't about to let them make it to the village, so he distracted them." He sat up straight and found that he was growing into the story. "Cyrus was famed for his bravery and called the thugs away to save everyone in the village. That's when he found Fran, and the two of them ran together through the forest." He leaned down to his sister to grab her attention as she wavered on the edge of sleep. She roused again, and he continued, "They ran as fast as they could, refusing to stop, leading the nasty thugs away so that everyone else was kept safe!"

"And they can never go back, can they?" asked Fran, her words slurred, her eyes now fully closed. Despite all the growing she'd done recently, she looked so small in that moment.

"No," cautioned Cyrus as his face dropped in sadness. "If they do, bad people might find the village. Besides, they made it to Corhollow, where a kind man called Osbert saved them, and they all lived happily ever after. A classic happy ending." He waited for a response that never came. "They saved everyone, Fran. They were heroes!" He straightened the bedcovers and pulled them to cover Fran fully.

"We were heroes," he repeated gently before smothering the candle beside them and leaving Fran to find a bed of his own.

Darkness fell upon the capital as celebrations continued with no sign of an end. Stood on the ramparts beside his king, Garrett wondered if the people of Easthaven had ever known such popular rule. There was Isidore the Liberator, King Zacharias who had won great seafaring battles against the Verderans, maybe even King Everard II who was Anselm's grandfather and was famed for his exploits in the Low Country after years of occupation. The common thread among them was that they were men of war, men who thrived in desperate times, while Anselm in contrast offered a story of peace and hope.

After brokering the difficult Treaty of Eriwald, he had encouraged trade for goods and culture among the four nations of the quadripartite. A freedom of movement and political harmony had enabled the people of Easthaven to experience liberty and opportunity previously unknown. Together, they had grown stronger and wealthier, and despite the harsh conditions of the most recent winter, Anselm had been able to share food and supplies with those less prosperous, a gesture that had cemented his legacy and earned him the enduring love of his people.

The evening air was mild, and Anselm had been keen to observe his people, both in the courtyard of his castle and about the city. Despite the distraction of food, drink, and celebration, his presence had not gone unnoticed, and Garrett observed a beaming smile on the king's face as he was regaled with birthday wishes and calls for good health from below.

"You're enjoying this, aren't you?" Garrett enquired, his eyebrows raised but with his mind ever vigilant to potential threats.

"You know, I rather am," came the King's straight-faced reply, before a smile broke out to tease Garrett's discomfort. "I appreciate your watchfulness, Garrett, but relax for a moment and look at what we've built."

"*You've* built," responded Garrett assertively, pacing along the walls to absorb the view.

"You, me, both of us. Does it really matter? We have peace, our people are prospering, and I've at least a couple in my employ that aren't trying to kill me!" He flashed a smile at his old friend, before taking him by the shoulder. "Have it your way, Garrett. Queen Adaline will no doubt be waiting anyway. You know how she can be." He nudged his friend towards the door, and they returned to the banquet hall where celebrations continued.

With long, golden hair and an elegant blue dress that shone with the sparkle of sapphire, Queen Adaline drew their attention from the moment that Anselm and Garrett arrived.

"Isn't she beautiful?" Anselm said, shaking his head. It was one of those questions to which Garrett wasn't sure how he should respond, but he had known the couple for more than twenty years and had witnessed the unfaltering affection between them.

"She's a great woman," he responded, hoping that this was the right approach, "though she might not be best pleased at you for leaving her with General Broderick. The man serves you for his skill in combat rather than conversation."

Anselm nodded, peering across as the large, greying general gesticulated wildly at his queen, the large vein on his head protruding even more than usual. It was truly a gathering befitting the occasion. Fragrant meats and cheeses were being served while accomplished musicians played lively, exotic melodies from the Verderan capital of Casarossa. Even Wendell seemed in good form, buzzing around the room with entertaining anecdotes, ensuring that nobody went without a drink.

Raucous laughter broke out, and Garrett was frustrated to see Augustus reach and grab Marcia from behind while being encouraged by the younger nobility. He wondered if the prince had taken anything from their earlier conversation, but as he made to intervene, the music ceased, and as the housemaid retreated with a forced smile, he noticed that Thaddeus sat alone, deep in thought.

"Who died, Thaddeus?" he questioned, dragging a seat to rest beside his friend.

"Nobody, yet," came a terse reply, the older man taking a final swig of his drink as King Anselm joined them. "With any luck, that's how things will stay."

"Oh, Thaddeus, always so glum," announced Anselm in good humour. "Get this man more wine!"

32

"Most kind, your Grace," Thaddeus responded, rising to provide a courteous bow. "No more for me, but please enjoy yourself. Right now, I think the Queen has greater need of me." He smiled before bowing again, and then he departed to join Adaline and Broderick in conversation.

"I did try!" said Anselm, face scrunched as Garrett's eyebrows raised in a telling expression. "You know Thaddeus. There's no helping the man sometimes. As for Broderick, he seems to treat conversation like war: always on the attack!" Though Anselm was characteristically jovial in his response, his smile soon dropped, and his eyes squinted as he surveyed the room, making it obvious to Garrett that Thaddeus's words had affected the king. Popular though he was, his royal efforts to provide for the majority had diluted the earnings of the wealthy for what he called "the greater good," while his hard-fought treaty was a constant balance on fine political lines with volatile neighbours.

Garrett recalled that their musicians hailed from Verdera under King Ferdinand's rule, and he made sure to keep Anselm close. There were many who could benefit from the king's demise, and where would that leave Easthaven?

"Wine," demanded the king, interrupting Garrett's thoughts. "The good stuff," he added. "Something from Nivelle. You know how I love a Cornessian vintage." The king's buoyant tone had returned, and Garrett was keen to encourage his good mood. In all likelihood, he was just being paranoid, and Thaddeus was not known for his cheery optimism.

"Of course," he responded, noting that he alone had heard the request. The serving staff were all busy, and Marcia was once again preoccupied with the attention of Augustus and his dandies.

"I've risked my life for you these past twenty odd years, but only for the privilege of fetching wine for your lazy arse!"

He nudged his king playfully, making towards the galleys as Anselm's deep laughter echoed around the room.

Lost in a warren of sacks, barrels, and jugs and surrounded by salted meats, Garrett had to admit that he had perhaps underestimated the task at hand. The kitchens had offered him little assistance, as they were in the midst of preparations for their grand finale, and as the scent of sweet pies and fruit cakes wafted into the storerooms, he wondered why he'd ever left the party.

Garrett laughed briefly, remembering his conversation with Anselm. This task was the frivolous whim of the king, but to Garrett, Anselm had also become a friend. He had so many memories of their time together. Anselm's marriage to Adaline. The day that Anselm and his queen had subsequently become parents. The momentous treaty and all that they had prospered since. It dawned on him that he loved the king as a brother and having pledged servitude in the face of adversity, he was embarrassed at being bested by so small a task as fetching wine. He wondered if Anselm would even notice the difference, but a sheepish voice sounded as he reached for the nearest carafe.

"The king's wine, milord," said a man, causing Garrett to dismiss his choice and turn to face the door. The man was partially concealed by shadow, but his apron exposed him as kitchen staff, young and handsome with a dark complexion, which was marred by scarring on his cheek. The man made his way from the entrance to meet Garrett with an empathetic smile before proffering the wine and turning hurriedly to leave.

The kitchens were clearly under pressure with the celebration, so Garrett called thanks to the man's back as he disappeared, leaving Garrett alone in the darkness. Still and silent, Garrett was startled by the eerie creaking of meats that hung from metal hooks around him and the sound of rodents scuttling in search of grain. He noticed his heart was beating faster and louder, his breathing sounding exaggerated. Worst of all, he had an inexplicable feeling that he was not alone.

Reaching for his sword, Garrett secured the wine and crept slowly beyond the shelves where he had been standing. This end of the pantry was somehow darker still, and he was forced to proceed on intuition alone as gentle suggestions of movement stayed his concern. Before him, a trace of moonlight illuminated the stone floor, angled towards the corner of the room where oak casks were primed for consumption. Garrett noticed that he'd begun to develop a nervous sweat and that his hands were shaking, palms clammy as he locked his fingers into a two-handed grip on the sword. This helped to steady him, but his right eye twitched as he measured the scene in front of him. It seemed that one of the barrels was out of place, angled away from the wall to as though to provide concealment. He raised his blade as Thaddeus's concern echoed in his head, and the suspense became unbearable as he edged slowly forward.

The next Garett knew, he was on his back. The speed of the attack had taken him by surprise, causing him to slip on the damp cobblestones. His head bounced hard against the floor, and it was all he could do to keep hold of his sword, spare hand fighting to protect his face from razor sharp claws as an unbearable shrieking filled the air.

"Get back!" he screamed, pushing the predator away to scramble to his feet. The shadow of the beast loomed threateningly, and a hissing sound echoed from the darkness, but Garrett's expression changed as his attacker finally moved into the light.

"You must be kidding," he said with head in hands. "We are definitely not telling Anselm about this!"

He sheathed his sword and walked away laughing, neither the cat nor her kittens following him.

"What happened to your face?" called the king as he and the queen stood ready to address their assembly. Garrett rolled his eyes but decided to ignore the question before hastening to fill Anselm's glass.

"A toast to my queen," thundered the king with his glass raised, his other hand embracing Adaline. "A toast to all of you. My dear friends and family, and even you, Garrett." He gave a boyish smirk that reminded Garrett of a much younger Anselm. "Together, we are stronger, and I can only pray for many more years in your company. For many more years as your king!"

The outpour of affection was unanimous, and Queen Adaline held her husband tightly as he tipped the glass to his mouth. Music reconvened, and Garrett scoured the room for Thaddeus in an attempt to improve his mood. He was keen to share the perfect moment with his old friend and so began to pour some of the king's wine into two crystal glasses, but they remained less than halfway full when sudden and hysterical cries startled the jug out of Garrett's hands, contents left strewn across the floor.

"No!" cried Adaline, dragging at her hair as tears streamed lines in the powder on her face. Anselm was nowhere to be seen in the commotion, but Augustus had now arrived at his mother's side, the two of them speechless with shock as a crowd began to smother them.

"Out of my way!" screamed Garrett as he pushed forward in desperation. He drew his sword and called for calm, but as people parted before him, he was anything but. Edging closer, he braced himself for the worst, but nothing could have prepared him for the sight of Anselm sprawled with blood bubbling from his mouth.

"You!" spat Wendell, glaring at Garrett. "Marcia, fetch the surgeon, and Broderick, summon your men. There is treason among us!"

Garrett was speechless, and his hands were shaking once more, but he approached the king with instinctive concern.

"Stay back," Wendell commanded, causing Garrett to stop, sword falling from his grip as the surgeon shouldered past in his haste to reach the king. "I heard you in the throne room, you and Thaddeus. You wanted this!" He stood, seizing his moment to address the room. "They spoke of life after the king, his weakness. They planned it all!"

"Seize them!" cried Broderick, as Garrett turned to find Thaddeus speechless in the melee, Adaline's cries ringing out once more. The surgeon had lifted Anselm into sitting position, but he was propped against the table, his body limp, his head sagging as blood continued to fall from his lips.

"Wait!" Garrett interjected, reclaiming his sword and using all of his effort to maintain a calm voice. "Why would I do this? I owe everything to Anselm. He is like a brother to me."

"He is your king!" Wendell barked in response, as startled onlookers answered the surgeon's frantic calls for assistance and the king was raised onto a table. Elaborate tableware crashed to the ground to clear space, but it was clear that Anselm's convulsions were already starting to slow. Broderick's troops were now circling ominously, and Garrett knew that time was running out. He searched the room, but no help was forthcoming. Thaddeus stood constrained, leaving all eyes upon him. He looked for the queen to protest his innocence but found her stooping over a pile of broken glass.

"The wine!" Garrett called out urgently as he backed away, lowering his sword again. "There was a man from the kitchens. He brought it to me. He must have added something. I can take you to him."

"Well stop talking then, Garrett!" said Prince Augustus, breaking his silence to beat Wendell to a response. "Broderick's men will come with you." He approached the table where Adaline was taking his father's head within her hands, the subtle movement of the king's chest confirming that he yet clung to life. "Wendell, keep an eye on Garrett, and do not return until vengeance has been served upon the culprit."

Garrett burst into the kitchens and saw the man immediately. Grabbing him from behind, he drew his sword up to rest on his throat. "Who are you working for?" he demanded, before turning the man's face to find that it was not the man with the scar. A flash of movement caught the corner of his eye as the rear exit crashed open, the would-be assassin fleeing for the busy courtyard, where celebrations continued under the night sky, the crowd unaware that the subject of their celebrations was even now hanging in the balance between life and death. Garrett followed and emerged into a crowd of blurred faces, but as his eyes adjusted, he noticed a parting in the crowd that led towards the exit. "It'll be easier if we split up," he suggested. "Wendell, come with me if you must, and bring some of Broderick's men."

As half of the men began to circle the crowd, covering access to the royal stables, Garrett—followed by Wendell and the remaining troops—took the most direct route towards the gatehouse. He thought to call for the guard but knew that the portcullis would be too slow to contain them. All around him, people were falling out of his way or shouting curses, but Garrett had sight of the runaway and was determined not to fail the king twice this evening.

Exiting the gates, he struggled to keep his footing while descending a steep hill into the narrow streets of the capital. Highcastle's earliest inhabitants had settled in tents, and while the city had sprung up around them, with Eldred's Keep overlooking the sprawl, it remained nostalgic in its jumbled charm.

Garrett had grown up in the city and knew these streets well. Countless were the days spent chasing childhood friends or escaping the attention of angry shopkeepers with pockets of stolen food. This all meant that he moved quickly, and he knew that the gap between him and his prey was closing with every stride.

"Stop!" he shouted, as the man with the scarred face slammed through the door of the nearest building. "Wendell, take the others and cover his escape!"

"But—," sounded Wendell, seemingly reluctant to let Garrett from his sight.

"No, Wendell, you have to go, or we are going to lose him!" Garrett rushed into the butcher's shop and slid across the blood-stained counter to access the back of the building. The storeroom reeked of meat and dead animals, and he spotted a heavy knife resting on the butcher's block. It was only steps away, but a heavy blow landed unexpectedly on the back of his head as he hurried towards the knife, and he could only watch from the bloody wood floor as a pair of boots grew distant in his vision.

As his head cleared, Garrett raised himself to claim the knife and continue his heavy-legged pursuit into the streets beyond. With the shame of the ambush equal to the pain, he was relieved when two enterprising street urchins offered directions in exchange for money. He ran as fast as he could, with adrenaline coursing through his veins, until Wendell and Broderick's troops came into view. They were also running but in the direction of a dead end, where the path met a steep wall—the wall that the would-be assassin was scaling in escape.

"You won't get away with this!" Wendell yelled at the runaway as Garrett drew level. He turned back towards the men and ordered, "Shoot him down!"

Broderick's men readied their bows, but Garrett suspected that it would all be in vain. His legs were still heavy, and he realised that he might never catch the younger man on foot. He knew that it was now or never and that he wouldn't be able to live with himself if the poisoner escaped justice. He hurled the butcher's knife more in hope than expectation, but to his surprise, his throw had been remarkably accurate. The blade tore into the back of its target, and Garrett knew the chase was over.

Wendell pushed past him to smother the body where it had landed. "Out of my way!" he shouted, struggling to form his words around deep, heavy breathing while Garrett rested hands on knees in similar condition. Wendell turned the body to expose the man's face, and Garrett experienced a brief moment of relief at the familiarity of its features before the adrenaline of the chase faded and he recalled Anselm in a similar lifeless form back at the castle.

"His pockets," said Wendell abruptly, calling Garrett back into the moment as he searched the body for clues. He imagined that they must have looked like common thieves, stripping a corpse in a back alley. He could sense Broderick's men watching him intently and felt the tension rising as Wendell grunted in frustration, tearing at the dead man's clothing. Then suddenly he stopped, and a disc of metal echoed as it clinked to the ground.

"What is it?" asked Garrett, moving closer. "A button?" But he saw that it was bigger than he had first thought.

Wendell climbed slowly to his feet holding the disc to the light with his left hand. "Not a button, you fool. It's a coin," he said, rotating the silver piece to catch the moonlight as Garrett looked on. "And not just any coin either: an Auldhaven Crown to be exact."

Garrett's skin prickled and his face creased as he considered the implications.

"We'd better return to the castle," said Wendell assertively, turning to look directly at Garrett. "It seems that the time for peace is over."

Garrett crashed through the kitchens and back into the banquet hall, but the king was nowhere to be seen. The rich smell of food hung in the air and glasses sat half-empty, but without people and music, the celebrations of the evening suddenly seemed very distant.

"The king's chambers?" suggested Wendell, propped against the doorway, groaning as Garrett sprinted back past him.

They climbed through the castle in haste and arrived to find the royal chambers manned by more of Broderick's troops. The men wore plate armour and were armed with halberds but stood aside as Garrett and Wendell made their way to the door. A terrible sense of dread overcame Garrett as he turned the handle and realised that the death of the scarred man held no comfort or salvation. Intricate wood furnishings and a bear hide rug sat before the warmth of a roaring fire, but as Garrett joined those gathered around Anselm's bed, his body turned icy cold.

Garrett stood forlorn before King Anselm, who was laid out pale and still under the surgeon's attention. His large, commanding figure suddenly seemed small within the grand framework of his canopy bed. Hearing the queen's gentle sobbing, Garrett moved to stand at her side in an act of comfort. Adaline's hand rested on Augustus, who knelt by his father. In that moment, Garrett realised he needed some comfort of his own. Anselm had always been good at that; he had a rare ability to lighten the mood in difficult times or find a positive when hope seemed lost. Garrett's heart sank when he realised he was already thinking of Anselm in the past tense. He of all people would be expected to stay strong, but there were so many things he still wanted to say to the king, so many promises unfulfilled, and so many questions yet unanswered.

Tears swelled and cries broke out around the room as the surgeon closed Anselm's eyes for a final time.

"The king is dead," announced Thaddeus, turning away from Anselm to land his gaze on Augustus. "Long live the king."

C yrus attacked in ardent defence of his king. The woods of Coldwynne had been an obvious place for an ambush, and though he was only a boy, he would fight to level the odds.

"Stay back!" he yelled, hacking and slashing as enemies poured at them from all angles. He was conscious to shield King Anselm, but he was renowned for his swordsmanship and keen to add to his bloody reputation. Darting forward, he sensed that the tide was turning, and his fleeing enemies received no mercy as he cut them down. This left just three as Cyrus leapt at the largest of his assailants, guarding against a pitiful thrust before turning the man onto his compatriot's blade. The inadvertent killer was stunned and without a weapon as the last of Cyrus's enemies chose his moment to attack. Pushing the weaponless man away from him, Cyrus met his enemy's blade in kind. He was a worthy adversary, but his aggression and strength counted for nothing as Cyrus's intricate swordplay tricked the steel from his hand before landing a lethal blow. The remaining man tried to crawl away with a knife in his hand and his sights on the king, but as Cyrus took him by the hair, the man knew he had taken his final breath.

"Take that!" shouted Cyrus aggressively as his sharpened stick tore leaves from a tree. His imagination was boundless, and Coldwynne Woods was the perfect playground. His parents had filled his head with legends, and Cyrus took every opportunity to explore the dense forest in pursuit of his own. Inspired by his surroundings, Cyrus would spend long hours climbing through branches, collecting stones, and paddling in the gentle streams. He might only be a boy, but people told him he was destined for great things; he just needed that moment, the call of adventure.

He walked on through the woods, swinging his stick through the air as he replayed his most recent fantasy. Chosen shield to the king was his favourite role, and his heart rate was only just beginning to settle when her voice startled him.

"Help!" came the call, and Cyrus listened intently as a woman's cries echoed throughout the forest. The voice was familiar, and he placed her at a clearing nearby in which he had often wandered, trees curving overhead, dappling him in sunlight. It was only a short distance, but he ran with purpose before sliding in behind a section of thick brush, fit to burst with excited energy and ready to make his name. Adventure was calling him at last.

"Shut it, woman!" came a man's voice, though Cyrus couldn't see the man or recognise his unusual accent. "Keep talking and you'll be next."

Cyrus couldn't see through the thick brush where he was hidden, but from the sounds of the struggle, he gathered that a man and a woman were being threatened by another man. The heady mix of fear and excitement was intoxicating, but Cyrus chose to pause for a moment, weighing his makeshift weapon and wondering what a hero would do.

"Argh!" came another desperate cry, and this time Cyrus instinctively raised himself out of the brush to attack. He jabbed his stick in the direction of two men locked in struggle but froze when one of them collapsed to the ground like an empty sack, his wife wailing as the other probed a blood-slick sword towards her, demanding silence.

He recognised the blonde-haired woman as Muriel from the village. She had always been kind to him, and her husband made the best cakes and bread. His name was Virgil, and he was an excellent baker—or at least he had been. The killer hadn't noticed Cyrus standing open-mouthed among the trees, but Muriel had, and she gestured to Cyrus with her eyes. The man was still armed, but he had discarded a small sack at the base of a nearby trunk, and as Cyrus looked a little closer, he saw the protruding blade of a small but deadly axe.

The man's back was entirely exposed as he began to grab at Muriel, and Cyrus's brow furrowed as he saw tears form upon her face. She protested wildly as the man pressed her to the ground, his weight upon her, and Cyrus used this moment to slip from his position and grab the axe. He edged towards them with gritted teeth, axe at his side. He would end this vile man's life. He would save Muriel and make his name. He had the weapon and the element of surprise; in the end, it was easier to kill him than not.

When Cyrus looked down, he found his hands shaking. His legs were suddenly frozen, and a wetness ran between his thighs. Muriel cried out desperately for help, and he saw her kicking and screaming at her captor. Cyrus knew she was calling for him, but he knew in that moment that he wouldn't be able to save her. He caught her eyes again as her attacker's sword crossed her throat and brought an end to her life.

Cyrus dropped the axe as he turned to run. He took the path to the village with adrenaline carrying him swiftly across the earthy track. Trees began to thin as he drew nearer to home, and for the very first time, he had to acknowledge that he was scared. How could he have thought himself capable of killing that man? He was just a boy, he'd never hurt anyone, and he wasn't like the people in the stories. It was all meant to be a game, only a game. His head was spinning, and by the time he reached the overlook to Coldwynne village, a faintness had overcome him. He was desperate to get back and warn his parents. He could still be a hero yet.

He stepped to the edge, peering down at his village, but all he saw was flames.

Smoke rose high into the sky, and Cyrus shook his head, wondering how he hadn't noticed it previously. Though the smoke hadn't reached him yet, he felt choked by it all the same, his chest tight with panic. His mind was full of spinning thoughts, and the ever-thickening smog from the flames was only adding to his headache. He didn't know where to go or what to do but felt suddenly stifled by the thick canopy that loomed above him. It seemed his only option was to run.

Taking the direction that led him farthest from the village, he began by following the path before deviating into the dense woodland to avoid being seen—by whom, he was not sure. Branches seemed to claw at him, and as birds fluttered from the trees, it looked as though the forest had come to life. He had lost his bearings and in doing so wandered dangerously close to the scene of the murders he'd just witnessed. Cyrus clutched his head in his hands, reaching for direction. He knew these tracks as well as anyone, but he was frantic, and his heart sounded like a drum being beaten in his ears. He gripped his head tighter to drown out the sound, squeezing hard at his temples to target the pain, before the call of sweet music cut through the noise and brought calm upon him.

It was the singing voice of a young girl, and Cyrus could tell she was close. Calling to her through the thicket, he pushed through the overgrowth with thorns scratching at his arms and branches lashing at his face. He regretted his decision not to keep the axe, but light finally emerged ahead of him, and there she was: picking flowers to make bracelets. Her name was Francine, and she didn't know that her parents were dead.

"Fran, you need to come with me!" he shouted, grabbing her arm. His words took her by surprise, but she sat up to greet him, pulling tight curls of hair away from her face to reveal a warm smile, one which faltered slightly when she saw the look on Cyrus's face.

"Francine, this is serious, there are bad people out here, and…"

He paused, not knowing how to finish the sentence as the small girl looked on with wide, confused eyes. She still had the ghost of a smile on her face as though wondering if this was just a game, as he would have done only a short while before.

"Fran, we have to get out of here. There are bad people coming to the village. This isn't play, it isn't funny, we have to save them. I need you to come with me!"

"But what about Mummy and Daddy?" she said with tears welling in her eyes, her mind seeming to finally catch on to the fact that this was not pretend.

"We can save them," he said, with no better idea of what to say. "We can save them, but we have to go." He had no idea where the killer was, nor those who had burned the village, but he took a moment to steady his own nerves before taking Fran by the hand to run as fast as her small legs would carry her. He could hear her gentle sobbing as they went, but his only focus was to find a way out. Cyrus refused to let his companion slow as they finally broke free from the trees and out into the open pasture.

"Keep going, Francine," he called back through heavy breaths. "We can save everyone. We can be heroes!" He looked back to her with a smile of reassurance, trying to believe his own words, but as his foot caught a stone, his balance was lost, and the ground rushed up to meet him.

Cyrus woke to the sound of screaming, perhaps his own or rather a lingering echo from the dream. His head hurt from his over-consumption, and his body hurt from the beating, but worst of all, he was agonized by the shame. It had been the same dream for years now, and he would never forget the look on Muriel's face as she had breathed her last. He closed his eyes again to think about it. He could have saved her. He should have saved her. Maybe in a way he had killed her himself?

He blinked hard in hope that his eyes would open to a different world, one where he was someone to be admired rather than a source of constant disappointment. What kind of warrior empties his bladder in fear when he is needed most? The cycle of self-pity was all too familiar, but another scream rose up, calling him back into the moment as he realised the first one must have been real too.

Leaping from his bed, Cyrus ran to check on his sister and found her resting as she had been when he left. Returning to his room, he fetched the sword from beneath his bed, taking comfort in the deadly weight in his hand. The grip was wrapped with dark leather, and the pocked bronze guard was simple but for a slight curve in the metal, turning upward towards the blade. It was a stretch to call it beautiful, but it was well-balanced, and Cyrus appreciated the weapon's deadly efficiency as he tested it through the air. Heading for the door, Cyrus noticed an all-too-familiar glow of hot, orange light. He bit the inside of his lip to determine if he was suffering some new kind of nightmare, but he instantly knew it to be a frightening reality.

The heat of the blaze was immediate, and as he opened the door, the full extent of the noise hit him like another unwanted blow to the head. He started calling for his father and brother, like a lost child, but his voice went missing in the chaos around him. In every direction, men were fighting for their lives. Punching and stabbing and strangling and gouging. The faces were a blur, but Cyrus knew he had to do something lest he be next. Following the path away from the house, he found it difficult to comprehend how quickly things had changed. In just a few hours, the songs had turned to screams, and instead of villagers, it was flames that now danced throughout the village. Blade primed, he continued cautiously towards the market square before taking cover behind an overturned cart where three men from the village stood resolutely, waving pitchforks at their intruders to push them back.

"Leave now, and we'll spare your lives!" called one of the men, stabbing with a pitchfork as he snarled at their enemies. Cyrus recognised him as Lowell, a well-built farmer with shaggy red hair who had supplied the vegetables Cyrus had prepared with Aunt Aggie only a few hours before. Lowell was a good man, and Cyrus felt drawn by the need to help, but it was a fool's errand. They were outnumbered and outmatched, and the twisted yellow smiles of their antagonists gave hint to the outcome that would likely befall them.

The clash of metal sounded out as Cyrus slipped away in search of Osbert and Edgar. They had stationed themselves at the opening of a narrow bridge where their group was fighting desperately to stop the advance. Cyrus began to run for his father but found Osbert locked in struggle, probing with a fire iron as their well-armed enemies advanced.

It suddenly occurred to Cyrus just how scared he was. He was the only one with a sword, but did he actually intend to use it? His hands were shaking, and his body was numb as the noise around him grew distant: He was back in his own world, trapped within his head and victim to his own fears and doubts, as carnage raged all around him. He was oblivious to the attack that knocked him to the ground, but as Cyrus looked up at the blade above him, he realised that a part of him would be thankful for the release that it promised. He let his arms rest at his side and prepared to slip away as the sword lowered towards his chest. Blood and ash stained the man's face, and he showed no joy in his actions, but as time slowed, Cyrus watched his jaw fall and his eyes open wide before Edgar tore his body away.

"Get up!" screamed Edgar, removing a crude kitchen knife from the man's back to reach down and help Cyrus to his feet. "Where is Francine? Is she safe? You have to get out of here. Now!"

His voice grew clearer with every word, and Cyrus found himself back in the moment and filled once again with dread.

"I can help," he said, peering down to find that he still had his sword in his hand. He raised it as a sign of strength, but Edgar knocked the blade down with the palm of his hand before turning away dismissively.

"I said I can help!" shouted Cyrus, grabbing his brother to pull him back and immediately registering how childish he must sound.

"You just don't get it, do you, Cy?" shouted Edgar, grabbing his brother by the neck. "All of those stories and legends, and you still don't get it."

He pushed Cyrus away.

"People like me and dad, we fight so that you can live. So that you can do great things with those smarts of yours that everyone is always talking about." His head dropped, and his voice started to shake in a way that caused Cyrus's lips to tremble. "So that you can save Fran. Save her Cy, don't let this all be for nothing."

"Cy!" came his father's voice, running to interrupt. "Take Fran and head south towards Mistcliff. Their warden is Eustace, and he will see you both safe." He forced a smile that was intended to reassure Cyrus but instead revealed pink wounds around his mouth and gaps where teeth used to be. "We'll join you when this is over."

Cyrus stood speechless as his father and brother plunged back into the madness, both of them raising makeshift weapons in the same motion as they entered the fray once more. His was the only proper weapon among them. It wasn't a battle; it was a massacre.

Overcome with the thought of never seeing them again, Cyrus raised his sword and backed away, turning to run, but he only made it a couple of strides before colliding with a man who had appeared behind him. He had not seen him coming and could only guess at his lethal intentions, but the first thing Cyrus registered was the man's blood trickling down his own hands. He caught his reflection in the man's glazed eyes. They had been enemies, but he was still a man. A man with a family, perhaps, with hopes and with dreams, for certain. A man who he would always remember as his first.

Panicked, Cyrus left his sword protruding from the body and continued towards the house. The door was open when he arrived. He couldn't remember if he'd left it this way but was relieved to find the house yet untouched by fire or foe.

"Leave us alone!" called a small, frightened voice, and as Cyrus darted into Fran's room, he saw that she had taken cover under the bedsheets.

"It's okay. It's only me, Cyrus," he responded, rushing to her bedside. "I know it's scary, but you have to trust me."

Her expression was one of fear and confusion as she pulled back the covers, and the situation was alarmingly familiar to Cyrus, who took his sister by the arm and began to drag her away from danger as he had done years before, just minutes ago in his dream. Cyrus noticed how much quicker she had become and took some comfort in thinking that she might be too dazed to fully perceive the bloodshed around them.

Hands clasped together, they made for the woods, Cyrus's chest aching at the thought of their father and Edgar and all the others making sacrifices to see them safe. He wondered what had happened to the people that they knew. Bertram and his tavern, or Lowell. Who would tend to the crops if not Lowell? His heart raced at the thought of Alana as he wondered what might have been. Names and memories whirled through his head, and Cyrus scolded himself for giving up on them. A sudden tug at his arm told Cyrus that Fran had stumbled and fallen behind him. He expected her to cry out in pain but turned to find her shaking silently.

"Are you okay?" he asked, reaching to help, but as his eyes drew level with his sister's, he jerked back, recognising the cold, lifeless form that had broken her fall. It was Aunt Aggie. It was hard to imagine her so quiet and still, but even in death, Aggie still carried a cheery look upon her face. She was tenacious in a way Cyrus had always admired, and as he looked down at what was left of her, he prayed to muster some resolve of his own.

He wanted to stay with her longer and bury her body, but when Cyrus felt himself sinking again, a rider emerged with a torch in his hand, set to burning their homes.

"Run!" Cyrus shouted as the eyes of the rider fell upon them.

The stretch of grassland between the village and the woods was only short, but in that moment, the distance had never seemed greater. They received the briefest moment of hesitation before the rider kicked his horse into action, recklessly disregarding the flame in order to speed his pursuit. Cyrus was no longer able to hold his sister's hand, though he could hear her desperate breathing close behind. The sun was beginning to rise behind the trees, bathing them in a gentle orange glow that could not have been more different from what they had experienced back at the village, new details of the treeline emerging with every stride. Cyrus could sense that the rider was gaining on them as he whooped to drive his horse forward, Fran struggling to stifle her cries. They finally made it to the treeline, but Cyrus knew they were not safe yet, so he snatched Fran from her feet to take cover behind a nearby tree.

"It's okay, just stay completely silent," he whispered in reassurance, one hand covering her mouth as the other locked fingers with hers. He could feel the warmth and condensation of her rapid breathing on his hands, but he was anxious to calm her with the rider prowling nearby. Fran's heartbeat seemed to accelerate with every step the horse took, and Cyrus clamped his hand around her mouth even tighter as the rider stalled before slamming a heavy boot into the wet mud. Cyrus hadn't had chance to look at him previously, but their hunter was a broad man with thick stubble and dark hair tied at the back of his head. His boots were black to match the rest of his ensemble, a jerkin covered in dust and ash with a doublet tucked into his trousers. He looked like Death to Cyrus, who adjusted to embrace Fran as they pressed their backs hard into the trunk of the tree.

"I know you're out there," came the rider's voice, deep and rasping as he choked on a scratchy cough that suggested years of pipe smoking. He had an unusual accent, but his mocking tone suggested that he was enjoying his moment, while Fran's grip only tightened around Cyrus's chest. The sense of responsibility weighed down on Cyrus who buried his face in his sister's shoulder. The footsteps grew ever closer, and he knew they had to do something, but was he the right person to decide? The right person to follow?

"Now, Francine!" he whispered, his nerve breaking as a twig snapped beneath the foot of their pursuer. He had Fran's hand in his again, weaving in and out of the trees in an attempt to disorient the man in black. His only thought was to put distance between them, but as Francine started to slow, it became clear that their best hope was to hide once more.

A medley of earth tones flew by in the weak morning light as Cyrus dug deep into his mind to find his bearings. Just as frustration started to cloud his mind, the trees parted, and a small stone bridge suddenly appeared in front of them like salvation.

"Over there!" he motioned to his sister, dropping into ankle deep water that snatched his breath away before taking cover beneath the stone structure. For the first time that morning, Cyrus was relieved to find luck on their side as water trickled lightly in gullies, its flow broken by exposed rocks.

"We'll be safe here," he whispered, pulling them both behind a vast boulder, which was propped against the corner of the stonework above. Fran's head pressed tightly into him as they made themselves small, and though he hated the circumstances, he took a guilty satisfaction in feeling needed once more.

"Why is this happening again, Cyrus?" she asked in a helpless voice, but the sound of hooves grew closer as Cyrus opened his mouth to answer, forcing him into silence once more.

"You can't run, you know?" said the man in black, his voice—which was already familiar despite its strange inflections—sending shivers through Cyrus's body as they sat concealed by damp rocks. "We'll find you eventually and have you killed like everyone else in your stinking village."

He broke out into another bout of painful-sounding chest coughs before spitting remnants into the water nearby. "Simeon will take his lands back whether you like it or not."

Hooves echoed on the stones above them and continued halfway across the bridge before the rider halted his progress, cursing their escape. Turning back towards the village, his threats became increasingly distant, but Cyrus noticed that Fran never loosened her grip on his hands. Cold, damp, and afraid as they were, her breathing eventually grew calm, and the nightmare of the morning gradually gave way to fitful sleep.

CHAPTER
V

"I t's an act of war!" boomed Broderick from one end of the table, the vein on his forehead visibly throbbing as his fists slammed onto the dark, polished wood.

Chaos reigned in the Grand Hall of Eldred's Keep as Easthaven's most illustrious leaders and nobility gathered to discuss King Anselm's murder. Two days had passed, but emotions ran high among the assembly, with voices raised in disagreement and signs of frustration already beginning to show. Outside, the sky provided a bleak reflection of their mood, and sheets of rain lashed the castle, only adding to the discordance of their animated exchange. Though a pervading sadness characterized the room, none wore it more obviously than Garrett, who sat slouched as his mind wandered from the mayhem.

"Eight years of peace, and I never trusted those Auldhaven dogs," Broderick continued with a chorus of vocal support from his generals. "King Simeon wears a serpent's smile while we have allowed his murderous intent to slither into the heart of our capital. We've grown vulnerable, letting people live off of our charity when we should have been investing in our defences!"

He sat to mixed reactions as fingers pointed and voices raised even higher, while his closest followers proceeded to applaud the sentiment. Garrett, meanwhile, remained silent. He had always appreciated Broderick's honest patriotism but was beginning to fear the influence of bloodlust in such a charged atmosphere.

It was no surprise to Garrett that it was Thaddeus who chose this moment to rise. "These are sad times for us all, but can we first maintain some respect for the late king and indeed his son whose job it will be to navigate this most delicate of political situations?"

He paused, inclining his head to Augustus, who sat opposite Broderick at the end of the table. The young man remained silent, his face blank of expression, before a small nod of encouragement gave Thaddeus cause to continue.

"As much as I enjoyed your rather confusing animal analogy, Broderick, I think it is my place to remind you all that this was the act of one man. There is tenuous evidence to suggest anything more sinister. It is not for me to determine guilt either way, but I would certainly hazard caution in our approach."

Augustus sat in quiet consideration, his right hand twisting a small knife into the table for distraction until it became obvious that everyone expected him to respond. Thaddeus was an admirable speaker, and Garrett was relieved to hear the voice of reason, though this reprieve was short-lived.

"What say you, Garrett?" ventured Augustus with more than a hint of spite. "It seems strange that you're even here with my father absent. Did you not swear your life to protect his?"

Garrett's head dropped with an audible exhale of air, but he knew better than to respond. It seemed that his hands wouldn't stop shaking these days, but as he steadied one with the other, he was momentarily grateful for the distraction.

"Perhaps we should give Garrett a moment," said Wendell, placing a steady hand of reassurance on Augustus's shoulder before standing as though about to perform for the room. "Failure is difficult to swallow, even at the very best of times, but when it costs a life…" He made a small *tsk* and then pursed his lips, head tilted thoughtfully to one side. "Well, I can only imagine—the disappointment, the shame, the hopeless feeling that there is nothing more you can do." He waited a moment before pointing an accusatory finger in Garrett's direction. A finger that Garrett had to stop himself from breaking. "But must we all behave as this man?" He turned back to the prince, all eyes around the table resting on him as he did so. "They think us weak and vulnerable. They think that they can take our king without consequence. Will we sit back in pity while they come for us?"

"They're attacking our villages and terrorizing our people!" shouted Broderick, silencing Thaddeus, who had readied a reply to Wendell's speech. "Augustus, my king," he continued in a pleading tone. "You need only say the word, and I will take our troops west to meet Simeon and—"

"Relax, Broderick, and please be seated," Augustus said as he slammed the knifepoint into the table before proceeding to tap the arm of his chair with impatience. "It seems that we have grown complacent of late. My father was a great man, but he was naïve to danger and slow to act."

A momentary pause seemed to suggest that Augustus's words had caught up with him, though his face continued to mask his emotions.

"This will not be my way," he continued. "In fact, this is the very reason for the promptness of his funeral arrangements. Desperate times require decisive action, and I am committed to seeing justice served. Wendell, can we afford this war?"

The Master of Coin rustled papers in front of him importantly. "It will come at a great price, your Grace, but I have suggestions that will help to fund your campaign. It has already cost us your father, after all."

"Indeed, it has," Augustus said, bowing his head slightly and then rising to circle the group, "but we must ensure that Simeon is repaid in kind." He stood still, resting a closed fist against his mouth. "I have considered the situation and have decided that doing as Broderick has suggested is our only course."

"My king!" pleaded Garrett, finally rising to join the discussion before it was too late. "We will be outnumbered three to one! Besides, your father fought for the treaty, and we must respect it. It is his greatest legacy. Send word to Ferdinand and Mathilde, or parley with Simeon so his intentions are clear."

"Wait, you mean as we did before, ignorant to the world developing around us?" asked Augustus, snapping the room into silence. "No! You will have your war, Broderick, as soon as I have my crown." He stopped behind Garrett's chair, clasping his hands upon the older man's shoulders. "As for you, Garrett, you may yet have your chance at redemption. You will accompany me as you did my father, and together we will take the fight to our enemies."

Augustus stood tall and said, in a cheerful tone that raised eyebrows around the room, "But now, I shall take my throne."

Rain poured upon the people of Easthaven as they gathered for the coronation of their new king. Every path, passage, and street was lined with people as the earth turned to wet mud beneath them. A nervous energy passed among the well-wishers as brass instruments sounded and royal banners flapped in the breeze, indicating that celebrations would soon be underway.

Augustus stood peering from the window of his chambers, arms outstretched as the chamberlain proceeded to dress him in rich silks befitting the occasion.

"Wine!" he barked at no one in particular, and his expression froze for a moment as he was reminded of his late father, who always drank with such enthusiasm. Augustus had waited long enough for this opportunity, but it made the loss no less painful.

A flicker of a memory brought a smile to Augustus's face: a small prince bouncing upon his father's knee as Anselm sat proudly upon Isidore's chair, crown sparkling in the sunlight. It was a perfect moment, but not one to last, and Augustus's smile faded as his father vanished to leave the boy weeping helplessly, dwarfed by the size and weight of the crown.

He shook his head; it was not becoming of a king to show weakness. Now more than ever, people were looking to him for strength and security. He inhaled deeply to bury his emotions and watched Marcia leave to fetch the wine, while the chamberlain adjusted his ceremonial robe.

"There," said the chamberlain, stepping back with a look of satisfaction to admire his work. "You certainly have the look of a king."

Augustus caught his reflection in a nearby mirror and found himself surprised by the fully-fledged man before him. A small patch of stubble adorned his chin, and his hair was cropped short to belie his boyish looks. The chamberlain was not wrong; the ensemble was spectacular. He wore richly coloured silks of red and gold along with a girdle lined with precious stones, his robe trimmed with elaborate furs. He *did* look like a king, he thought, and in that moment, he wondered what his father would have made of him.

"Your wine, my king," gestured Marcia gently, drawing him back into the moment.

He glanced to gauge what she thought of his new look, but he was met with the same cold and evasive behaviour as always— eyes averted from him as though he didn't deserve her attention. He, the king!

"About time," he replied, taking the glass forcefully from her hand, a splash of red landing dangerously close to his boots.

He paced about the room swilling his wine, stopping to take a mouthful as Marcia began to scrub the hardwood floor.

"Ugh!" he grimaced, considering the taste. "What is this pond water? Something from your own personal collection, commoner? Are you trying to poison me now?"

Marcia stopped her task, speechless in the face of the new king's anger.

"Answer me, woman!" Augustus continued, moving to intimidate the girl with his presence. "Would you have served this to my father? Is this wine fit for a king?"

"No, my lord," came Marcia's whimpered response, still on her knees as the prince loomed over her. "I will fetch another, perhaps one of your father's favoured vintages from Nivelle?"

Augustus felt his face bunching into a scowl. It seemed she hadn't learnt her lesson at all. What did he have to do to get her attention? Whatever the answer, his patience had run out.

"You're right, lowborn; this wine is far from befitting a king. And yet…" He paused, tipping his glass so that the remainder of the wine trickled onto her. "It's still wasted on you."

He placed the empty glass on a table, straightened his robe, and made for the door as wine dripped slow and pronounced from Marcia's hair.

"Make sure this is clean by the time I return. A mess like this would be no way to welcome your new king."

Garrett adjusted the prince's extravagant outfit as he helped Augustus onto his horse. He had to admit that the young man looked impressive, if perhaps unsuitably dressed for the conditions. Augustus's stallion was named Allegro, and he was the most majestic creature that Garrett had ever seen. He was pure white but with a shine that suggested silver, like the glow of a unicorn that had often occupied Garrett's childhood dreams. His body was lean but strong, and he stood with great height and poise to match. He was fit for a king and every bit equal to the occasion.

Garrett eventually mounted his own horse, drawing level with Thaddeus and the dowager Queen Adaline, already astride their own steeds, to complete their train. Ahead of them, General Broderick rode at the spearhead with his men on either flank guarding the procession. Augustus reached across to kiss his mother's hand before beginning their short journey, the portcullis retracting before them. The atmosphere seemed unusual to Garrett, who felt a heavy sense of loss present in the crowd. Flowers rained down on Augustus as he proceeded at a gentle canter, but the celebrations were subdued, and many stood dressed in black.

"You see? They love me already!" said Augustus, turning in his saddle with a wide smile upon his face.

Garrett chose to nod rather than comment as they arrived at the basilica. The volume of the crowd fell away as Thaddeus and Wendell assisted the riders from their horses, and Broderick's men turned to form a guard at the foot of the grand staircase. Augustus flashed a final princely wave to enthusiastic applause, while Garrett took the queen by her hand as they continued through the holy doors.

Reserved for royal attendance and occasions, the Basilica of Highcastle was a truly breath-taking piece of architecture, from the broad aisles that welcomed their group to the inconceivably tall and intricate apex at the centre. Poor weather provided dim light but for occasional strands of colour extending into the room through vibrant glass windows, which complemented the rows of candles that lined the walls.

Rain continued to beat down on the dome above them, but this only drew attention to the magnificent arched stonework of the ceiling, each drop reverberating as friends, family, and other nobility watched Augustus approach the apse.

Ahead of them, the Master of Prayer, Cornelius stood with arms extended to welcome the group. He was a wiry old man with long grey hair and beard, dressed in immaculate white robes with elegant gold trim. All but Augustus took their seats, with Wendell and Broderick on one side of the aisle and the others opposite.

"Men and women of Easthaven," the Master of Prayer began, gesturing for Augustus to kneel before him. "We are gathered today for a most momentous occasion…"

Adaline nudged Garrett in his side, breaking his concentration.

"It's all so soon," she whispered in a sad tone with tears gathering in her eyes. "He's just a boy."

Garrett heard a cough from the row behind them and decided to rest his response as the ceremony unfolded before them.

"I don't blame you, Garrett," Adaline continued. "You should know that. Anselm loved you, and I know you loved him back."

Garrett shifted his eyes in the Queen's direction to indicate that he was listening, but he continued facing ahead in silence.

"I won't deny that he can be a foolish boy, but he's all that I have left, Garrett. Promise me you will keep him safe. Promise me."

Choral music began to swell as the Master of Prayer placed the crown onto Augustus's head. It was a simple design, but it shimmered gold, reflecting all other light in the room and drawing attention to an opulent inlay of ruby gemstones.

"I promise," said Garrett, inaudible to all except Adaline, as the room erupted with applause. Augustus rose to his feet a king.

The basilica doors opened, and the king made his way back down the aisle to find that the rain had passed. Garrett took his place at the king's side before each row of people began to join them, in order from front to back, following Augustus towards the atrium. Outside, the sun beamed down on the impressive staircase of the basilica, and as all others descended, Garrett remained at the top, close to the king, mindful of his promise to Adaline.

"Good people of Easthaven, welcome to a bright new era!" began Augustus, laughing jovially at his joke as he gestured to the sky.

Garrett looked on, impressed at the young man's confidence and yet equally concerned with an apparent lack of sadness at his father's untimely death.

As though Augustus had read Garrett's mind, he continued, "I know am not alone in my sadness at King Anselm's passing, but from my father's great work, we have a platform to build on."

Cries of support and sympathy echoed throughout the audience before the king showed raised palms, gesturing them to stop. "Together we will be stronger!" he shouted with narrowed eyes demonstrating a steely determination that saw fists raised into the air in the crowd before him. "No longer will our enemies think us weak or vulnerable!"

Raindrops started to fall once again, and Garrett saw Wendell and Broderick applauding wildly, eyes wide as the young king drew his sword from its sheath. The sky turned grey as clouds blotted out the sun, and Garrett rested his hand on his sword while Broderick's men struggled to contain the frenzied energy of the crowd.

Still Augustus pressed on, "We will take the fight to Simeon and see justice served! King Anselm will be avenged, and our enemies will know better than to underestimate us!"

Augustus paused and glanced at Wendell who gestured back with a nod of approval, the look of a proud father.

"But with great deeds come great sacrifices," continued the king, signalling to quell the boisterous atmosphere that he had so expertly created. "War comes at a price, and an army cannot feed on victory alone." He brushed rainwater from his eyes, as expressions of concern began to appear in the crowd. "Taxes will inevitably increase, and we can no longer support your hunger with charity."

Garrett moved closer to the king, motioning for the horses to be prepared as defiant hand gestures began to replace shows of support.

"Know that you will have all played your part in this historic campaign," Augustus finished, as Garrett helped him onto the back of Allegro. "We ride for the Low Country at first light!"

The first signs of daybreak appeared above Eldred's Keep as Broderick assembled his troops in flawless formation to welcome their king. Two thousand men gathered in the courtyard, armed and in silent attention but with purposeful looks upon their faces. They wore light armour typical of Easthaven, designed to allow free movement in battle: quilted jackets of deep red with breastplates carrying the royal insignia of a blazing sun.

An air of impatience was developing as Thaddeus and Garrett stood observing Broderick rouse his men.

"This is madness, you know?" urged Thaddeus, resting his forehead in his hands as the king emerged to survey his army. "It risks everything his father built and endangers us all."

"You're right as always, Thaddeus, but the boy is king now, and you can hardly blame him for wanting to avenge his father and make a name for himself, all in one fell swoop." Garrett placed a hand on Thaddeus's arm as a smile crept across his face. "Send all your prayers in hopes that we return. I made a promise to the queen to protect Augustus, and I would ask that you do the same for Adaline whilst I am away."

"Of course," responded Thaddeus, watching as the king mounted his horse to indicate their departure. "Be safe, Garrett, but be the voice of reason you were to his father. You have nothing to prove to anyone—"

"Garrett!" exclaimed Augustus interrupting their exchange with his sword pointed to the exit. "I'm so sorry to interrupt your cosy little chat, but don't you think it's time we move before more of our people die?"

Garrett waved a reluctant gesture of acknowledgment to his king before meeting Thaddeus in a strong embrace. "Goodbye, old friend. I will see you, in this life or the next."

Garrett forced a smile before climbing onto the saddle of his mount and following the silent procession out of the castle gates.

It felt like they had been walking for weeks. Cyrus knew from the sun and the moon that it had only been two days, but Francine had really started to slow and was beginning to complain. They were hungry, cold, and had struggled to dry fully from their recent escape. Sores had begun to appear on their feet, patience was wearing thin, and in truth, they were wandering more in hope than expectation.

Since leaving their seclusion under the bridge, they had followed Osbert's instruction to head south. Their route had taken them through woodland, over verdant hills sprinkled with the colours of spring, and out onto the open plains of Freyburn, which seemed to stretch endlessly before them. Night-time was the hardest. With no blankets for warmth, it was vital that they found shelter. A protruding rock on the incline of a hill had provided cover for the first night, and Cyrus had even been able to maintain a small fire, though he had scolded himself for failing to provide food.

By the second night, however, they had reached the vast and exposed grasslands of the Lowland Steppe, rolling fields of green under an enormous cloudless sky. This was a featureless landscape in which Cyrus had felt himself losing hope and direction in equal measure. After many hours of walking, they had caught the trail of some deer, which led them to a small patch of vegetation and a solitary tree. At first, Cyrus had thought it a trick of the mind, a mirage on the hopeless horizon, but the oasis was real, providing them with a trunk to rest against and a few straggly bushes with red berries on which to feed. Once more, Cyrus had gathered firewood to burn, but with the setting sun and rising winds, it had been impossible to sustain the flame. He had felt Fran shake with cold, her stomach growling fiercely and her tears falling onto his sleeve as he held her. In that moment, his stories of adventure hadn't seemed so exciting anymore, and he had rocked her in gentle silence until they were both taken by sleep.

They woke feeling sore and more tired than before, but after another meagre handful of berries for breakfast, Cyrus had encouraged a reluctant Fran to continue their journey.

Neither of them spoke of what happened in Corhollow. It was as though they had repressed the memories as Cyrus had previously tried to do with their memories of Coldwynne. Instead, they spent the morning in a cycle of grumbles and protests, harsh responses and periods of silence as the monotony of their surroundings bore down on them. That was, at least, until afternoon broke, and with the sun at its highest, the atmosphere started to change. A warm breeze carried the sweet scent of spring, and a spattering of peaks and knolls added texture to the landscape.

"Over here!" called Cyrus excitedly, gesturing Fran to the crest of a small hill while shielding his eyes from the midday sun.

"Can you hear that, Fran?" he continued, his smile breaking out as the distant sounds of village life hummed in the air. "This has to be Mistcliff. We made it!"

Fran threw her arms around her brother, her smile turning to a wince as it stretched the cracks in her dried lips. "Water and food and even people!" she added, wrestling to untangle the curls in her matted hair while climbing to join Cyrus at the highest point.

Cyrus breathed a sigh of relief as farmland sprawled below them: two expanses of land lined with crops and separated by a track that led to the village.

"I'll race you to the bottom!" cried Fran, somehow finding the energy to sprint ahead.

Cyrus ran to join her, careful with his footing on the steep hill.

"Slow down!" he called, shaking his head at how much he sounded like Osbert, a thought that amused him briefly before he realised with a jolt of nausea that he might never hear his father's voice again.

The wind rushed past them as the landscape became a blur, and for just a moment, they were children again. Fran was as he always saw her in his mind: a young girl without a care in the world. Her hair streamed behind her as she reached the track that would lead them towards town. She called out in exhilaration, and though Cyrus couldn't decipher the words, he loved to hear the joy in her voice, so he allowed the sound to wash over him as though it would clear away all of his troubles.

"I win!" came her voice, and he was back in the moment. She had decided to stop halfway up the track, arms raised in victory as the sounds of the village rolled in. The ring of metal echoed from the forge, and raised voices called out as if sharing Fran's celebrations.

Then suddenly a man appeared between the village gates. Cyrus could only distinguish dark hair at first, but as he started towards them, his features grew ever clearer to reveal the urgent look upon his face. Cyrus could tell that the man was calling for someone, but as he looked around him, he realised that the man's warnings could only be aimed at them.

"What is he saying?" asked Fran, turning as the man continued to close their distance.

"He's telling us to run," came Cyrus's reply taking his sister by the hand and standing firmly at her side.

"You have to get out of here!" shouted the man as he drew level with them, hands on his knees as he breathed heavily with exertion. He raised himself to run his hands through his long, dark hair, eyes twitching between Cyrus and the village. "Auldhaven— their troops—they're here, and they mean to kill us all. You have to leave!"

"Just like Corhollow," muttered Cyrus weakly, peering beyond the man to nowhere in particular. "We need to find Eustace," he said, his voice breaking with the panic that had descended upon him. "Is he in Mistcliff?"

"He was," said the man, his eyes full of fear as they twitched between the village and the space beyond Cyrus and Fran. "You'll have to see what Simeon has left of him."

With that, he pushed between them, running in the direction from which they had arrived.

"What are we going to do? Are we going to die?" asked Fran, the look of fear and expectancy obvious on her face.

An all-too-familiar sense of anxiety crept over Cyrus, but he knew that his sister needed him to be strong, so took a moment to gather his thoughts before answering her. It was the right choice, and his words came out far more confident and assured than he was feeling.

"It's up to you, Fran, but we can't run forever. We need to eat, and we need water. Perhaps we can find Eustace and find a way out of here. Will you come with me?"

Fran nodded without hesitation, brushing teardrops from her face, and Cyrus heard her sniffling as they headed for the village. When they arrived, it was as though they had never left Corhollow. Soldiers terrorized unarmed village folk, and Cyrus rubbed at his eyes to clear the faces of friends and family from each corpse lining the road. He felt like a harbinger of death for every place he had ever been, but he emerged from his despair as Fran forced them into cover behind a low fence.

"Can you hear that?" she asked, pointing to the village gates with uncertainty in her voice, turning her head slightly as if angling her ear towards the sound would help to clarify its origin. After a moment, she said, "Horses!"

The first Cyrus saw was a cloud of dust, but as their hooves beat down, closer with every step, he saw that she was right.

"They're carrying King Anselm's banner!" he whispered, shaking his sister's shoulders with a mixture of relief and excitement before repositioning to ensure that he remain concealed. "We're saved, and we can tell the king about Corhollow. Perhaps we can still save the village!"

He knew it was blind optimism, but as the riders soared past them into the village, Cyrus felt a sense of hope that he thought had left him back in Corhollow.

The horses and their heavily armoured riders came three across and ten deep, sweeping into the market square and bringing terror onto the faces of their opposition. Scythed down in front of Cyrus's eyes, Simeon's troops were instantly scattered and divided while Cyrus lived every cut and every thrust, exhilarated by the action as though he was watching one of his stories unfold right in front of him.

In the middle of it all rode a tall man on a black horse. His dark hair was short and plastered to his head with sweat, his beard well-maintained against his pronounced cheeks and jaw. He had lines etched across his face, a medley of scars, and the early signs of wrinkles, but his ferocity showed no signs of age.

"Onward!" called the man, indicating the narrow lanes of the village with his sword. "Clear the way and leave none of Simeon's men alive!"

Cyrus crept above the fence to watch the riders follow the man's orders, spreading about the village and cutting down all that stood in their paths. This man and his cavalry were so captivating that Cyrus didn't even notice when a new rider entered the scene.

"Good work, Garrett," came the voice of a younger man, a voice of unmistakably good breeding with perfect diction and more than a hint of pomposity. "Now let's clear this mess and move to the next village. We have Simeon in retreat, and Broderick's troops will join us shortly to press victory."

Cyrus's eyes narrowed as he struggled to absorb the features of the young man who had positioned himself beyond the warrior,

Garrett. He was too young to be King Anselm, but he sat astride a beautiful white steed in dazzling plate armour that signified title and position. He had short golden hair, a light dusting of beard, and a boyish face, though Cyrus thought the boy must be around his own age.

"Cyrus," whispered Fran, tugging at his sleeve to draw his attention, but he was too fixated on the young man in front of them.

If the man wasn't Anselm, where was the king, and why was this boy's face so familiar?

"Cyrus," Fran tried again, as Garrett and the newcomer continued their conversation with Cyrus listening intently.

"Cyrus!" she whispered more loudly, punching his arm.

"I know," said Cyrus solemnly, turning slowly to face her as it dawned on him.

"It's like you're here and there at the same time," she said with her brow furrowed, pointing at the boy on the white horse. "That man is your reflection."

"King Augustus!" came a cry as one of the riders raced back into the market square. "Simeon's men, it was a—"

An arrow caught the man through his back, causing him to fall from his horse as armed men from Auldhaven poured into view from all angles. Garrett reared his horse, dashing to cover the young king with riders from Easthaven appearing to even the odds.

The king? thought Cyrus. *But what happened to Anselm?*

He lowered himself to cover Fran as a body fell limp in front of the fence that shielded them from view. His eyes twitched from one tussle to the next, the last cries of men calling to him, and in that moment, he realised that there is nothing heroic in death.

76

"Drive them back!" cried Garrett, hacking to sever the head of his enemy. He was lost in the heat of battle and lost in the moment, but he wouldn't lose another king. Simeon's men were well-armed and well-trained, but the advantage of being astride horses was working in favour of Augustus's troops, and Garrett could sense that the tide was turning.

"To the left flank!" he cried, gesturing to a point where enemy archers had begun to gather. The market square was small, and he knew better than to be pinned by enemy fire.

Archers loosed arrows in panic as horses rushed towards them, with men trampled and riders thrown from their mounts as wayward shafts cut through the air at random. Garrett turned his horse to find one of Simeon's men grappling to wrestle Augustus from his horse. The king was without his sword but fighting to release a knife from his belt in retaliation.

"To the king!" Garrett shouted, ushering his horse forward, but an arrow lashed into the hindquarters of the beast, and the world turned onto its side. An excruciating pain spread through his legs; the full weight of the horse rested on top of him as chaos continued all around. His sword was within reach, but it took the very tips of his fingers to recover it with an enemy bearing down.

"Die, scum!" screamed a toothless man as Garrett met his attack with an impulsive block. The horse had stopped moving, trapping Garrett, who writhed for freedom while parrying for his life under the unrelenting assault. He could feel the sword loosening in his hand with every strike, and when it crashed to the ground beside him, he sensed the end was near.

Cyrus had only known these people for a matter of moments—that's if you could say that he knew them at all given that he had never spoken to them. Still, he felt the power of every blow they received, including the one that took the blade from Garrett's hand. Cyrus knew nothing of this man, but he wasn't ready for his story to end. In his actions, Cyrus saw the fighting spirit of everyone he had loved and lost, of every hero from his years of storytelling. He couldn't let him die.

"No!" Cyrus screamed, causing the toothless attacker to twist momentarily. Garrett took this moment of distraction to tear the arrow from his horse and drive it into his adversary's gut.

"What are you doing?" called Fran, pulling him back into cover. "You'll get us killed."

Her voice was distant, and Cyrus remained transfixed by the action. Garrett continued to struggle away from underneath his mount, while the king had fallen from his saddle and was stabbing a knife into his enemy's chest repeatedly, blood spraying his face and breastplate.

"We have to do something," said Cyrus to Fran, as the king rose in a daze and ran for one of the narrow passages away from the market square. "Stay here and stay covered. I'll come back for you."

Tears welled in Fran's eyes once more. "But what about you?" she asked, pulling him back by the arm.

"I'll be fine," he answered with the last of his composure. "I'll be back for you, I promise."

Fran's grip loosened, and Cyrus darted away to follow the king's path. It was little more than a gap between rows of houses just like those back in Corhollow, or at least they were like those that had been in Corhollow before the attack, anyway.

Frightened faces peered out of windows as Cyrus ran by, and he arrived to find the king slashing desperately with a knife as three men backed him towards the edge of a cliff. The king's contorted expression was somewhere between fear and madness, with blood covering his upper body and the ominous sound of rocks falling away behind him.

"Stay back!" he screamed, but as Cyrus ducked behind a tall bag of grain, all he could hear was laughter in response.

"You hear that, boys? The king has given his orders," said one of the men in a voice that rang with familiarity in Cyrus's ears. "Maybe his Grace would like to drop his little knife, and we can discuss this politely?"

The three men continued laughing in unison, and though Cyrus couldn't see them, he imagined the sniggering faces of the villagers in Corhollow when Edgar had humiliated him. He remembered the mocking laugh of the man who had killed Fran's mother and the grin of the man that faced down Lowell and the others as they had pillaged the village.

The men laughed and laughed until one of them stopped, and the dry rasping cough of a habitual pipe smoker left Cyrus in no doubt as to the man's identity. Cyrus leapt out and immediately lost his balance, stumbling forward before his blade tore into the back of the first man, who folded without ever seeing Cyrus's face.

"You!" exclaimed the same man in black who had chased Cyrus and Fran out of Corhollow, lashing out with his sword.

Cyrus dodged the man's wild swipe to stand like a mirror image beside the king. Their likeness was uncanny, and as Augustus removed his robe, Cyrus knew that they were virtually indistinguishable.

"Enough!" shouted the man in black, drawing Cyrus's mind away from the resemblance between the king and himself.

The man in black darted at Cyrus blade first as his partner raced towards the king. Cyrus deflected the attack with a surprising level of skill that he attributed to adrenaline. They had switched places, and he now had the opportunity to push his adversary back towards the cliff-edge, but he could see the king locked in struggle, his arm around the other man's neck as they fought for control of the knife.

"Hold on!" Cyrus shouted, driving forward as the wide-eyed expression on his enemy's face betrayed his fear. Over and over, Cyrus swung in anger, and with his teeth clenched and face turning red, the man in black lost his footing on loose gravel, inviting Cyrus's sword into his midriff and forcing him to his knees. Cyrus kicked his beaten foe to the ground, raising his blade for the kill, but as the edge lowered, he heard the king cry out, and he turned to find that it was all too late.

Cyrus's jaw dropped as the king fell away over the edge, dragged down by the clawing hands of his enemy. They never let go of each other as they fell, and Cyrus wondered if they would continue fighting until the ground below gave the last word.

He couldn't believe this was happening, that he had just watched the king die before his eyes, but as Cyrus made for the ledge, a sharp, stabbing pain suddenly spiked in his lower back. He felt his legs turn to stone, and his brows lowered in confusion as he touched his back and found blood on his hand.

The next he knew, he was on the floor, and the man in black lay beside him, blood gurgling in his efforts to force one final laugh before he was silent and still.

Tears formed in Cyrus's eyes as he tore at the ground to crawl away.

He had to get to Fran.

He had to save her.

He dragged himself inch by inch to where the king's robe lined the ground, but as he fell to his back in utter exhaustion, a boot appeared above him, then all was black.

It took the last of Garrett's energy to crawl out from beneath his horse. He tested his leg, and though the pain brought a grimace, nothing was broken, and he was able to stumble away.

"Look out!" came a cry, causing him to stoop instinctively as an axe flew past and into the shoulder of one of Simeon's men. The man's face went pale as he dropped to the ground beside Garrett, and a young rider approached.

"Garrett, are you okay?" the rider asked. "I think that's the last of them. It was just a fraction of Simeon's army, which means that the rest of them must be gathered nearby. Should we regroup and prepare to advance?"

"No," said Garrett assertively, working the muscles in his upper leg. "We should wait for Broderick's reinforcements and plan our next step. Right now, our priority is the safety of—"

Garrett's head jerked and rotated, almost owl-like, until his eyes settled on a single white horse, bloodstained but still upright among the slaughter.

"The king," he said, his heart racing. "Where is the king?"

The young rider stood wide-eyed in panic until their silence was broken by strained laughter.

"We have your king," came the voice of the man with the axe in his shoulder, a trembling smile exaggerated by the moustache upon his lip. "Our men took him, and his fate will soon rest in Simeon's hands."

The man winced as Garrett grabbed him aggressively by the throat. "Where are they taking him?" demanded Garrett with spit lashing the face of the dying man as Garrett dragged him from the ground and applied pressure to the axe. "Tell me, and I'll end this quickly."

"Eriwald," came a gasped response, teeth gritted against the pain as Garrett pushed harder. "Simeon is using the city as a base to reclaim the Low Country. He had no idea that Anselm's son would be here, but I saw our men take him. Please, let me—"

Garrett buried a knife in the man's chest before letting him fall to the floor. "Tell Broderick all we know," he commanded the young rider, making hastily for the king's horse. "Tell him to reinforce these towns and villages against further attacks."

He climbed into the saddle and called back as they galloped away from the village. "Tell him I won't return until I have the king!"

C old water slapped Cyrus in the face, causing him to draw his breath in sharply as his eyes opened slowly to let in the daylight.

"Wake up, your lordship," came a sneering voice as Cyrus struggled to settle his breathing.

Heavy drops of water began to drip from his hair and eyes. A man's face came into view, revealing a long scar that ran from his forehead to his cheek across his left eye, which was permanently closed.

"Eat this," continued the man, dropping a piece of charred meat where Cyrus sat. "I can't have you dying before we get you to Simeon." He narrowed his eyes at Cyrus as he scratched at his own greasy golden hair. "And no funny business. I'm the nice guy around here, but there is a group of rather unpleasant men over there that think we'd be better killing you now to save ourselves some effort. Am I clear?"

Cyrus nodded as he registered a group of armed men gathered around the fire nearby, the smell of cooked meat carrying in the air as his stomach groaned with hunger.

"Excellent," finished the man, flashing a yellow smile at Cyrus as he gestured towards his men. "Now if you don't mind, I'm going to go and share a drink with that horrible bunch over there."

Cyrus watched the man re-join the group as laughter rose into the air and drink swilled from tankards as they crashed together. They had chosen to camp by a river, which flowed high against the bank but with a gentle motion that helped to calm some of Cyrus's anxiety. He noticed that the men had a wagon and two horses tethered to a tree, but each man sat with a pack of supplies, the glare of the fire reflecting ominously on an assortment of steel.

"I see you met Brogan," came a voice, startling Cyrus, but heavy chains restricted his movement as a shot of pain tore through his back to remind him of the battle at Mistcliff. The voice belonged to a man, certainly older than Cyrus was, and it seemed to have sounded from behind him.

"Ah yes, the chains. You get used to them after a while," the voice continued, but the man remained out of view, hidden by the width of the tree to which Cyrus realised he was chained.

The man chuckled to himself. "He said he was going to keep an eye on me when he introduced himself, and—forget the sword he was carrying—I damn near died of laughter right there!"

Feet appeared to Cyrus's left as the man shimmied himself around the tree and into view. "The name's Seth," he said, the chains restricting his efforts at a handshake. "This isn't how I imagined meeting you, but it's a pleasure all the same."

The man looked to be near Osbert's age, with his head shaved but for the top, where hair sat in a tight knot upon the crown of his head. Cyrus noticed gold in his mouth when he smiled, replacing one of his front teeth.

Unsure of what to say, Cyrus responded with a lazy nod of the head before turning to hide a frown at the man's over-familiar behaviour.

"It's okay," he continued. "I understand. I was sad to hear what happened to your father. He was a truly great man." Seth sighed as his voice turned sad. "Of all the ways to die."

Cyrus's stomach dropped. "Die?" he asked, lowering his voice as Brogan looked back at them before returning to his drink. "What do you know of my father?"

"Well, only that he was poisoned."

"Poisoned?" exploded Cyrus, pushing outward at the chains as pains shot through his body, leaving him lightheaded.

Seth's eyes twitched between Cyrus and their captors as he shuffled around the tree to close the gap between them. "Relax," he said as his eyes dropped in sadness. "They bandaged the wound on your back, but it sounds like you lost a fair bit of blood, and your face is full of bruises."

"The boot to the face," muttered Cyrus, working his jaw to uncover a number of new pains.

"Right," came Seth's response with a nod. "Well, either way you've taken a real knock to the head. Your memories will return in time, your Grace."

Cyrus closed his eyes tight and took a deep breath to compose himself before tilting his head towards Seth in response. "Why are you calling me that, and what do you know about my father?"

"You really don't remember, do you?" Seth answered gently, shaking his head. "Your father was poisoned during his birthday celebrations. Now you're king, Augustus, and—"

"Shut up over there! Some of us are trying to enjoy a quiet drink!" shouted Brogan.

Cyrus's confusion turned to a disbelieving snort of laughter at Seth's story. "I think you have me confused with someone else," he said. "I'm no king. I'm just a village storyteller. I'm nobody!"

Seth went to speak and then paused for a moment, biting his lower lip as he considered Cyrus. "Well, I think I'd keep that from Brogan and his friends if I were you. It's the only thing keeping you alive." He looked Cyrus up and down. "But if you aren't Augustus, then why are you wearing his robe?"

Cyrus glanced down to find himself covered by the bloodstained robe Augustus had thrown to the ground as they fought together on the ledge.

"I don't know," he whispered, his eyes rolling upward as he tried to piece the events together. "But my name is Cyrus, and I live…" He stopped for a moment as recent events replayed in his mind. "I lived in a village called Corhollow."

"Ah, Corhollow!" said Seth with a wide grin. "Yes, I know it well. Trade has taken me through those lands on many occasions. Who is your father?"

"Osbert," said Cyrus, straightening his back against the tree in hopes that Seth might have some information on his family's whereabouts.

"Good old Osbert," he responded nodding in recollection. "One of the finest swordsmen I have ever seen. His skills are legend throughout the Low Country."

The corners of Cyrus's mouth climbed into his first real smile since the events at Mistcliff.

"It has been years since I saw Ozzie," Seth continued. "But hang on a minute?" He turned his head to the side, narrowing his eyes in thought. "Osbert only had one son, Edwin or something."

"Edgar," said Cyrus. "His name was Edgar." His head drooped as hope seemed to be snatched from his grasp prematurely. "Osbert adopted me and my sister, Fran, eight years ago after our village was attacked, but it seems that Simeon still wasn't ready to let us live in peace."

"No, it doesn't seem so," agreed Seth edging the final few inches around the tree to rest at Cyrus's side. "I heard Brogan and his men discussing how the village had been burned to the ground." Seth must have noticed how Cyrus's face dropped because he nudged him with a shoulder, clearly trying to raise Cyrus's spirits. "But your old dad was a survivor," Seth continued, "and you know how handy he is with a sword. I'm sure he made it out and saved your brother and sister."

"I left my sister in Mistcliff," Cyrus said miserably.

"You did what?" It was the older man's turn to close his eyes in disbelief, and Cyrus imagined that he would have put his head in his hands if he could.

"We were coming to speak to the warden, Eustace," said Cyrus. "I thought I could do something, maybe even save the villagers."

A round of raucous applause broke out from Brogan's gang as one of the men finished his drink and balanced the tankard on the top of his head, much to the delight of the others. The light was starting to fade, and Cyrus grabbed at the meat that Brogan had left with shackled hands, wondering how long it had been since he had last eaten. The meat was so burnt it was nearly inedible, but Cyrus wasn't going to be picky at a time like this.

"I fear that Mistcliff suffered a similar fate to Corhollow," continued Seth, "but she might have survived."

"Maybe," came Cyrus's muted reply. He wanted to scream at the injustice or threaten Brogan for standing in the way of his search, but recent events had caught up with him, and his body sagged as he wiped grease from his mouth before dropping the leftover bone in defeat.

Seth considered the discarded bone for a moment before a smile reappeared on his face. "Can I have that?" he asked, eyes suddenly alight with mischief.

"Why?" responded Cyrus, nudging the bone towards Seth.

"Because in my experience, hope tends to find you when you need it the most."

"What are you talking about?" demanded Cyrus impatiently as Seth leant across to him.

"You never asked, but I'm a blacksmith by trade," he said, squinting at the bone as he turned it in his hands.

"And?" asked Cyrus, but even as he asked it, Seth forced the sharp end of the bone into the lock around his hands. Cyrus's eyes widened.

"Who do you think makes these things?" Seth asked, grinning as the lock clicked open and Cyrus's hands fell loose.

"Wake up. It's time," whispered Seth, as Cyrus opened his eyes to find that darkness had descended upon the campsite, their dwindling fire providing the last of the light. An ensemble of snores, snorts, and wheezes replaced earlier revelry, with the exception of Brogan, who sat facing the river, singing quietly under his breath.

"Are you going to be able to go through with this? You're cut pretty bad," said Seth, but Cyrus only nodded soundlessly before letting his head fall slack, just as they had discussed.

"Perfect," he heard Seth say, the chains clanking as he adjusted himself. "Brogan," he called out, loud enough to gain his attention without rousing the others. "We need you over here. I think the boy has stopped breathing!"

"What?" Cyrus heard Brogan respond impatiently, cursing under his breath as he made his way over to the tree where they were bound.

"He said he was having real pain from that cut in his back earlier, but he isn't responding anymore. You'd better check him." Seth's voice was earnest, entirely believable. Cyrus was impressed.

"Oh, I'll check him all right," said Brogan, leaning down to search Cyrus for a pulse. "King Simeon will kill me if—"

Seth snapped across from where he was sitting, slamming the pointed edge of the bone into Brogan's right eye before grappling him to the ground to cover his mouth. It was all so quick and silent, but Cyrus watched as Seth choked the life out of their captor, his legs kicking until his body went still.

"I'd been looking forward to that," said Seth gently, taking Brogan's sword from his sheath. "Are you ready?"

Cyrus twisted loose of his chains and made to stand but was lucky when Seth caught him as his legs gave out.

"Take it steady, boy," he added, "and perhaps you'd be better off without that robe?"

Cyrus agreed and cast the heavy garment from his shoulders, using it to cover Brogan's body. When he turned back to Seth, Cyrus found his new companion staring at his back, wincing with deep lines around the corner of his eyes.

"Your cut," Seth finally said, reaching for a branch that was on the ground beside him. Cyrus couldn't figure out what he wanted with a branch, but before he could ask him what he was doing, Seth continued, "It doesn't look so good. You should get going."

"What?" asked Cyrus with a raised eyebrow. "What about you?"

"Oh, I'll join you shortly," Seth added, "I just have something I need to do first."

"Are you crazy?" Cyrus asked, his mouth falling open.

Seth paused for a moment, scratching his head as he seemed to consider his reply. "Do you know why they kept me alive?" he asked.

Cyrus shook his head in response.

"Simeon is raiding all of the towns and villages of the Low Country. Yes, he wants his land back, and yes, he wants to send a message to the people, but he is here to gather the trades that he needs to support his army." Seth stopped to point the branch at Brogan's wagon, his men sleeping by the fire. "You see that cart over there? It's full of the tools and materials he needs to make weapons." He paused to calm the growing frustration in his voice. "The tools that *I* would need to make weapons."

Cyrus remained silent, adjusting his hips and back in an effort to find some comfort in his new upright position, as Seth continued.

"I will not be part of this. I will not contribute to Simeon's war effort. Too many good people have suffered already. But you have to go!"

"Come with me," pleaded Cyrus, grabbing Seth by the arm, even as the man made towards the fire.

Seth sighed as he turned to release Cyrus's grasp. "I had a family once," he started. "A wife and a daughter."

Cyrus watched as the older man took a deep inhale of breath and his jaw trembled.

"It has been ten years now, but he took them, and it still hurts just as much today as it did then." Tears welled in the corner of his eyes, glistening in the moonlight. "I won't see this happen to others. Get moving. There is something I must do!"

Seth pushed Cyrus away as he crept towards the campfire and set light to the branch, waving Cyrus to leave as he pressed flames against the wood panelling of the wagon. The last Cyrus saw was the grin on Seth's face as the wagon was set ablaze, his laughter alerting Brogan's men to his presence.

A commotion of sound rose up as Cyrus ran. The men were all shouting different things, calls to kill or to save the wagon as the clash of steel echoed behind Cyrus, whose only thoughts were of running ahead and of the pain in his back. He followed the path that ran beside the river, but his wound prevented him from running at any speed, and his right leg dragged through the dirt as he staggered into the darkness.

On and on he went, and as the sounds of the ruckus grew distant, the agony in his back seemed to close in, reaching into his legs, his arms, and up his neck. It seemed that every glimmer of hope was simply a precursor to worse luck. He had lost everyone he'd ever loved, and he was still running, but to what end?

A light appeared in front of him, and Cyrus wondered if this was the end, but the sound of hooves filled him with more earthly concerns. Pain surged through him as he turned to hobble away, seeking cover, but his right leg trailed limp at his side as the hooves grew nearer. The thought of Fran and the others kept him moving, but Cyrus knew deep inside that they were probably all gone.

Despite the fact that he knew he should remain silent, he cried out as a spasm of pain knocked him to his knees in the dirt, his shadow growing larger as the light drew nearer. Louder and louder the hooves came, and Cyrus gathered all of his courage to turn and face the dazzling white horse galloping towards him.

He had never held much belief in religion, always considering it to be just another story, but in that moment, Cyrus raised his head to the sky, and a pair of hands reached down to take him.

B rilliant white light poured in as Cyrus's eyes adjusted to his surroundings. He was in a bed, one far grander than his own back in Corhollow. Four intricately carved posts supported the structure, one at each corner, and from them hung elaborate red cloths with gold stitching. Cyrus thought it felt more like a tent than a bed with all its drapery, but the soft cushioning was kind on his back, which throbbed with a dull ache.

He winced, raising his body to rest against the ornately carved headboard to look around the room. A fire crackled in its grate beyond the foot of the bed, and two dark wood chairs were positioned on either side of an imposing bear-hide rug. Mahogany-framed paintings lined the walls, and the faces of stern men looked back at him as if wondering who he was and why he was there.

Cyrus smiled wistfully at a stag's head mounted upon the wall, recalling his recent hunt and knowing he could never be responsible for making decoration of such a majestic creature. His smile lowered as he remembered Corhollow. He had hated that last day, the humiliation that he suffered at the hands of Edgar, but what he wouldn't give to be back there once more…

"You're awake, my king," came a delicate female voice that rang with a distant familiarity.

Cyrus turned to see a girl opening the wooden shutters on each of the windows. She wore a long white gown, and her hair was bright auburn, falling in waves down her back.

"You've been out for some time," she continued, her silhouette in contrast to the sunlight gushing into the room.

Cyrus rubbed his eyes as the girl approached the bed, her features becoming clearer with every step. She had pale skin and green eyes, but he found himself most drawn to the freckles that lined her cheeks. At closer glance, her face was not familiar, but her presence was curiously soothing, and her voice pulled at his subconscious like the waking memory of a dream.

"Who are you?" he asked as the girl glided towards him, seeming to emit an almost angelic light.

His question caused her to stop and purse her lips as she considered him, and Cyrus became aware that his top half was uncovered but for bandages around his waist and back.

"You really aren't yourself, my king," she finally answered with eyes narrowed in appraisal. "I'm Marcia, and I'm your maid. Do you mind if I look at the wound on your back? The surgeon said it wasn't so deep and that you were healing nicely."

She made her way over to the bed, and Cyrus was relieved when she tore back the covers to find that he was wearing short woollen trousers.

"Onto your side please, my king," she said as she took him under the arm and turned him to inspect the wound in his back. "Yes, much better. No blood on the dressing at all."

Cyrus grimaced and jerked forward involuntarily as Marcia seemed to prod the wound before letting him return to his back.

"Seems you are healing up very nicely," she continued with what seemed to be a sigh and a subtle roll of the eyes. "You'll be back to your old self in no time."

"Thank you," said Cyrus.

"Excuse me, my king?"

"No, nothing just—thank you. I presume you have been looking after me all this time, and well, I thought I was dead so…" He paused to look around the room again. "I'm sorry, Marcia, another stupid question I'm sure, but where am I?"

Marcia's eyes narrowed further, and her head tilted as she looked at him. "You really don't remember?"

Cyrus shook his head, encouraging Marcia to continue.

Instead of answering his question, she said, "The queen is resting. She has barely left your side these last couple of days. She spoke to you, read you stories. We both did."

All of a sudden, the pieces fell into place.

"Your voice," he began, as his mind began to clear, and he was momentarily parted from his concerns. "I heard you in my dreams."

"You did?" asked Marcia, eyes wide as her cheeks flushed pink.

"King Cecil," Cyrus continued, as the memories continued to flood back with her every word. "I remember you telling me the story of The Boy King, Cecil."

95

"Oh, sorry. It was nothing," answered Marcia, bowing her head as she backed away from the bed, seemingly taken aback by the turn in conversation. "Just something I've been meaning to practice. I'm sorry, I didn't think you could actually hear me."

"No, it's fine. Interesting choice of bedside story, but it certainly helped me sleep!" joked Cyrus, his cheeks beginning to ache from his foolish smile. "From what I can remember, it was perfect. I used to enjoy the same story with my father when I was little."

"Me too!" said Marcia in a rush, raising her head to make rare eye contact and revealing a smile. "He believed that it was the queen that killed Cecil in the end. He said she grew fearful of her son's murderous nature and killed him for the greater good. I don't know what to believe, but it was always so exciting!"

"Huh," uttered Cyrus, biting his lip as he considered this exciting new addition to the tale. "I loved stories when I was younger. My father always used to say 'there is no story worse than—'"

"—that of a story untold," finished Marcia, smile broadening upon her face, but as their eyes met again, an awkward feeling enveloped them again.

"Thank you, my king," she said with another bow. "I'm glad you enjoyed the story, but I should probably fetch Garrett and Thaddeus now. They will want to know that you're awake."

Cyrus made to protest, but Marcia flashed a curious look in his direction before making hastily for the door.

The name Thaddeus didn't mean anything to Cyrus, but Garrett had a familiar ring, perhaps from a dream or another of Marcia's stories.

"You're awake, Gus!" came a cheery voice as two men appeared in the room, interrupting Cyrus's thoughts. The first—the one who had spoken—was the older of the two, with shoulder-length grey hair, a well-trimmed beard of the same colour, and deep wrinkles on his eyes and forehead.

"I bet you're glad to be back in Eldred's Keep. You've been on quite the adventure," said the second man, but as Cyrus's eyes glanced across towards him, he found himself transported back to the market square in Mistcliff.

Crouched behind the fence, he watched as the man with the dark sweat-slicked hair cut down swathes of Simeon's men from horseback. He cried out as the same man lay trapped beneath his horse, and then watched him drive an arrow into his attacker's torso.

"Garrett," said Cyrus without thought, realising that the man was no dream and was in fact now at his bedside.

"Yes, Gus, I'm here. You gave me quite a scare back in Mistcliff, but here you are, and Easthaven has a king again," he said, opening his arms to gesture at Cyrus.

Cyrus chewed at his fingernails as he replayed the events of the last few days in his mind. Had he and the king truly looked as alike as he had thought? It already seemed so distant, and as he pictured Augustus falling from the ledge, his face was a nothing more than a blur.

"I'm not King Augustus," he said. "I know we look alike, but I saw the king die. He was killed in Mistcliff."

"Augustus, you've had a bump to the head. These things take time," said the kind-faced older man that Cyrus assumed must be Thaddeus.

"No, I'm serious," added Cyrus, frustrated that nobody seemed to be listening to him. "The king fell from the cliff. I guess you all want me to be him, but he's gone, and I can't explain why we look so alike."

Silence descended upon the room but for the spit and crackle of the fire.

After taking a moment to consider what Cyrus had said, Garrett said, "Close the doors."

Cyrus watched as Thaddeus peered into the hallway, looking in both directions before drawing the doors shut and standing with his back against them.

"The king is dead?" asked Thaddeus, glancing briefly at Garrett and then back at Cyrus.

"Yes," responded Cyrus, relieved that someone was taking him seriously at last. He dragged his legs off the side of the bed so that they hung towards the ground. "Before you ask, my name is Cyrus, and I'm just a village storyteller from Corhollow, but I must say, I've never heard a story like this."

"Corhollow in the Low Country?" asked Garrett, scratching at his chin as he strolled around the bed, looking at Cyrus appraisingly.

Cyrus nodded as Thaddeus came away from the door and towards the bed, his stare extending beyond Cyrus as though he was in deep thought.

"And your family?" enquired Garrett, his eyes narrowing with every question.

"I have a sister. She's not my sister from birth, but we have been living with the warden in Corhollow as siblings for most of her life. Before that we lived in Coldwynne," explained Cyrus.

"Coldwynne?" snapped Garrett, as his head turned to the side and he bit his bottom lip.

"It's near—" started Cyrus.

"It's fine, I know where it is," responded Garrett, looking to Thaddeus, who had paused to listen. "What do you make of this?" he asked his friend.

"I think we are at war," Thaddeus said, tapping at his mouth with a finger as he gazed up at the ceiling. "I think we need a king now more than ever, and I believe we have been sent one," he finished, bringing his eyes down to meet Cyrus.

"You're not serious, surely?" asked Cyrus as his jaw dropped and his head shook. "The king, he must have friends and family." He stepped off the bed, and though his legs were numb, he was able to remain upright with support from the framework. "The girl, Marcia, said the queen had been here waiting for me to wake. A woman knows her own son!"

"What you have told us about Augustus is tragic news," said Thaddeus, "and there will be a time to mourn his passing, but no man is bigger than this country and its people." He lowered his voice in a way that reminded Cyrus of one of Osbert's lectures. "Right now, we must think of the greater good. We can't say how this will play out, but we have to try."

"The injury to your head will buy us time," added Garrett, as their plan seemed to grow in momentum. "As for the queen, leave this to me. I'm sure she will be too happy at having you—" he winced before correcting himself, "at having Gus back that she will hardly notice."

Cyrus felt his legs shaking. He wasn't sure if this was borne from his injuries or his nerves, but he decided to sit back on the bed, not knowing what to say for the best.

"It's a lot to take in for all of us," said Thaddeus, his voice consoling as he perched himself on the bed beside Cyrus. "Take your time to think about it."

Already, though, Cyrus wondered if he really had a choice in the matter.

Garrett made for the door, and Thaddeus placed his hand on Cyrus's shoulder, though it was hard to tell if it was for comfort or simply to help the old man to his feet.

"Let's discuss this again tomorrow," added Thaddeus as he joined Garrett to exit the room. "I suggest we keep this between us until then."

"But—" Cyrus said, a mind full of questions on his lips, but before he could get even one of them out, the door closed behind the two men.

The afternoon sky turned grey with clouds before early evening broke, bathing the royal chambers of Eldred's Keep in gentle pink light. Cyrus had spent the entire day within the same four walls, pacing the stone floor, wincing occasionally at the pain in his lower back, watching the hum of activity in the courtyard below, or simply laid out on the bed, wondering if this was all just another dream. Thaddeus and Garett had offered him a kingdom, and yet he felt more prisoner than king. It seemed he was just a playing piece in their game, to move and use as they pleased—a game to which he didn't even know the rules.

Hardest of all were the thoughts of home. Had any survived in Corhollow? Had Fran made it out of Mistcliff? He grew frustrated at himself for not asking about them when Thaddeus and Garrett had been in the room. No doubt they'd have thought his concerns insignificant anyway, especially when compared to the problems faced by a king, problems that they now intended him to face! He felt his anger swell towards the two men and the king selfish enough to get himself killed, landing Cyrus in this situation.

As frustration had turned to anger, so anger turned to sadness, and Cyrus found himself struggling to fight back tears. His head was so full and his chest so tight with emotion, he wasn't sure what to think or feel; all he knew was that he was in pain, and not just from his wound. It seemed as though he had spent his whole life running, and it occurred to him now just as it had in Mistcliff that maybe he was the problem. Death and suffering seemed to follow him like a shadow wherever he went.

Cyrus approached the largest window in his chambers and considered what difference it would make if he were to throw himself onto the cobblestones below. Might it save lives? Could he prevent the suffering of others?

He scanned the courtyard. Carts rolled into the square loaded with fresh foods, and maids rushed back and forth, busying themselves while armed men stood exchanging stories. It was everything he had ever imagined a castle to be, and yet his imagination was no match for the scale of what he saw or the frantic pace of life as people seemed to swarm across the stones like ants to their nest.

From the corner of his eye, Cyrus noticed a large adolescent jabbing a wooden sword at a smaller boy. He couldn't hear their words, but he sensed from their postures that the larger of the two was aiming to provoke the other into a reaction. Cyrus watched with frustration as the smaller boy held his own sword at his side and attempted to move away from the bully, but the larger boy would not let him leave. It was as though Cyrus was watching his own struggles play out before him. By not acting, the smaller boy was allowing himself to be intimidated, allowing himself to be beaten.

Cyrus sighed, turning away from the window, but as he did, the smaller boy pivoted to smash his antagonist on the knee with his sword, sweeping him from his feet. Cyrus turned back around and looked to where the larger boy had landed, but his imagination didn't show him the boy. Instead, it conjured an image of Simeon.

Cyrus had tried to run. He had never wanted to be part of this, but it was clear to him now that if he wanted an end to his problems, he would need to take action.

A gentle knock on the door startled him out of his thoughts.

"Augustus, my king, it's just me, Wendell," came a voice from the hallway outside of the royal chambers. Cyrus froze in hopes that the man might leave, but after a few moments, a bald man entered, his smile emphasized by bright red cheeks.

"They said you were on your feet my king, but I didn't dare to believe it!" He rushed over to Cyrus and threw an arm around him for support. "Please rest, and let us discuss your wonderful victory."

Cyrus pushed him away instinctively, raising his palms to maintain the space between them before following the man's suggestion to sit by the fire. Not wanting to give away that he was not in fact the king, he remained silent, staring at Wendell.

"Your very first battle, and a decisive victory at that. Simeon will be licking his wounds now, I'm sure," said Wendell, taking the seat opposite Cyrus, who found the man's tone to be quite simpering. "You've made Easthaven strong again, and when you destroy the remainder of Simeon's army, you'll be remembered as the greatest king this country has ever had."

Cyrus nodded in an attempt to buy himself time. In that moment, he was, at least in Wendell's eyes, everything that he had ever wanted to be—a celebrated war hero, a leader of men—and yet he knew himself to be an imposter. There was also something about Wendell that made him even more uncomfortable than the knowledge of his own deception. No doubt the man's bloodlust was unnerving, but Cyrus concluded it was Wendell's sheer pomposity that made him truly uneasy. Maybe the man had his suspicions already about Cyrus's true identity?

"It was a great victory," Cyrus agreed finally, his voice taking on an uncharacteristically jaunty tone befitting a king, while the memories of dead bodies from both sides of the conflict caused him to grimace internally.

"Indeed, it was, my king," responded Wendell, bringing his hands together in a dramatic clap. "I can't wait to hear of your plans to pursue Simeon."

"My plans?" responded Cyrus, more in his own voice as he was caught off-guard, concerned that Wendell might be referring to a previous conversation with Augustus. He was also surprised to find that the Wendell was missing two fingers on his right hand, distracting him even further.

"I know you were keen to bring Simeon to justice, for your father's sake," Wendell said before pausing for a moment, frowning slightly as he pulled long sleeves to cover the hand in question. "I just assumed—"

"Yes, of course," said Cyrus, mustering all of the poise he could manage while considering the possible causes of Wendell's disfigurement. He didn't know why, but he was keen to avoid losing control of the conversation—the 'upper hand,' he supposed, but this was not the time for quips.

He cleared his throat and tried to speak once more in an assertive tone, asking himself what King Anselm would say, or Zacharias, Isidore, or any of the great kings of old?

"My wounds will soon be healed, and with some planning, we will take the fight to Simeon. He will pay for his actions." Cyrus sat back in the chair, happy with his response. Maybe he could do this. Maybe he could be a king, or at least pretend to be one.

Cyrus had hoped that this would be the end of Wendell's questioning, but the bald man seemed dissatisfied with his answer. "I understand, my king, but we have Simeon on the run. We should press our advantage."

"In time," answered Cyrus, beginning to tire of the questioning. "Now, if you don't mind, I really should rest."

Despite having been clearly dismissed, Wendell pressed on, "Of course, my king, but Broderick and his men are growing restless and—"

"My lord," came a soft voice from the doorway, silencing the bald man. "The queen wishes to see her son and will be here any moment."

Cyrus turned as Marcia angled her body to gesture Wendell back through the doors. She stood upright with her hands clasped behind her, and Cyrus couldn't help but notice how her gown clung to her lean body.

"Ah, of course," said Wendell, standing slowly with the same smile he had worn when he entered the room. "Rest well, my king, and perhaps we can finish our conversation tomorrow?" The man's eyes glinted, and though Cyrus knew he wasn't free of the conversation, he was glad for the respite.

Cyrus nodded, and Wendell made for the door as Marcia stepped out of the way to let him pass.

"It's a good job you didn't leave Wendell to the bedside stories," Cyrus said to her once the bald man was gone. "I think I'd still be asleep!"

He chanced a glance at Marcia, who smiled, and Cyrus couldn't prevent the corners of his own mouth from lifting as his troubles seemed distant once more. She had a gentle way about her that somehow made him relaxed yet nervous at the same time. He knew she was there to serve him, but he wondered if she had felt something for Gus and whether she might be able to feel something for him.

Involuntarily, his mind raced back to Corhollow and his conversation with Alana at the spring festival. He could scarcely remember her face in that moment, but he was sure he would need to do better this time to avoid the embarrassment he had suffered then. He was the king now, after all.

"I thought being stabbed was bad," he continued with a straight face, "but it was nowhere near as painful as having to sit and listen to Wendell."

He hoped for a smile and wished for laughter, but her cheerful snort was entirely unexpected, pulling both of them into a moment of carefree amusement before Marcia seemed to remember herself, clearing her throat to restore normality.

"Your mother will be here shortly," said Marcia. "I will check on you tomorrow, my king."

"Looking forward to it already," responded Cyrus, surprised at how naturally his response had come to him as the maid gave a half-smile before leaving, the smallest hint of confusion still lingering behind her eyes.

Cyrus rested his head against the back of the chair, supporting it with his hands. What was he thinking? Had he totally forgotten about his family, his life? None of this was real, and yet here he was, drawn to this girl, smiling and laughing without a care in the world, already settling into this false identity. He had spent the entire day trapped inside his head again. Fear and doubt had chipped away at him, and yet in one smile and that silly little snort at Cyrus's joke, Marcia had made him feel alive. It wasn't as if he hadn't met beautiful women before, but Marcia—well, she was different, something more. She understood him, she found him funny, and she even had stories!

Cyrus felt rather than heard the presence of another in the room, and as he looked to the doorway, he saw a woman with long blonde hair observing him. She was smiling widely, but her eyes looked swollen and pink as though she had been crying. He had heard much of the queen's beauty, but none of the stories had done her justice. Her golden hair hung straight with two sections plaited to create the impression of a crown, while she wore a long gown of deep red and a necklace encrusted with ruby gemstones. There were small signs of her middle-age—and perhaps the worry her son had caused her—such as subtle lines around her eyes, but she was still a great beauty. Cyrus was struck by how instantly he was drawn to her, how maternal she seemed to him, even though he had never met her.

"My son," she said, sweeping over to him. "I thought you might never return."

Cyrus had been dreading the queen's visit, but nothing could have prepared him for the wave of raw emotion she brought with her. From the minute she addressed him, he felt like an imposter once more, and it was his turn to play with people's lives and emotions.

Despite how sickened he felt with himself, he managed to say, "It's good to see you, Mother."

He stood, and she cupped his face in her hands, drawing him close. The queen was a tall woman, and it suddenly occurred to Cyrus that his pretence was under possibly its greatest threat at her scrutiny. He braced himself as she gazed upon his features. Perhaps she was seeking a scar or a mark that would set them apart, but as their eyes met, he saw only the smile of relief upon her.

They stood without speech as the queen took Cyrus's hands into hers, and he felt the full warmth of a mother's love wash over him. Tears formed in her eyes, and Cyrus noticed that his lower lip was trembling as the moment consumed him. Finally, the queen threw her arms around him, half laughing and half crying as she held him tight. His head rested on her shoulders, her arms squeezed around him, and Cyrus was suddenly back with his own mother in Coldwynne. He realised it had been that long since someone truly held him. Osbert had tried his best, but his way was with words, and Cyrus had always been the one to hold Fran.

He knew he was stealing affection meant for another now, but did he not deserve it, after all? Cyrus let his head hang loose upon her, overwhelmed by thoughts of all the people he had ever loved, all those he had left behind, and he began to cry steadily until she left him to rest.

Cyrus considered himself a capable storyteller, but even so, as he walked the corridors of Eldred's Keep, he wondered how he would ever find the words to describe them. The surgeon had visited him in the morning to recommend exercise, and after a full day in the royal chambers, he was relieved at the chance to satisfy his curiosity with a look around the castle.

The grey brickwork of the castle seemed to extend beyond his vision in every direction: long passageways beset with thick, wooden doors leading to who-knew-where and tall ceilings that served to make him feel even smaller than he already did. A new face appeared with every step, maids offering curtsies, armed men in salute, and kitchen staff gesticulating wildly as they spoke of their newest recipes that the king absolutely must sample. If the courtyard had been an ant nest, the inside of Eldred's Keep was a rabbit warren.

It felt unnatural at first, but Cyrus soon grew accustomed to the reactions of those around him. He had grown up with people acknowledging him and occasionally even pitying him, but the respect and affection in the castle was new and addictive, a strange rush. He reminded himself that his real strength in storytelling was an ability to bring characters to life, and this was no different. His limping step gradually became a confident swagger, and as he passed through the castle, he started to enjoy it, but there was one room in particular that he was desperate to discover.

As Cyrus peered up at Isidore's chair, he marvelled. Perched upon a great dais, the black iron throne was intricate and imposing, and Cyrus found himself wide-mouthed as he considered the number of great men who had presided over the cavernous expanse that surrounded him. It shocked him to think he now had the same power as those very men.

Interrupting his revelry, a now-familiar voice came from behind him, "Magnificent, isn't it?"

Cyrus turned to find Garrett and Thaddeus with smiles upon their faces. It was Thaddeus who had spoken, and Cyrus was surprised by how familiar the man's voice already sounded.

"That's an understatement," he answered after a few seconds.

"This room has played host to many great kings," said Thaddeus, his voice echoing about them, "but it is the man who brings power to the throne, not the other way around."

Garrett nodded in agreement as Cyrus contemplated Thaddeus's meaning. "So where does that leave me?" he finally asked, extending his arms towards the two men, inviting an answer. "I'm not great or special. I don't even have royal blood."

"Time will tell," responded Garrett in haste. "I will help Thaddeus to help you, but you will show us what kind of man you are—what kind of king you can be."

"The country is in need," added Thaddeus. "This is your first trial. Will you rise to it or walk away?"

Cyrus paused as the biggest decision of his life bore down on him like a physical weight. He had spent the past day thinking it through; he knew what was right and that a remarkable opportunity stood before him. In truth, he knew this was what he had always dreamt of but never thought possible. He also knew he had already deceived the queen, and his eyes lowered as he realised that the decision was already out of his hands.

"My family," he said. "I need to know whether they are alive or not."

"We can arrange that," said Thaddeus in a tone that reassured Cyrus. "A great king is one that loves his family but cares for all of his people as though they were also his kin."

Cyrus breathed heavily, accepting his fate. "You really think we can do this?"

"We have to try," said Garrett, his face resolute.

"Okay then," said Cyrus with a sigh. "Where do we start?"

C yrus spat blood into the sand.

It had been days of training—the same time, the same lessons, and the same opponent, but his frustration grew as all of his efforts continued to deliver the same outcome.

"Better, much better," shouted Thaddeus, clapping his hands in encouragement, but Cyrus could only shake his head as he dragged himself to his feet for the third time that morning.

The pain in his back grew more distant with every hour, hidden almost completely by the adrenaline of combat, and Cyrus knew that his swordsmanship had improved significantly with direction from Thaddeus. The old man had shown him how to handle the blade, how to move and plant his feet for an effective attack, yet for all of his instruction, Cyrus seemed no closer to besting his opponent, and his patience was wearing thin.

"Again," he called out to Thaddeus, strolling to his starting position at the centre of the training circle. Cyrus was a little taller than his opponent, but the dark-haired man before him had a muscular upper body and thin, quick legs with the strength to handle even Cyrus's fiercest attacks. He wasn't graceful, but he had a well-drilled, unyielding style and a permanent smirk on his face that infuriated Cyrus.

"Attack," shouted Thaddeus, and Cyrus leapt forward with an aggressive series of strikes. He had tried to implement Thaddeus's many lessons, but nothing had worked so far, and it was time for something a little more rudimentary. The man in front of him was capable but rigid, and Cyrus was sure he could find a gap in his opponent's defence.

"What are you doing?" shouted Garrett, who stood with Thaddeus watching on, but Cyrus continued to slash repeatedly at his enemy as they edged towards the outer limit of the training circle. Cyrus felt his hands start to shake under the constant clash of swords as the exchange wore on, but he kept pushing forward, determined to end the contest with a smile of his own. He felt himself transported to the contest at the spring festival, driving his brother back as the crowd cheered him on. Attack after attack, he crashed down on his opponent as the sword became an extension of his angst and fury. He looked to see if the man was still smirking, but all he saw was a cold, lifeless expression; his skin was pale, his eyes glazed, and his features belonged to Edgar.

"No," called Thaddeus, bringing his hands to his face as Cyrus hesitated, allowing his opponent to deliver a forceful blow to his stomach.

"I can't do it," responded Cyrus, still on his feet but folded over. "I can't beat him."

"Not like that, you can't," said Thaddeus as he made his way into the training circle and gestured for Cyrus's opponent to stand down. "He's too strong. You need to learn to fight with your brain." Cyrus straightened himself as Thaddeus continued, "What happens when you attack high?"

"He blocks and attacks low."

"Correct," answered Thaddeus. "We humans are creatures of habit, and swordsmen are no exception. Pick your attacks and anticipate his next move. All I can do is help you to read the signs."

Cyrus considered this for a moment before nodding in approval.

"Good," added Thaddeus. "Let's make this the last of the day, and Gus…" He pulled Cyrus back by the arm and looked at him seriously before finishing, "You can do this."

Cyrus smiled from one side of his mouth and walked over to take his place, as before, at the centre of the training circle.

"Attack," called Thaddeus, and although his voice was starting to sound frustratingly repetitive, Cyrus raised his sword as his opponent came at him. This time, it was Cyrus on the defence, parrying blows as he danced into the space around him. With a strong grip on the handle of his sword, he found he was able to absorb even the heaviest attacks and block resolutely, sending his opponent back with a jolt. Within a couple of exchanges, Cyrus noticed he was already finding his rhythm, and more importantly, the rhythm of the attacks coming at him. It was every bit as predictable as Thaddeus had said, and as he watched sweat pour from the brow of his foe, he knew exactly how the contest would end.

"Now, Gus!" yelled Thaddeus, and Cyrus stepped onto the front foot to strike high. As anticipated, the attack was met with a solid block, and Cyrus saw the smirk reappear as his opponent dropped to one knee to swing his sword. It was an attack that had defeated him many times, an attack designed to steal his legs from under him, but this time it was also an attack he was expecting.

Cyrus leapt over the sword, leaving it to slash at empty air, before landing to ram a shoulder into his opponent's torso, causing him to crumble.

"Yes, Gus!" yelled Thaddeus, punching the air before composing himself.

Cyrus smiled widely, glancing across at Garrett, who raised his thumb in approval. Cyrus was enjoying this rare moment of victory, but he dusted himself down in order to help his opponent to his feet and share a respectful handshake. There was no smirk on his face anymore, Cyrus noticed, trying to contain his own smugness.

"You did it," said Garrett, as he and Thaddeus approached the combatants.

"He certainly did," added Thaddeus, simultaneously gesturing Cyrus's opponent to leave. "And tell me, Gus, who was King Cecil?"

Cyrus cuffed sweat from his forehead, composing himself to answer the question. "King Cecil was the fourth king of Easthaven. He took the throne at the age of six and was known as The Boy King until he was murdered in his bed as a teenager." He took a dramatic breath as he found himself back in his comfort zone, and a smile developed on his face as Marcia's words replayed in his mind. "Some people even say that his own mother killed him, fearful of her son's fiery temper and bloodlust."

"You see, Garrett?" said Thaddeus, chuckling to himself. "My best pupil, whether he has a book or a sword for a weapon. I'd never heard that last bit about Cecil's mother. Fascinating!"

"It certainly is," said Garrett as he smiled on. "We'll make a king of him yet."

Thaddeus winced as he considered Garrett's statement. "We'll see about that. This morning was practice swords, but the real knives will be out this afternoon."

"I'm not sure if I'm ready for this," said Cyrus, his hands shaking as he stood at the entrance to the grand hall of Eldred's Keep. The doors themselves were solid oak with imposing wrought ironwork. It was a design intended for decoration, but they made Cyrus feel as though he was entering a prison.

"You'll be great, my king," said Marcia as she stood beside him. "Garrett and Thaddeus say you've made fantastic progress." She smiled warmly at him.

Cyrus didn't respond but instead shook his body as he tried to get comfortable within the ensemble he had been given. As a boy, he had often used pots as crowns and blankets as robes, but it wasn't so much fun in reality. The deep red robe hung as a heavy reminder of Augustus's passing, while the gold belt seemed to fall loose around the long stockings and scratchy tunic that Thaddeus had forced him to wear.

"Okay, I'm ready," he said, pressing his hand against the door to enter, but Marcia called out to halt his progress.

"Your robe, my king."

Cyrus turned, and Marcia reached to adjust the robe around his shoulders. Her hand was small, and hairs raised on the back of his neck as her soft skin brushed against his cheek. She was close enough that he could smell her sweet floral scent and look deep into her green eyes as she tended to him. The freckles upon her cheeks were scattered without design, but to Cyrus they were perfect, her own map of constellations no one had ever studied.

"There, much better," said Marcia as she raised her head to Cyrus, catching his gaze upon her.

For a moment they stood, just staring at one another, their quick breaths in harmony, and then Cyrus reached to place his hand on top of hers. Her palm rested on his heart, which was beating so hard that he could feel its rhythm in his own fingertips. It seemed suddenly that nothing else in the world mattered, and he imagined that time must have slowed as his lips were drawn towards her...

"Excuse me, my king," said Marcia, tearing herself away with her eyes lowered. Her face was bright red as she refused to meet his gaze. "The council will be waiting for you."

And with that, she turned and paced down the corridor.

Cyrus threw his head back and looked up at the tall ceiling in a mixture of embarrassment and disappointment, his heart still pounding relentlessly. It had all seemed so natural; could he have misread the situation so badly? The connection between them when they touched, the way he looked at her, the way she looked at him. He had a kingdom at his disposal, and yet he still couldn't get a girl he liked to give him the time of day. The heavy door opened behind him, and Cyrus turned to see Thaddeus waiting in the doorway with the council gathered around a large table behind him.

The group went silent as Thaddeus whispered, "How nice of you to arrive, my king, just as the others were about to leave." Thaddeus shook his head at Cyrus with a mocking smile as the council stood for his arrival.

"Please don't stand for me.... I mean, please be seated," said Cyrus as he sat in a seat meant for Thaddeus before being encouraged towards his own at the end of the table. He had started to feel confident in his new role, but as the assembly of experienced, accomplished, and battle-hardened men sat expectantly before him, he felt doubt creeping back in.

"Thank you for joining us, King Augustus," started Thaddeus, standing to address the room. "It is a pleasure to have you back with us after such a successful campaign." Noise erupted as each man proceeded to clap, cheer or drum their hands on the tabletop. Thaddeus waited for quiet before continuing, "Your intention was, of course, to stifle the advance of Simeon's troops, and I am pleased to say that General Broderick has returned to us today for an update."

"Yes, thank you, Thaddeus," started Broderick, whose polished plate armour reflected streaks of light into the eyes of those before him. "I was sorry to have missed your magnificent victory in the village of Mistcliff." He knocked a clenched fist against his chest in salute to Cyrus, who simply nodded, not knowing the correct response. "Since this time, my troops have secured many towns and villages in the Low Country against raids from Simeon's men."

"Any sign of Simeon himself?" asked Garrett.

"No, since seizing control of Eriwald, the coward seems content to sit within the city and let his dogs do the dirty work for him." At this, many of the men grumbled angrily around the table.

"I heard tell that he is preparing an army," said Cyrus, speaking instinctively as he remembered Seth's warning.

"It certainly seems that way," responded Broderick, throwing his palms down onto the table to rest his weight. "We don't know the full extent of his intentions, but Eriwald belongs to Easthaven, and his actions demand a response!"

"Think of the people," added Wendell, standing to support Broderick. "Their homes attacked, their properties burned."

"And what is it that you suggest, Wendell?" asked Garrett, sitting back in his chair.

"I suggest that we enlist all that are healthy and capable to march upon Simeon and bring this conflict to a swift conclusion."

"Aye," added Broderick, a vein bulging on his forehead. "Just give me the troops, my king, and I will see this ended."

"So, you propose leaving our capital unguarded and laying siege to another of our cities against near insurmountable odds?" asked Garrett, his arms extended and his face screwed up.

The room descended into a chaos of noise as esteemed members of the council shouted and gestured across the table. It was quite a sight to Cyrus, who had always imagined a more dignified affair, but their behaviour went some way to settling his nerves.

"Okay, okay!" he finally shouted, restoring the room to silence. "Thank you all for your input." He decided to stand as the others had done before him. "It seems to me that there is much we still don't know."

He looked to Thaddeus and Garrett and could see nervousness in their eyes, which knocked his confidence briefly. He straightened up to his full height and recovered, "If history has taught us anything, it is that reckless kings are rarely remembered fondly."

At this, he saw Thaddeus break into a smile.

"I will not lay siege to Eriwald, nor will I leave our capital to the mercy of others—"

"But the people!" cried Wendell, rising to stand.

"That's enough, Wendell," continued Cyrus commandingly. The man shrank back into his seat almost immediately. "I admire the passion and bravery of my council, but it is my decision that we should parley with King Simeon to understand his interests and determine our next steps." He raised his hand to silence Broderick who looked set to respond. "Broderick, I suggest that you return to Mistcliff and continue to lead your troops. They are our vital line of defence against Simeon's advance and a valuable source of information in this conflict. I will make for Eriwald to parley with Simeon myself."

"I will ride with you, my king," said Garrett. "Simeon is more likely to welcome a small party, and we may yet be able to avoid war."

"With me?" answered Cyrus as the weight of responsibility suddenly dawned on him. "Yes, of course," he said, forcing a confident smile. "Broderick, send word of my arrival to Simeon. Garrett, I will leave you to make our arrangements."

"Well, I guess that concludes the matter," said Thaddeus as he made to open the doors once more. "The council is excused, and may we all pray that our king is successful in his negotiations."

The room emptied to a drone of grumbles as Wendell, Broderick, and his captains sidled out, leaving Cyrus alone with Thaddeus and Garrett. Cyrus sat silently, drained by his efforts as it dawned on him that he would soon come face to face with the man responsible for all of his suffering. Would his composure hold in the face of a killer?

"You did well, boy," said Thaddeus resting a hand on his back.

"I'd say he's about ready for his next commitment," added Garrett.

Cyrus let his head drop to the table. The simple life of a village storyteller suddenly didn't seem so bad after all.

"How many more of these?" asked Cyrus as he shifted uncomfortably upon Isidore's Chair. It occurred to him why stories tend to focus on the imposing nature of thrones, rather than the level of comfort that they afford. It made him uncomfortable enough to sit so high above everyone else, but hours of hopeful nobles with requests to collect higher taxes or with plans for land development had left him feeling extremely restless.

"One more, my king," said Wendell, calling up to Cyrus as he shuffled the papers in his hand. "A warden from the Low Country, so quick work, I'm sure."

Cyrus sat up in his chair, Wendell's words having grabbed his attention. "I'm sure he will be at least as deserving as those who have come before him, Wendell. Did you take his name?"

"No, I'm sorry, my king. I didn't think it relevant."

"Of course not," said Cyrus, struggling not to roll his eyes. "Please send him in."

Cyrus trained his eyes on the doorway as a man stepped through. He wore a dark, broad-brimmed hat that shadowed his face, but Cyrus could see strands of dark hair falling upon his shoulders, and he wore a brown tunic and wool trousers in the style that Osbert had favoured. Could it be possible that his father had survived? Cyrus had managed to escape with Fran, and Osbert was a renowned swordsman after all.

Panic suddenly descended upon him. Osbert would surely identify him, and Cyrus sensed that Wendell wouldn't let him escape alive if that happened, especially considering he might already have his suspicions.

"Thank you for seeing me, my king," said the man as he removed his hat. "My name is Merrill, and I come with an urgent request from the Low Country."

Cyrus sat back in his seat, disheartened but somewhat relieved.

"Make it quick, Warden," said Wendell. "It has been a long and challenging day for our king."

"Yes, of course," said Merrill, fumbling with the hat in his hands. "I am warden for the town of Ironwell, my king."

"Thank you, Merrill. Take your time," said Cyrus kindly, shooting a glare at Wendell.

"We're hungry, my king," the man continued. "We cannot thank you enough for the men stationed in our towns and villages, but it is too many mouths to feed."

"War is tough on us all," commented Wendell, rolling his eyes, but Cyrus raised a palm to silence him.

Merrill glanced between Wendell and Cyrus and then continued, "We understand your decision to withdraw the food and supplies that kept us during the winter, but Simeon's men have burned much of our crop, and," the warden wiped tears from his eyes as he tried to suppress his emotions, "I can't feed my boy. I can't feed my people."

Cyrus felt his face prickle and had to bite his lower lip to prevent it from trembling as he took a moment to consider Merrill's request. He was disappointed that the man hadn't been Osbert, but he saw a man of similar values and quality before him. Yes, he had a crown and a throne now, but Cyrus knew he had more in common with Merrill than anyone else he had met in the castle.

"Thank you for coming, Merrill," he began. "These are trying times for us all." He took pause for a moment while he scratched at his stubble. "We all have a part to play in this, but I will not see the people of Easthaven lost to starvation. What was it you said to me earlier, Wendell? Think about the people?"

Wendell nodded, narrowing his eyes as he seemed to consider Cyrus's next move.

"We will send food and supplies to support our people." Cyrus stood as he continued to grow in confidence. "What's more, I will send a trusted aide to ensure fair distribution and the wellbeing of our brothers and sisters in the Low Country." His eyes searched for Wendell, who seemed to take a deep breath as his fate became clear. "Wendell, I trust that you will not disappoint me?"

Wendell pursed his lips and nodded his head. "Of course, my king, a very fine idea." He forced a smile, but his red cheeks were lost to the newly pink tone of his skin. "I will make the necessary arrangements to leave tomorrow."

"This evening please, Wendell," instructed Cyrus in an assertive tone, struggling not to grin at the surprised look on

Wendell's face. "I would also ask that you carry Merrill with you, since he has travelled a great distance to be with us."

"Of course," added Wendell in his most agreeable tone, inclining his head in deference. Cyrus could still see the flicker of annoyance under his eyes, but Wendell's words didn't betray his true feelings. "If you'd care to walk with me, Warden."

"Thank you, my king," called the warden as he fell to one knee before Cyrus. "Your people will live to love you for this."

"My only hope is that they live," finished Cyrus as Wendell and the warden proceeded to leave. He wondered if he had lost himself in the moment, but he felt reassured to see Thaddeus and Garrett smiling as they approached the dais.

"You're a natural," said Garrett as he gazed up at the throne.

"He certainly is," added Thaddeus. "Victory with the sword, respect in the council, and the love of your people. Not bad for one day."

"What do you have planned for tomorrow?" asked Garrett, but Thaddeus answered for him.

"Tomorrow, he must prevent a war."

Cyrus sighed.

The shutters in the royal chambers crashed open, and Cyrus shielded his face as the early morning sun spilled into the room. He felt as though he had only just closed his eyes, and he rubbed at them as he yawned loudly.

"Come, my king," said Marcia in an uncharacteristically assertive tone. "Thaddeus and Garrett will be waiting for you."

"Yes, of course," responded Cyrus as his brain caught up to remember the task ahead of him. "Today we ride for Eriwald."

"Indeed, you do, but not dressed like that." Marcia gestured to a dressing table where the royal armour rested in preparation. "I will help."

Cyrus stepped out of bed, stretching the aches out of his body as he found himself relieved at the idea of a day on horseback rather than another on the throne.

"Okay, so where do we start?" he asked Marcia with a smile, which he noticed she did not return in kind. His smile turned to a frown as Marcia passed a black quilted jacket across to him without ever making eye contact. He slipped into the coat, considering Marcia's sudden change of mood and felt suddenly embarrassed at the events of the previous day.

"You know, I'll miss these conversations," he added awkwardly in an attempt to lighten the mood, though his effort fell short of being either a joke or an expression of his feelings.

"Yes, my king," came Marcia's reply as she heaved a breastplate over his jacket and pulled the leather fastenings and buckles tight with a jolt. He couldn't help but notice how strong she was for someone so slight of build.

"It's quite magnificent," said Cyrus as he watched Marcia add his robe in the reflection of a mirror. The shining steel breastplate sparkled with a sun insignia and made him feel every bit a warrior and a king. He felt her hands around his shoulders again, just as they had been the day before, but her touch was cold, and there was an urgency to her work as she finished before turning away.

"Marcia," he called as he caught her arm, "is there something wrong?"

Her body tensed, and she took a moment to consider his question before turning to face him with a smile. "I'm fine, my king. Nothing at all."

It was clear to Cyrus that her cheeks were working hard to maintain the smile, and he was frustrated at himself for making her uncomfortable.

"If this is about yesterday, I'm sorry." He stepped towards her with his arms extended in peace. "I must have misread the situation, but I don't want to leave things like this."

Marcia stepped back and paused again for a moment, fidgeting with her hair as she chose her words. "I'm not your plaything!" she shouted suddenly, backing towards the door. "One minute, I'm just another lowborn, and then all of a sudden, I mean something to you?"

Cyrus shook his head, desperately trying to understand her meaning. He tried to close the gap between them, but she continued to retreat.

"You're leaving again, and I have no idea which Augustus to expect when you return." He saw a tear roll down her face. "I'm sorry, my king. It's stupid. I'm just a maid, and we could never…" She let the end of her sentence hang incomplete before lowering her voice to finish, "Be safe, my king."

Cyrus watched in silence as Marcia gave a sad smile before turning and walking out of his chambers. His head already felt like it was about to explode, and he hadn't even left the castle.

Cyrus rode silently, his thoughts still fixed on Marcia. He wondered what kind of life she had lived in the castle and what kind of king Augustus had been before Cyrus arrived. He felt annoyed at himself for even trying to save the true king, but he knew these were treasonous thoughts, and a pang of guilt soon followed. He wanted to find a way to make things right with Marcia, but what she said was true: he was the king now, and she was in his employ. Cyrus found no humour in the irony that becoming someone had made him even less successful with girls.

They rode at speed, with two of the royal guard at the spearhead, then Cyrus, followed by Thaddeus and Garrett to the rear. Their journey took them due west from Highcastle, traversing the rich, rolling countryside of central Easthaven before small villages surrounded by forest and farmland appeared, signifying their arrival into the Low Country. For all his concerns in the castle, Cyrus felt a certain relief at the familiarity of his surroundings before his mind shifted to Fran. She was smart and resourceful, and he sensed that she was still out there somewhere, perhaps nearby. It would take no more than a couple of days to reach Mistcliff and scour the surrounding areas. She might even have returned to Corhollow, and Cyrus's heart sank at the thought of his sister alone among the remains of their village.

"You seem distracted," said Thaddeus, drawing his horse level with Cyrus.

"I know that look," added Garrett with an eyebrow raised. "Girl troubles, if I'm not mistaken?"

"Something like that," Cyrus muttered distantly, his thoughts divided between Marcia and Fran.

"Ah yes, the struggles of youth. I remember them vaguely," joked Thaddeus with a smile that Cyrus was unable to return. "But remember, you are no normal boy anymore. Your relationships will not be so simple, and of course, your priorities are very different. Do not forget why we ride today, young king."

Cyrus inhaled deeply to show his appreciation for the significance of their journey, and the distraction of conversation helped him to focus on the task ahead.

"He killed my parents, Thaddeus," he said flatly in a voice he barely recognised as his own. "Or at least his men did. He has taken happiness from me at every opportunity and cost Easthaven dearly."

The seriousness of his convictions seemed to register with Thaddeus and Garrett, who slowed their horses to a stop, while listening on intently.

"Don't worry. I know exactly why we're here."

"Well, good," said Thaddeus, arms gesturing before them. "Welcome to Eriwald."

Cyrus glanced down from their vantage point to see an enormous walled city before him. He knew it was second in size only to the capital but couldn't stop his head from shaking in disbelief at the scale of the city from above.

"I remember the first time I saw Eriwald," said Garrett, shielding his eyes from the sun. "Amazing what men can build, eh?"

"Quite," added Thaddeus. "It has always been an important stronghold in defence of the threat from Auldhaven, and indeed Cornesse to the north, but it really has flourished as a centre for trade since the treaty."

Cyrus knew his history but nodded along with Thaddeus's summary, still lost for words.

"I understand it has been a fairly peaceable occupation so far," continued Thaddeus. "We believe the magistrate, Kendrick, was killed, but the local guard surrendered their position to join Broderick's troops in return for the protection of the people."

"A small mercy," added Garrett, cracking his knuckles as he scowled towards the city. "It's naught more than a prison to our people."

"But they live," added Thaddeus. "The portcullis will open for us today, and we have an opportunity to speak with Simeon. Perhaps there is still a way to resolve all of this."

"I can think of one," spat Cyrus, caught in the heat of the moment.

Thaddeus studied Cyrus critically. "Yes, well, I trust that we will be thinking with our heads rather than our hearts when we enter the city. Remember that we are here on a mission of peace."

Cyrus felt his mood cool with Thaddeus's calming words as one of their guards raised a white flag and proceeded down the earthy track that led to the city gates. It was only as they levelled out in approach that Cyrus began to observe Simeon's influence. Enormous green banners hung from the walls, and as Cyrus arched his head, he met fierce expressions from those who patrolled the ramparts. Bowmen followed their every move as the horses stepped onto a stonework bridge that crossed the moat beyond the city walls. Dressed in green hooded tunics with black bracers, the archers watched on with deadly intent as voices from within called to let Cyrus and his company pass. It took all of Cyrus's courage to maintain regal composure as they sat in wait before continuing through the entrance.

"Well, I don't know about you, but I feel welcome," said Garrett, nudging Cyrus in an attempt to lighten the mood, but Thaddeus's reaction suggested that this was not a time for jokes, and the group proceeded in silence.

The first thing Cyrus noticed was how organized Eriwald was in comparison to Highcastle. While the capital had grown up unsystematically around an early settlement, Eriwald had started out as a large military outpost, with the area inside the walls later developed to meet the demands of trade. The streets were straight and wide, the buildings were uniform, and all of the attractions of the city were signposted. It certainly lacked some of the capital's charm, but Cyrus found himself speechless at the variety of shops, inns, and taverns on offer. It was unlike anything he had ever seen, but there was an unusual atmosphere in the air that he couldn't place.

"It's so quiet," commented Garrett, peering at the upper levels of the buildings surrounding them, where shadows seemed to move in the windows.

"Well, it was," said Thaddeus, nodding ahead of them as a number of Simeon's troops approached on horseback.

"Gentleman," called the foremost of them, a man of tanned complexion with a wispy brown beard. "I am General Lambert, and I would like to welcome you to Eriwald."

He tipped his broad-brimmed hat in mock greeting, and even though Cyrus was new to being a king, he inwardly bristled at being welcome to his own domain.

"King Simeon awaits your company. If you would like to follow me?" General Lambert turned and gestured in the direction from which he had just come.

Cyrus nodded, his mouth a hard line, and the group followed behind as they made their way up a long, cobbled path with more of Simeon's men watching on.

"Where are they taking us?" he asked Thaddeus and Garrett quietly, trying to maintain a look of confidence as they proceeded under the watchful eye of armed guards lining the streets. It was silent but for the sound of hooves, and Thaddeus snatched a moment to reply.

"The castle, I shouldn't wonder. It's far smaller than Eldred's Keep, but I doubt we will see the inside. Simeon will want to meet us in the courtyard, for the irony if nothing else."

"Because of the monument, the Pillars of Peace?" asked Cyrus, recalling the stories and his recent lessons with Thaddeus, a surge of excitement running through him until he remembered the purpose of his visit, which served to sober him.

"Indeed," replied Thaddeus. "Remember what I told you: Simeon is every bit as smart as he is ruthless. You should be on your guard at all times."

They passed through the castle gates and into the courtyard, where a number of stable hands waited to tether the horses. Lambert descended from his mount, and the group followed his lead as the sun retreated behind the castle, dusk setting in.

"This way please, gentleman," ushered Lambert, as two of his underlings fell behind the group from Easthaven to form an escort. "You are most privileged to receive an audience. King Simeon has been very busy of late." Lambert raised his hand to rest it against his forehead, a brief chuckle escaping him. Once again, Cyrus felt indignation flame in his chest. Lambert added, "I'm sorry—of course I'm only telling you what you already know."

A voice came from behind the general. "Yes, thank you, that's more than enough, Lambert."

Cyrus was pleased to see that Lambert immediately snapped to attention, like a small child caught in a naughty act. "My king," Lambert said with a salute.

"Last time I checked, yes," answered a lean, middle-aged man sitting on a stone bench before them. He was not as intimidating as Cyrus had expected, but he had an air of confidence about him that commanded attention.

Simeon took a loud crunch from an apple before continuing, a long grey strand of hair that was otherwise dark falling to cover his eyes. "I hope you appreciate your welcome as much as we enjoyed ours." Another crunch of the apple as Simeon inspected the core before flicking it away and rising to his feet. "Your people were most accommodating upon our arrival. Well, all except…what was that man's name, Lambert?"

"Kendrick, my king."

"Ah yes, Kendrick. Well, needless to say, he was not the most gracious of hosts, but the good news is that he is gone now."

Cyrus noticed Garrett clenching his hands into fists as Simeon began walking towards them. With armed men in every direction, the precarious nature of their situation was all too obvious, and Cyrus instinctively rested a hand on the pommel of his sword.

"My, how you've grown, Augustus," said Simeon, stopping to stand at eye level with Cyrus. "So much of your mother in your appearance, and yet you seem to have inherited your father's bloodlust." He called Lambert over to the group. "I'm sure our guests would be happy to hand over their swords while we speak. I find that sharp blades often lead to sharp words, and this is a day for peace."

Cyrus looked to Thaddeus for guidance and received a quick nod of approval as the group began to unsheathe their weapons before passing them to Lambert.

"Garrett, my old friend," added Simeon, stepping back with his arms extended. "We've known each other for a long time, haven't we? Please don't spoil a nice occasion by insulting me."

Cyrus quirked his eyebrows in question, but Garrett smiled as he handed a pair of knives over, and Simeon gave him a wink of acknowledgment. The atmosphere was strange, and Cyrus could sense the history between them. He found himself wishing Garrett had managed to hold onto his knives, just in case.

Simeon walked across the courtyard to a magnificent cherry blossom growing in the centre of four evenly sized pillars which were positioned as if they were the corners of a square, each six feet tall. Simple, yet beautiful, with elegant vertical lines carved into the stone, a scroll-like ornament at the top, each plinth at the pillars' bases a different colour.

"To business then," Simeon continued, and Cyrus found himself already tiring of the other king's antics. He'd been so overwhelmed by the city and the occasion that he had scarcely considered the prospect of facing the man who ordered the death of his parents and countless others.

"It's good to see you, Simeon," said Thaddeus, pausing to consider his next words. "I can't help but notice that you have taken up residence somewhat east of your border. Dare I ask the…nature of your visit?"

Simeon turned with a smile as he leaned back against the trunk of the cherry blossom. "You never were one for small talk, were you, Thaddeus? The night is young—"

"Enough," shouted Cyrus, stepping forward and stamping a foot down to assert himself. "Why are you here, Simeon, and why did you have my father killed?" Cyrus thought about the double meaning of his own question—of course he was meant to be asking about Gus's father, King Anselm, but the question rang true for his own father as well, all those years ago back in Coldwynne.

Simeon nodded slowly as he pushed himself away from the tree, seeming entirely unaffected by Cyrus's questions. He took this moment to purposefully remove long, dark leather gloves, folding them slowly as all in attendance watched intently.

"Oh, Gus, so young and impatient. That really isn't how this works." He picked a handful of white flowers from the cherry blossom and brought them to his nose to inhale the scent before turning back to Cyrus. "Okay, fine, but only because you're new. I am here because the Low Country belongs to Auldhaven. As for your father, a lucky coincidence, I'm afraid. No blood on my conscience there."

"Liar!" shouted Cyrus, and Garrett had to hold him back by his arm as Lambert and his men raised their swords in defence. Simeon's face betrayed no worry.

"It seems the young pup needs some training," said Simeon to Thaddeus and Garrett as he gestured to his men to lower their blades.

"He is emotional, Simeon. I'm sure you can forgive him that," Thaddeus said, narrowing his eyes at Cyrus. "And yet, he has a point." Thaddeus turned to Simeon, running his hands through his grey hair. "I'm quite sure that I saw you sign a treaty for peace in this very courtyard just eight years ago, or does my memory serve me incorrectly?"

"Ah, your beloved treaty," answered Simeon with a sneer, closing his eyes to breathe in the warm early evening air. "Need I remind you that Easthaven was once a part of Auldhaven?"

"A long time ago, Simeon, and we didn't come here for a history lesson," snapped Cyrus.

"Patience, my boy," continued Simeon, seeming to enjoy Cyrus's frustration. Simeon's continued implication that Cyrus was nothing more than a baby was grating on him. The man continued,

"We will always have our disputes over land, and since the Low Country forms a border between us, this will forever be one of the more contentious issues."

Thaddeus stepped forward to interject, and Cyrus was glad to have the benefit of his advisor's composure and wisdom. "You would do this in the shadow of the pillars?" Thaddeus asked, gesturing towards the monument. "You know very well what they symbolize. The four nations of the Treaty of Eriwald, each indicated by a coloured stone, the edges of each stone etched with the values agreed upon that day: respect, trust, integrity, and participation."

"Who delivers the history lesson now?" joked Simeon, causing Lambert and his men to snigger as Thaddeus persisted.

"I was there at Anselm's side when he placed the red stone. Maxim, of course gave us the blue of Cornesse, and Ferdinand brought yellow on behalf of Verdera. That leaves just one: the green stone. A symbol of peace from a canny young king with a full head of dark hair, as I remember!"

"Watch yourself, Thaddeus," said Simeon, his smile turning to a snarl as he slicked grey strands of hair back onto his head. "Need I remind you that I had just lost my wife to one of your skulking cutthroats?"

"You ordered the very same fate for King Anselm and continue to murder hundreds of our people," called out Cyrus, his frustration boiling over at Simeon's attempts to play the victim.

"I told you, I did not order Anselm's death!" shouted Simeon, demonstrating an unpredictability to his character that had previously seemed only calm and calculated. "God knows he deserved it, but it was not by my hand." He steadied himself, taking a deep breath and continuing, "As for your treaty, the conflict between our two nations was never the business of Cornesse or Verdera." He seemed to weigh the cherry blossom in his hand, looking to the delicate white flowers for inspiration. "I admit that I was not myself after my wife's passing, and what choice did I have with three kings ready to march upon me?"

"Peace is good for all, Simeon. Can you not see how we have prospered?" questioned Thaddeus.

"Oh, I see how you have prospered! Perhaps there is no greater example than Eriwald. But like leaves on a tree, good things rarely last forever." He blew the cherry blossom from his hand and onto the floor before twisting the flowers into the ground with a heavy black boot. "Maxim and Anselm are dead, while Ferdinand is rumoured to be at death's door. It is only a matter of time before his bloodthirsty sons assume control, and when that day comes, I would see Auldhaven equipped to face them."

"But we are stronger together," pleaded Thaddeus. "See your troops removed from our land, and there will be time to meet with Ferdinand and his sons."

"We have all had our time," answered Simeon. "Last winter was harsh in our mountainous lands to the west, and I will need the green pastures of the Low Country to feed my people."

"We pay our tax on the land!" said Cyrus, his voice starting in an angry tone that soon turned to despair as he added, "Besides, you burned the fields, the villages, and the people."

"All unfortunate consequences of war," responded Simeon as he pursed his lips and his eyes looked to the ground. "But you know what men are like when the killing begins."

"What is it that you want, Simeon?" asked Cyrus. It occurred to him that, despite everything, he didn't truly desire to fight the man. All he wanted was to do some good in order to end the suffering.

"No more than I am entitled to," began Simeon as his tone became more purposeful. "Surrender the Low Country to me, and no more blood will be spilled."

"Come now, Simeon, you must know that we cannot agree to that," said Garrett, stepping forward with a smile that contrasted the assertive nature of his statement.

"Perhaps not," Simeon continued with a deep sigh. "But I will give you one month to reconsider that position. If you are of a similar mind at the end of this period, then we will finish our negotiations on the battlefield."

"Preposterous!" bellowed Thaddeus, struggling to maintain his calm demeanour. "This is a blatant breach of the treaty."

"Perhaps," answered Simeon with a toothy grin, "but since we are breaking the rules, let me say this: if you choose to fight me, I will not end my campaign in the Low Country. I will march on Highcastle and see our nations pieced together once again. Do not tempt me."

Garrett and Thaddeus were silent, staring at Simeon with fire behind their eyes as talk of peace began to seem like a distant hope. Cyrus felt entirely despondent as the task before him grew with every moment. He was just a boy from a small village. How could he possibly face these challenges, these threats?

"We will consider your offer," Cyrus finally said, surprised at himself for being the first to speak but feeling some responsibility to do so. "What of our people, those within these walls?"

"He's a fast learner, this one, Thaddeus," said Simeon. Thaddeus didn't respond, and Simeon turned back to Cyrus. "In the spirit of…" He peered at the pillars while considering his words. "Peaceful cooperation," he smiled before continuing. "I have already arranged for my men to assemble those who wish to leave. I will instruct that the portcullis remain open for your safe departure, and we will call this a coronation gift, young king. What say you?"

Simeon extended a hand, and Cyrus inhaled deeply as he tried to interpret the man's words and intentions. He felt frustrated and outmanoeuvred, and his anger began to resurface. He knew Lambert and his men remained nearby, but they would not be close enough to prevent him from attacking Simeon, if that was what he decided. Then he remembered that neither he nor Garrett nor Thaddeus was armed, and he felt defeat overcome him like a wave.

"I accept your offer," said Cyrus begrudgingly, reaching to shake Simeon's hand. "We will consider the fate of the Low Country and answer within the month."

"A smart choice, Augustus," came Simeon's response. "This could very well be the start of an excellent relationship between our two nations."

Cyrus nodded silently before turning back to Thaddeus and Garrett. "Prepare the horses. That's enough talk for one day."

"Aye, my king," said Garrett, and Cyrus watched as the older man clumsily untethered their mounts, his hands seeming to shake involuntarily as he fumbled with the rope.

"Lambert," said Simeon, returning to sit on his bench and enjoy the last of the dusk light. "Kindly return our visitors' belongings and see that the people are brought to the city gates. They will enjoy a royal escort this evening."

Their departure was a solemn affair, and though the same two guards led the way, their group was much changed.

"How many are there?" asked Cyrus as they reached the same overlook on which they had stood only hours before. A trail of people followed behind them, the men carrying tools, mothers carrying crying babies. Cyrus felt he carried the hopes of all, and it seemed incredible to him that he'd gone into the parley with Simeon with even a modicum of hope.

"Around five hundred, we think," answered Garrett, drawing up beside him. "Thaddeus is at the rear and can give you a more exact number in time, but we have saved a lot of lives today."

"It wasn't a total failure then?" asked Cyrus, his eyes lowered and his tone downtrodden.

"Not at all," said Garrett, reaching across to place a reassuring hand on Cyrus's shoulder. "They will name you liberator of Eriwald for this. Your legend swells!"

"But Simeon handed our people over. There were no heroic actions here today."

"Leave heroism to the stories, young man. You know how it goes."

Cyrus nodded, turning his horse to lead on. "And what next, Garrett? Will my first act as king be to surrender our lands, to forsake my own people?"

"That is ultimately your decision as king," answered Garrett, his dark horse trotting alongside the magnificent white stallion upon which Cyrus sat.

Cyrus lowered his voice so only Garrett could hear him. "But I'm not really king, am I? I need your guidance on this. I can't make this sort of decision on my own!"

Garrett sighed, "My guidance will only take you so far. If we choose to fight, this isn't a war we can win on our own."

"So...we need an alliance then?" questioned Cyrus, narrowing his eyes as an idea began to form. "Simeon fears Verdera, King Ferdinand and his sons—"

"They are of a similar age to you," added Garrett, finishing Cyrus's train of thought. "They are known to be fairly..." he bit his lip before continuing, "uncompromising. But it is certainly worth a try."

"One month," pondered Cyrus aloud, shaking his head as he measured the enormity of their task. "How will we travel to Verdera? Must we cross the entire country on horseback?"

"That I can help with," said Garrett with a broad smile. "I hope you like boats because there is someone I'd like you to meet."

The bright orange sun rested high in a cloudless blue sky as gulls cawed overhead. The smell of salt stung Cyrus's nostrils as he stood watching cargo being loaded and unloaded from ships that lined the docks. It was as frantic as Eldred's Keep, only noisier, with creaking ropes, ringing bells, rolling barrels, and hollering traders creating their own unique composition. To Cyrus, it was wonderful mayhem and a fascinating first taste of coastal life, so far from the life he'd always known growing up in the Low Country.

After leaving Eriwald, the group had divided as Thaddeus escorted the liberated peoples towards the capital, where Cyrus had promised temporary accommodation within the castle walls. Meanwhile, Cyrus, Garrett, and their guard of two had continued across the craggy landscape of southern Easthaven, through the ranges of the Esterloch Hills, until the blue ocean appeared in the distance and Garrett had announced their approach to the port town of Aldsea.

As a remarkable contrast to their experience in Eriwald, Aldsea was absolutely brimming with life. A constant backdrop of lively sea-shanties, laughter, and animated conversations in languages that were all new to Cyrus. The town's wood-beamed buildings stood facing the ocean, leaning towards the water as if drawn by the horizon.

It was perhaps the most exciting place Cyrus had ever been, but he had told one too many stories about pirates and bandits to let his guard fall completely. For Garrett, on the other hand, it looked like a homecoming. He had instructed Cyrus to travel discreetly under the cover of a dark hood, and their roles had seemed to reverse as the older man drew respect and recognition with every step as he escorted Cyrus inconspicuously to where the ships were docked.

"Been here before then?" asked Cyrus with an accusatory eyebrow raise.

"Once or twice," answered Garrett. "Though I don't remember a lot of it."

The two of them laughed briefly before Cyrus's face dropped in sadness as he saw a small girl collecting shells in a pool of shallow water.

"I hope there is news of my family when we return," he said with concern as to whether or not his sister would resurface.

"Keep hold of that hope, young man, and you never know," Garrett said as he dismounted his horse, handing the reins to one of their guard. "Thaddeus should be back in Highcastle now, and there were many in Eriwald who might know the fate of your village. We will keep searching."

Cyrus stepped down from Allegro, running his fingers through the horse's perfect white mane. The heat of the sun bathed his pale skin, and he closed his eyes as the warm sea breeze washed over him.

"But for now," continued Garrett, as if keen to ruin Cyrus's moment of peace, "we have another challenge ahead of us."

Cyrus opened his eyes to survey the harbour, blinking in disbelief as the most magnificent vessel came into view. Constructed of dark oak, with four masts, a prominent beaked prow, and a squared-off stern, it was like every ship he had ever described in his stories, but more like a floating city in size.

"Wow," he uttered as his jaw fell slack. "Who owns that ship?"

"Well, technically you, but—"

"Garrett, you old fool!" came a voice tinged with laughter as a hefty man in a black tricorn hat blustered over before throwing his arms around Garrett in a warm embrace.

"Old, yes," answered Garrett with a broad smile, "but at least I've been able to keep the weight off. No need to ask if you've been eating well, my friend!"

Enthusiastic laughter broke out between them, and Cyrus rolled his eyes as he watched on in awkward silence.

"Sorry, Gus," said Garrett as he reached out to invite Cyrus into the conversation. "I want you to meet an old friend of mine." The other man stepped forward, pulling on his white shirt and dark waistcoat until they covered a previously exposed midriff. "Roscoe, this is King Augustus. Gus, this is Roscoe."

"A pleasure, young king," said Roscoe, his voice becoming more serious than it had been when he was jesting with Garrett.

"And might I also add what a privilege it is to be responsible for your safe passage during this important journey."

Cyrus lowered his brows in confusion as Roscoe attempted to kneel, before making his apologies and calling a further three men forward to join them.

"This is the rest of our crew, my king," Roscoe said. "They aren't much to look at, but you can trust them with your life."

The motley bunch stepped forward in a parade of mismatched colours, ill-fitting breeches, waistcoats, and bandanas as Roscoe tipped his hat in an attempt at reverence. "Behold, the crew of the Dirty Dagger," he finished, gesturing to the right of the large galleon where a single-mast, barnacle-encrusted sail ship bobbed unpredictably in the water.

Cyrus turned to Garrett, who tilted his head with a smile that only confirmed his fears.

"We're traveling with pirates?" Cyrus exclaimed, with little consideration for Roscoe's presence. It would have seemed a fine and exciting idea back in Corhollow, but the reality was not so appealing, and Cyrus knew that things were rarely as grand and heroic as the storytellers made them seem.

"My king," cried Roscoe, hand on heart as he retreated in a dramatic show of offense. "We all have a past, do we not? I admit I've been known to acquire goods through *questionable* means in my time, and I regret to say that there are very few business partners who live to endorse my finer qualities, but Garrett has promised to make an honest man of me and of my crew."

It wasn't the most convincing argument Cyrus had ever heard—nor did Cyrus believe that Roscoe's pirate days were necessarily something he had left in his past—but he did think it somewhat ironic to continue questioning the man all while Cyrus himself was pretending to be a king.

He sighed. Desperate times often call for desperate measures, and Cyrus scolded himself for judging Roscoe based on a first impression.

"It's fine, Gus," interjected Garrett, raising his hands to pause the pirate. "Avoid playing cards with the man, and he'll do you no harm. His biggest crime is his jokes, most of the time."

"Yes, yes! A joke for the young king!" called Roscoe in excitement. "How do you make a pirate furious?"

Cyrus rolled his eyes again by way of response as Garrett jabbed him in the arm playfully.

"You take the P!" finished Roscoe with a booming laugh while his crew stood with blank expressions that spoke for their illiteracy.

Despite himself, Cyrus chuckled. "Why aren't we taking the other ship?" he asked, turning to Garrett. "You said it was mine?" He looked at the much larger, grander ship wistfully.

"The Adaline?" answered Garrett, peering at the prow of the imposing wooden structure. "It's a fine vessel indeed, and one that Anselm commissioned as his flagship, but these are unpredictable times, Gus, and let us not forget that assassins walk among us." He looked back at Cyrus, resting both hands on his shoulders as he lowered his voice. "The Dirty Dagger is not registered, and Roscoe is not known to associate with the crown. He is the best sea captain I know, but most importantly, he can help us move in secret."

Cyrus looked across at Roscoe, who gave him a wink as if drawing attention to the gold hoop ring in his eyebrow. The crew remained nearby, but their posture had slouched, and Cyrus noticed one of them picking his ears as though no one was watching.

"Okay," he said, with a grimace. "If this man has your trust, then he has mine."

"Excellent," said Roscoe with a celebratory clap. "Well, we are all loaded and set to go, so let's get you on board, and the boys will show you to the royal quarters."

"Land ahoy!" called Roscoe from above deck.

Cyrus's head shot up from his thin pillow. He had spent most of the last two days below deck, laid out on a pile of scratchy blankets, and vomiting periodically into a bucket beside his bed—if you could call it that—as the sun bore down and sea spray crept through the rickety hull. The hold of the Dirty Dagger would have been spacious but for the assortment of ropes, timber, and more casks than even the cellars of Eldred's Keep held.

"We are arriving, Gus," said Garrett as he descended a small wooden ladder from the main deck above. Cyrus noticed his protector's hair had started to grow through; his stubble was turning to beard with patches of grey, and he seemed relaxed in the face of their task. Cyrus conceded that there probably was a certain freedom to life on the water and rolled over in frustration at his sickness before a large rat scuttled over his makeshift bed, and he decided it was time to join the rest of the crew.

"King Augustus, how lovely to see you!" yelled Roscoe from the prow, sheltering his eyes from the blazing sun. "Even better to see a little colour back in your cheeks."

The hefty pirate called orders to his crew as they methodically worked a sequence of ropes and rigging to slow their arrival into port. "I hope we didn't keep you awake last night, only, it has been some time since my last journey with Garrett, and we had plenty of catching up to do."

Cyrus looked across at Garrett, who seemed to do everything possible to avoid his stare, possibly embarrassed by the raucous laughter that anyone onboard the ship—and possibly anyone in the ocean—would have struggled not to hear.

"I'm just glad we have finally arrived," Cyrus said.

"Well, arrived we have! And you will never see a more beautiful welcome than the city of Casarossa," Roscoe said, gesturing towards the mass of land they were approaching.

Cyrus found his sea legs to join Roscoe and watch the city unfold before them, finding that the nearer they drew to land, the less pronounced his nausea became. The port of Casarossa was an impressive horseshoe shape, narrowing to limit the passage of vessels at any one time. Small fishing boats rocked gently within the harbour walls, and larger ships lined the docks with a throng of activity becoming clearer to Cyrus's eyes and ears as they edged closer, the energy reminding Cyrus of Aldsea.

"It's magnificent," he uttered as the sun's rays beamed down on him, gulls diving for fish in the water and exotic breeds of colourful birds resting in palm trees that added variety to the dazzling white stonework of the city limits.

"Aye, it is," agreed Roscoe, stuffing tobacco into a clay pipe. "And you are yet to see the wonders within. I've happily lost months of my life to this city."

147

"Something that we can ill afford on this visit, old friend," said Garrett sadly, joining them as the Dirty Dagger passed into the harbour. "You know the rules. This is business, Roscoe." He raised his eyebrows, and Roscoe rested on a barrel with a deep puff of his pipe. "Secure provisions for the journey home and await our return."

Cyrus was slightly taken aback by the authoritative tone of Garrett's voice given how jovial he had been in Roscoe's company up until this point. It meant it was time to get to work.

Roscoe blew a thick smoke ring into the air before nodding at Garrett with a yellow grin that Cyrus found frustratingly infectious. "Okay, boys, you heard the man," he shouted, summoning his crew. "Let's bring her in and let our esteemed passengers go about their business."

Cyrus watched the crew prepare for their arrival until the approach of a large rowboat caught his eye.

"Who are they?" he asked as Garrett appeared at his side. The boat contained six muscular oarsmen, but it was their equal number in armour that provided greater concern. The sun gleamed off shining breastplates and crested helmets with upturned brims.

"Ferdinand's men," answered Garrett, lowering his voice as the new arrivals manoeuvred alongside.

"A royal welcome?"

"No, they aren't expecting our visit." Garrett narrowed his eyes at the deadly assortment of cutlasses heading towards them. "Let me do the talking and try to remain calm. They are hot-headed people around these parts, but remember, we travel in peace."

"Permission to board," called one of the men in a thick accent Cyrus had often attempted when portraying Verderans within his storytelling. He knew now that he had never gotten it quite right and spent a brief moment rolling the words over in his mouth before he was interrupted.

"Permission granted," responded Garrett, signalling the crew to lower a small rope ladder and summoning the two royal guards whose hands hovered over the handles of their swords.

"Thank you, kind sirs," said a broad man with a waxed moustache as he ascended the ladder. Within a matter of seconds, his black leather boots with gold buckles took their first steps on deck and he looked around appraisingly.

"A beautiful day for a sail," said Garrett, reaching to shake the man's hand. "Bright skies, brisk winds."

"Quite," said the man, rolling his eyes and ignoring Garrett's outstretched hand. "The sun will always shine on honest men, but are there any to be found on this vessel?"

"But of course," came Garrett's instinctive reply. "My name is Garrett, and—"

"There will be time for pleasantries later," interjected the newly arrived Verderan, with the rest of his armoured colleagues now gathered on deck. "Let me simply tell you that I am Captain Lorenzo, and it is my job to maintain the order of things around here."

Cyrus looked across at Roscoe, who was uncharacteristically quiet and glistening with sweat either from the heat or from the captain's arrival.

"I can assure you we are newly arrived," said Garrett. "You'll find no evidence of unlawful activity on this vessel." Cyrus was glad to see that Garrett was keeping his cool a bit more than his pirate friend.

Lorenzo paced the deck for a moment, landing each step heavily as if hinting at an intention to inspect the hold. "Is that so?" he probed, hovering over the ladder from which Cyrus had earlier emerged. "The problem is that I have been seeking a particular ship for some time, a ship that was used to transport a great deal of stolen rum, a ship whose description very closely matches yours."

Cyrus glared at Roscoe, whose eyes were shifting between the men as if considering options for escape. He couldn't believe they had travelled onboard a vessel with such a chequered past, but Garrett's words of caution rang in his ears, and Cyrus felt his heart pounding as he realised the need to act.

"And you would place your accusations at the feet of a king?" he asked in his most pompous voice.

His question was met with an immediate round of laughter from the Verderans. "I doubt you even command this ugly little boat," said Lorenzo as he moved to stand eye-to-eye with Cyrus, and Roscoe muttered offense at the man's words. "You'll be presenting me with your royal seal then, milord," he sneered.

Cyrus felt overcome with panic. He had heard of a royal seal: a document which proved a king's identity, a page that allowed freedom of movement between kingdoms. He had described them vividly in his stories, but he had never seen one, and he certainly didn't have one in his possession.

"You need only ask," interjected Garrett, drawing Lorenzo's eyes as he handed him an elaborate looking scroll. "Since we seem to have arrived at the pleasantries at last, my name is Garrett, and I am chosen shield to King Augustus of Easthaven."

The group of Verderans went silent as Lorenzo turned a stunning shade of pink as he read the parchment before falling to one knee. "But the boat, your highness?"

"These are dangerous times. I thought it better that our king travel undetected," Garrett interjected again, raising his eyebrows at the Verderan who had lost a lot of his earlier confidence. "An interesting test of Verderan hospitality, wouldn't you say?" He smiled, and on the surface, it looked pleasant, but Cyrus knew he was enjoying Lorenzo's discomfort, and he didn't blame Garrett one bit.

"Please forgive me," spluttered Lorenzo in a panicked voice, rising to his feet. "A simple mistake, of course. It must have been a different ship." He removed his helmet to reveal curly, sweat-drenched brown hair. "Perhaps I can be of assistance during your time in the city?" He bowed his head as though in prayer.

"Oh, I dare say you can," answered Garret, his smile broadening. "We're here to see the king."

CHAPTER XII

C yrus looked back at the ocean through a crescent arch, the Dirty Dagger a distant speck as his forearms rested on the balcony of the royal palace of Casarossa. "Think we can build one of these in Highcastle, Garrett?" he asked, turning to inspect the domed ceiling and elaborate geometric designs that added colour to tiled walls.

"We give you one kingdom and you already want another," said Garrett, grinning and nudging Cyrus with an elbow. "Perhaps Simeon should fear you!"

Cyrus turned back to the ocean and thought of Marcia as another warm breeze lapped at his face. He imagined the romance of sharing the view with her. Like him, she had probably never left Easthaven or perhaps even Highcastle. He regretted their argument but knew that he would not give up on her so easily, adding yet another to the list of challenges ahead.

"Sorry to keep you, gentlemen," came a voice as Cyrus turned to see two nearly identical young men enter the throne room that opened onto the balcony. Heavily tanned, both had long hair as black as night, and while one had neatly cropped stubble that framed his jaw, they wore the same striped breeches of red and yellow with dark doublets and puffed upper sleeves.

"No problem at all," said Garrett. "We're sorry to have arrived unannounced, but we do so in the gravest of circumstances."

"So I'm told," said the man with the stubble. "Well, you speak with royalty now. I am Prince Rafael, heir to the throne of Verdera. This…" he gestured to the other man, who Cyrus concluded must be the younger of the two, "is my brother Alonso."

"A privilege to see you both," said Garrett. "You may not remember me, but we met when you were only children. My name is Garrett, and I am here as escort to King Augustus." Garrett nodded in Cyrus's direction.

"King Augustus," said Alonso, pacing the room as he joined the conversation. "So sorry to hear the sad news about your father. His are big boots to fill."

Cyrus sensed a lack of sincerity in Alonso's voice but knew how important an alliance would be for their cause, so he chose to respond with a courteous nod.

"Please excuse my plain speech, but we have already arrived at the reason for our visit," ventured Garrett, snatching the attention of the room. "Anselm was murdered by an assassin who is believed to have acted on King Simeon's orders."

"Simeon?" exclaimed Rafael, exchanging a look of surprise with his brother. "On what grounds?"

"We have our evidence," said Garrett calmly as Rafael wandered over to the throne of Verdera before taking a seat, crossing his legs and scratching at his chin in thought. Something

153

about the brothers made Cyrus uneasy, but in that moment, he found himself lost in envy at the rich silk upholstery and quilted cushioning upon which the prince sat.

"He is in breach of the treaty," continued Garrett with added urgency to his voice. "The army of Auldhaven invaded the Low Country, and Simeon has threatened all-out war if we do not cede the Low Country to him."

"And why is it that you thought to bring this problem to our palace?" asked Rafael, leaning forward to rest his elbows on his knees. "I see no sign of Simeon's troops at our borders, nor is he famed for his prowess at sea."

"He shows no regard for the treaty your father swore to protect," Garrett said, his brow furrowing.

"So, it's an alliance that you seek?" surmised Alonso from the other side of the room, and Cyrus realised that the brothers had subtly split, leaving he and Garrett between them as their guards remained in the corridor beyond.

"A union, as was agreed in Eriwald eight years ago," said Garrett with clenched fists. "Perhaps we should discuss this matter with your father?"

"We will not bother our father with this matter," boomed Rafael, rising from the throne. "King Ferdinand is indisposed. The heat and dust treat him poorly this time of year."

The older prince walked across the room to place a hand on Garrett's shoulder. "We will discuss this matter and let you know our decision in due course. Until then, you will be our guests in the palace."

"You are most kind, young prince, but—"

Rafael interrupted Garrett, summoning the Verderan guards into the room. "Lorenzo, please see our guests to suitable quarters. King Augustus, Garrett," he said ushering them both towards the door, "eat, drink, and enjoy the many delights of our city. Your presence will be requested as soon as we have made our decision."

"How do you think that went?" asked Cyrus quietly as he followed Lorenzo out of the room.

"Not great," responded Garrett grimly, and the doors to the throne room slammed shut behind them.

The next three days passed in a blur as Cyrus felt as much a prisoner in the palace as he had on his arrival to Eldred's Keep. He dined on fresh fish and exotic fruits with meals brought to his chambers at the same time each day without exception, but on rare occasions when he left to explore the palace, one of Lorenzo's guards always lingered nearby.

Frustration grew with every passing moment as the implications of failure began to dawn on Cyrus. Could he possibly lead a country to war, with or without this alliance? The thought of surrender made his stomach turn, but it certainly seemed to be the easier option.

Despite the monotony of his time in the Verderan palace, Cyrus's chambers were spacious and every bit as lavish as the throne room. Decorative arches framed every door and window, where lengths of silk hung in place of wooden shutters to bring much-needed shade. The walls were painted with horizontal bands of intricate shapes and patterns, and thick, white columns of marble supported the angle of each wall. A dark wood canopy bed provided the centrepiece with ornate gold coverings, but every piece of furniture was dressed in the finest materials, and Cyrus was reluctant to set foot on the majestic carpets that covered sections of the tiled floor.

Beyond the confines of his quarters, Cyrus spent time on a small balcony with views of the city or in the tranquil courtyard garden at the centre of the palace, where colourful fruits and flowers added a sweet scent to the air and water trickled gently from a fountain into a star-shaped pool. While he was free to move about the palace, Cyrus saw little of Garrett during those three days, and when they were together, he found conversation strained by frustration and the constant presence of Verderan guards. After his initial hopes for a short visit, there was no further sight of the princes nor the king, and Cyrus noticed large sections of the palace under heavy guard, which made him suspicious to their hosts' agendas.

A fourth day in the palace dawned with an immediate sense of claustrophobia as the extravagant trappings of Cyrus's chambers started to lose their charm. It seemed an answer would never arrive and that the patterned walls and elaborate stitchwork were little more than a ruse to keep him distracted from more pressing concerns.

Jaded by the confines of the palace walls, Cyrus decided to explore the city, the famous market in particular, which sat within view of his balcony. It took some persuasion at the palace gates, but Lorenzo consented to let Cyrus pass, sending a junior guard with a fuzz of patchy facial hair as his escort.

After days of comfort in the shade of the palace, the heat was the first thing to hit Cyrus. It was still early morning, but the sun blazed high in the sky, and he pulled a light hood over his head, both to protect his pale skin from burning and to conceal his identity. The air was humid; dust and sand seemed to settle on every surface, and the fusion of smells from cooked foods and pipe smoke made it hard to breathe.

Cyrus found his senses overwhelmed as he had on arrival to Aldsea days before. The traders of Casarossa called to offer clothes and food, weapons, jewels, and everything in between, peddling their wares in a myriad of languages as customers gesticulated enthusiastically in negotiation. The scene before him was beyond his most vivid imagination, and Cyrus weighed a small money pouch in his hand, clutching it tight as he entered the main thoroughfare of the market, which extended to a maze of connecting alleys. It occurred to Cyrus how much he had missed human contact, and while his troubles were growing by the day, he knew to appreciate the realisation of his dream of travel as he witnessed new cultures and peoples. He noted that the citizens of Casarossa came in all shapes and sizes, and though most were bronzed by year-round sun, some even had black skin, a shade Cyrus had never seen before. These were migrant peoples from the Kanthu Islands to the north, tribal lands beyond the reach of Anselm's treaty.

Since the comfort of the palace catered for his needs, Cyrus felt himself drawn to curiosities, with a number of stalls dedicated to unusual trinkets and ornaments. His eyes widened at faded pages of ancient texts and scraps of tapestry depicting historic battles or great seafaring journeys. It was almost too much to take in, and Cyrus walked through the sticky heat in a daze, people bouncing off him in the hustle and bustle of the busy streets, while his escort tried to stay in sight.

The morning passed quickly, and with hunger developing, Cyrus turned to return to the palace. Keen to retreat from the midday sun, he walked hurriedly in the direction from which he had arrived, until the sandy path split in three, stopping him in his tracks.

"Excuse me," he called out as buyers pushed past him, ignoring his call for help or answering in languages he couldn't understand. The returning feeling of claustrophobia hit him almost immediately as he wiped sweat from his brow and longed for the sanctuary of the palace. The dream of new experiences had quickly become a nightmare, and smiling faces now snarled at him while the colours of the market whirled to create a blur.

"Please help," he called, stumbling down the central path, his voice barely audible above the clamour of the marketplace. "I need to find the palace," he finished, standing on his toes to peer above the crowd, but there was no sign of the attendant that Lorenzo had assigned.

Then finally, a voice he could understand. "Lost your way?" called the man, interrupting Cyrus's spiralling concern. The man had a bright white smile and a gap between his front teeth, with a length of yellow cloth wrapped neatly around his head. "The market of Casarossa is like a woman," he continued, taking Cyrus by the arm. "She'll tempt you in, take your money, and never let you go."

Cyrus took a few steps with the man, clasping his pouch of money even more tightly than before. "It's true that I'm lost," he finally answered, as the man released him. "I need to return to the palace."

"The palace?" asked the man, his smile somehow managing to broaden. "Well, why didn't you say? I sell only the very finest pieces. Items of distinction. Indulgences for the discerning."

Cyrus was about to dismiss the merchant when a flash of light caused him to shelter his eyes. A threadbare carpet covered the ground before him, fading in the sun along with an assortment of pots, pans, and candlestick holders.

"I see one piece in particular has caught your eye," continued the merchant, reaching to retrieve a small rectangular object before passing it carefully with both hands. "You have very fine tastes, young man, for this is the fabled Mirror of Amabel."

Cyrus took the mirror slowly and with equal care, turning from the sun for a closer look. The frame was dull silver in colour, and there were signs of rust in the intricate floral design that framed a reflective glass face. Even so, Cyrus marvelled at the craftsmanship of each unique flower, cut skilfully into thin metal with vines flowing between them. It was small enough to fit into the palm of his hand, and despite black spots of age around the corners of the glass, the mirror still gleamed like new.

"A wonderful piece, indeed," continued the merchant, arriving at Cyrus's side to hover over him. "Look to the mirror in your hour of need, and the reflection is said to show you the way."

"It's just an old mirror," said Cyrus, sneering down at his hands. The object had captivated him from the very first moment, but he had regularly negotiated trades with Osbert back in Corhollow and wasn't about to lose the upper hand.

"It is an antique," answered the merchant, palms pressed to his chest in offence. He reached to take the mirror, but Cyrus closed his grip around it, backing away. Fran had always been fascinated

159

with mirrors, and he knew that it would make a wonderful gift when he saw her again. If he saw her again…

"I'll give you two Easthaven marks," Cyrus said, offering two bronze coins.

"Five."

"Three," said Cyrus reaching back into his coin pouch for one more coin. "And that is my final offer."

"They should imprison you for this!" said the trader, snatching the coins. "It's as good as theft. I already regret coming to your aid!"

"People have suffered worse in doing so," answered Cyrus sadly, placing the mirror in his pocket and adjusting his hood. "I'll pay you another bronze piece if you can direct me back to the palace," he added, but their deal was cut short when he noticed Garrett breaking through the crowds, hastening in his direction.

"Augustus," came his call, and Cyrus noticed the merchant's eyes narrow as he realised that he had been bargaining with royalty.

Garrett reached Cyrus and said, "Ferdinand is ready to give us our answer. We must return to the palace now."

"But the bronze piece, my king," said the merchant, reaching out in expectation.

"Here," answered Garrett impatiently, placing a small pouch of money in the man's hand. "For your…" he paused, considering his words, "discretion."

"Thank you, kind sir," said the merchant as he bowed and backed away, leaving Garrett to escort Cyrus back to the palace.

"I'm sorry, young prince, but perhaps I misunderstand you?" Garrett stepped towards the throne where Rafael was sitting, his brother stood at his side. "You mean to say that you will turn a blind eye to Simeon's actions?"

"Please calm yourself, Garrett. I'm merely saying that it is not in our best interests to meddle in disputes about a stretch of land half a world away."

"But the treaty," voiced Cyrus, panicked by the prospect of failure.

"Yes, the treaty," answered Rafael. "A fine idea upon a time, but Simeon is an ambitious man, and it seems he wishes to renegotiate."

"We have received no word from Simeon," added Alonso. "On that day, we will consider what plans he has to reshape the world. These things change with the wind, but for now, the ocean brings only warmth to our fair city."

"Casarossa is so very beautiful this time of the year, wouldn't you agree?" asked Rafael with a smile that pushed Cyrus's patience beyond its limit.

"The city is a façade," he shouted, loud enough that Lorenzo's guards rushed into the throne room, halberds primed. "You have many fine and beautiful things here, but a kingdom cannot exist on vanity alone. Where is your valour, your honour?"

"You dare question my honour?" roared Rafael, drawing his cutlass as Cyrus's heavily outnumbered guards stepped forward in defence of their king. The tension in the room was palpable, everyone silent but for the sound of heavy breathing as eyes twitched in anticipation of the next move.

"Perhaps we should all take a moment of calm," said Garrett gently, showing his palms to the princes in a sign of peaceful intent. "Is this the will of the king?"

"Our father is not a well man," answered Rafael, gesturing the Verderan guards to stand down. "We are his voice and final word on the matter."

Cyrus narrowed his eyes at the princes as he felt anger rising within him. He knew the cause was lost, and it took a hand of reassurance from Garrett to calm his worsening mood. "Then we shall take our leave," he stated, with a great deal of effort to maintain composure in his tone. "We appreciate your kind hospitality of these past few days."

Cyrus struggled not to scoff as he reflected that the days they had been kept in the city had been a waste of their time, as had the entire journey. They should have just returned with Thaddeus.

"Our pleasure," answered Rafael with a twist in the corners of his mouth.

"Oh, I'm sure," said Cyrus, lips pursed as he nodded at the princes, considering his next words. "Let us hope that waves continue to break peacefully at your shores. The tide can turn so quickly, and it would be a shame to see all of this…" he gestured about the throne room, "drowned."

Garrett gave a sad smile at Cyrus's words, bowing silently before instructing the royal guard to sheath their swords in readiness to leave.

"Thank you, King Augustus," finished Rafael, staring out onto the balcony beyond Cyrus. "Change can indeed happen in an instant." He paused as a timely boom of thunder sounded in the sky. "A storm is coming as we speak. Perhaps it is time for Lorenzo to escort you back to port. You have our very best wishes for safe passage home."

Cyrus, Garrett, and their retinue returned to the Dirty Dagger, where Roscoe sat smoking his pipe in waiting, as though he knew they were coming. Their small ship bobbed in the harbour as it had before, but thick grey clouds had gathered in the sky, and the air was heavy with the ominous prospect of rain.

"A joke perhaps, my king?" asked Roscoe, smiling wryly, in an attempt to lift the mood after he took in the expressions on Cyrus and Garrett's faces.

"Not now," answered Cyrus with a sigh, walking towards the front of the ship. "I fear the weather will have the last laugh on this day."

Cyrus cursed as his foot slipped on the thin wooden rung of the ladder. It was hard enough climbing in and out of the Dirty Dagger's hold at the best of times, but one-handed and with rain lashing down, it was a truly thankless task.

"How are we looking down there?" shouted Roscoe through the darkness, holding his tricorn hat with both hands as he turned to shield from the deluge.

"Not good," called Cyrus in response, emptying a full bucket of water into the ocean, "But on the other hand, I think this might go some way to resolving your rat problem."

"Aye," answered Roscoe. "Every cloud, eh?"

"Captain!" cried one of the crew, a lanky young man with long sideburns and a beard braided with colourful beads. "We are way off course and—"

The ship listed wildly, throwing Cyrus to the ground, his head narrowly avoiding the mast pole.

"Everyone okay up there?" called Garrett, emerging from the hold with a bucket of his own. "Say what you want about this weather, but I think you'll have less rats at the end of it!"

"Yes, yes," answered Roscoe, finding the quip less funny the second time. "It's when they start deserting us that we know we're in trouble."

"As I was saying, Captain," continued the young crew member as Garrett disappeared below deck once more, "we've lost our bearings, and visibility is poor."

"Yes, I can see that," said Roscoe managing a smile at his wordplay. "It has been a day and a half since Casarossa, which puts us dangerously close to Mirramar by my reckoning."

"The islands of Mirramar?" asked Cyrus, holding the mast pole tightly as he climbed to his feet.

"Aye," answered Roscoe, raising his voice above the howling rain. "Hundreds of small uninhabited islands, near impossible to navigate."

"Where King Zacharias won his great victories against the Verderans?" Cyrus asked.

"Huh?" Roscoe said, his face bewildered.

"I said, where King Zacharias won his great victories against the Verderans?" Cyrus said again, a bit louder.

"Not my strong subject I'm afraid, young king, but I do know that there are more hulls on those jagged rocks than a shipbuilder's workshop."

A loud cracking noise filled the air as the Dirty Dagger tipped heavily to one side. Cyrus held on tight as his feet scrabbled against the slippery surface of the ship's deck and voices of panic called out around him.

165

"Steady!" yelled Roscoe as waves crashed up at the side of his vessel, seawater seeming to engulf them as the ocean claimed piles of rope and a solid oak chest. Sails flapped violently in the gale, and the wooden structure of the ship seemed to groan under pressure as the Dirty Dagger jerked forward.

"We're running aground, Captain," shouted another of the crew members, though Cyrus couldn't see which through a sideways sheet of rain.

"The hull has been breached!" added Garrett, reappearing from below with another full bucket. "A crack in our port side."

"Gods!" cried Roscoe, arms upward as he called out at the sky. "This is my reward for an honest living?"

"Your orders, Captain?" called the crew member with the braided beard.

"I hear you!" screeched Roscoe, squinting as he peered at the land mass emerging before them. "It seems we have some luck at last. You see, over there? A break in the rocks."

Cyrus made his way to Roscoe's side and saw an alcove just big enough for their ship, with the welcome sight of a sandy shoreline.

"Bring her to land," instructed Roscoe. "And don't kill us on those rocks, or I'll murder all of you!" He laughed maniacally, with heavy raindrops falling from his face as the crew worked to adjust their sails and beach the ship.

"Is there anything I can do to help?" called Garrett as he joined them on deck.

"Aye," answered Roscoe. "Prepare to drop anchor. We'll be spending the night here, and with any luck we will live to see morning!"

"And me?" asked Cyrus, keen to be of use.

"I hate to ask, young king, but perhaps you can try to salvage blankets from below. I won't see you without royal comforts while travelling in my company." Despite the dire circumstances, Roscoe still managed to grin at Cyrus.

The ship struggled against raging winds as Cyrus descended the small ladder once more. Much of Roscoe's contraband was now overturned in ankle deep water, but many of their blankets remained dry, suspended above the ground on hammocks. Moonlight streamed into the hold as Cyrus waded on, his spirits lifted as he peered through a gap in the hull to see the rain slowing and the solace of the bay much closer than before.

"Easy does it," he heard Roscoe call from above. "You may want to get back up here, young king. It's about to get a little bumpy."

Cyrus rushed back up the ladder, a bundle of blankets in his left arm, arriving in time to see the prow of the ship rise as it broke through the first of the sand and shingle. The relief of safety was tempered by an almighty scraping noise as the Dirty Dagger beached.

"Hang in there, old girl," said Roscoe sadly as he caressed the wooden balustrade nearest him. The deck trembled as the scraping noise grew louder, while the crew fought to stow the sails and slow their momentum. Inch by agonizing inch, they crept up the sand until their advance was finally brought to a halt.

"Secure us," called Roscoe, and Garrett immediately released the chains to drop anchor with a clank. "Make ready to disembark. We shelter in the sea caves this evening."

Cyrus followed Roscoe's sightline to a shadowy cliff face further up the beach with crude arches cut into the rock. "Will we be safe in there?" he asked, his voice sounding small and shaky, the din of their arrival still echoing in his ears.

"I wish I could promise it, young king," came the captain's response, shaking water from his hat as the rain slowed to a drizzle, "but at least they seem to be dry for now. Bring those blankets, and we can all get some rest. My crew can attend to the damage tomorrow."

Garrett dropped the rope ladder into the sand below, and the crew disembarked one by one, the sound of wet clothes and boots squelching up the beach.

"Search for some kindling, boys," ordered Roscoe, sniggering as they entered the mouth of the cave. "We can still make light of this!"

Cyrus woke to the smell of smoke as a grey plume rose from the dying embers of a small fire. His back was sore from sleeping on an uneven surface, but the large rocks beneath him were dry and smooth, shaped—like the cave itself—by many years of the ocean's artistry.

Sunlight poured in through the mouth of the cave, and Cyrus was sticky hot, wrapped in a bundle of damp blankets he had salvaged the night before. As the smell of smoke passed, it was replaced by muggy air that alluded to the storm, but seabirds could be heard in the skies beyond the cave, and Cyrus was forced to discard the thick covers as he sat up to look around.

The cave was only small, and he recalled the challenge of accommodating all eight of their party as he rose to his feet, his every move reverberating within the low ceiling and dark stone walls. Their survival had been a blessing, but it dawned on Cyrus that they were stranded, and his head ached at the thought of Simeon's approaching deadline.

Little more than two weeks left now, he thought. His attempts at peace and alliance had both failed, and here he was marooned in the middle of the ocean. He had been crazy to even think of himself as a king, and his mistakes would now cost people their freedom, perhaps even their lives.

Stifled by the humidity of the cave, Cyrus made for the beach, and the clamour of activity grew louder with each step. The sun shone bright white as he emerged, and he raised his hand for shelter as his eyes adjusted to the new day.

"Good morning, young king," called Roscoe, as fresh and vibrant as ever. "I trust your quarters were to your liking?" His gold tooth glinted in the sun as he smiled.

"Take it easy on him," said Garrett, jogging barefoot up the beach with his trousers rolled to the knee until he met Roscoe. "He had a tough evening."

"Where are we?" asked Cyrus, scratching his head as he squinted out beyond the Dirty Dagger to where clear blue water lapped calmly at the shore.

"Mirramar, as we thought," answered Garrett, sweeping wet hair away from his brow. "The good news is that we seem to have landed upon one of the larger islands. We've already found coconuts and some exotic fruits, and Roscoe's men are working on repairs while I've been fishing a little farther down the beach."

169

"Like I told you," called Roscoe, "scraps of wood all up the shoreline. We could have built an entirely new ship!"

"That's good," muttered Cyrus as his eyes dropped to find wet sand gathered on his boots. "Seems you've all been busy." He felt guilty that he'd stayed sleeping in the cave while everyone else was contributing to finding a solution for their predicament.

"Of course," answered Garrett with his biggest smile. "Need to get you home. We've a war to win."

Cyrus paused for a moment, observing Roscoe's crew as they called instructions to each other. The young man with the braided beard was suspended from the rope ladder, hammering new sections of wood into place over the cracked hull, while Roscoe stood in frustration, puffing at his pipe which refused to catch light.

"Is there anything I can do to help?" asked Cyrus as he surveyed the crescent-shaped cliffs extending out into the ocean, sheltering the bay in a form reminiscent of the harbour in Casarossa.

"Eat something and relax," answered Garrett. "You're a king, remember?"

Cyrus rolled his eyes and huffed in response as he walked towards a small fire on the beach where Roscoe was now sat, rotating fish on a crude skewer over the flame.

"You know, you'd call this place paradise under different circumstances," said the smiling captain, gesturing about them with his spare hand. "You're lucky, young king. You've known a life in the castle, a place to call home."

He handed a broad green leaf to Cyrus, from which the dead eyes of a charred fish looked up at him.

"But people like me," Roscoe continued, "we live for moments like this, searching the oceans for that special place, somewhere to settle down."

"We can't stay here!" exclaimed Cyrus, worried by the longing tone in Roscoe's voice.

"No, of course not," said the captain, chuckling as he slid a skewer through the last of the fish. "It's just another memory in a lifetime of fleeting moments. Besides, I'm a new man now, as I told you, and I'll be needing your royal endorsement when we get back to Easthaven."

Cyrus removed tiny fish bones from between his teeth, wiping his mouth before forcing a smile. "So, we will make it home then?" he asked, hope behind his question.

"Aye," answered Roscoe. "The Dagger will be patched up in no time, and then we just need to work with the tide. We'll sail out of here with the sunset, I should think."

Cyrus wasn't sure what answer he had hoped for. To leave Mirramar was to confront his fears, his responsibilities. The enormity of the situation had subsided with his circumstances, but it never really went away.

"I'm going to help the boys finish up the work," Roscoe continued, rising to his feet. "I don't pretend to understand your royal concerns, young king, but I do know that Garrett is a great man to have at your side in times like these." The captain's face developed a sincerity that Cyrus had not seen before, a kindness twinkling in his eye. "Speak to him…and more importantly, don't tell anyone about our conversation, or I'll skewer you next!" He winked.

Cyrus smiled as Roscoe jabbed the fish at him before turning towards the Dirty Dagger.

"Home," murmured Cyrus under his breath. It wasn't clear to him where that was anymore, but he knew he'd have to fight for it. He took a moment to strip the last of his fish before discarding the remains onto the fire and climbing the sandbanks to a rocky overhang where Garrett sat overlooking the ocean.

"Good chat?" Garrett asked as soon as Cyrus arrived, his smile turning to a grimace as he arched his back and brought his bait out of the water still intact. "Sometimes it seems like you're just destined to fail, right? No matter what you try."

Cyrus sat, his legs hanging over the ledge, as Garrett lowered the bait back into the ocean once more. "I've let everyone down," said Cyrus, shaking his head. "I thought I could do this, but I'm just a stupid boy who was so caught up in wanting to be a hero that I let the really important things pass me by."

"You've tried your best," answered Garrett gently.

"Not just Casarossa and Eriwald!" spat Cyrus. "I've been like this my entire life: useless. If we survive this, it will be the food that you caught and the skill of Roscoe's crew that saved us."

"We all have a role to play."

"Yes, but what exactly is mine? You asked me to show you what kind of king I am. Well, you see now—I'm a failure." Cyrus reached into his pocket and withdrew the mirror that he bought at the market, turning it in his hands for distraction. "I'm nothing but a pretender, Garrett."

"No," said Garrett assertively. "You're trying, and there's a difference. Believe me when I say that you deserve this opportunity, and I believe now more than ever before that you can do this."

"But I'm nobody."

"Renown is not the measure of a man, but it is true that most of us are simply waiting to achieve something of note." Garrett placed the simple wooden fishing pole beside him, turning to Cyrus. "It's about having dreams and making the most of our chances."

"Easy for you to say," answered Cyrus petulantly, his face screwed tight at the prospect of another lecture.

"It is, but that's because I speak from experience," said Garrett, rubbing his palms against the thigh of his trousers as his legs dangled beside Cyrus's. "Twenty-something years ago, I was just an apprentice stable boy. I worked for an awful man called Riddian, appalling breath, worse than the horses." Garrett chuckled briefly then cleared his throat to continue. "I only had the job because he caught me trying to steal from him. I had no education, and I came from a poor family, so I thought it was a good chance to learn a trade."

"What does this have to do with our current situation?" asked Cyrus, struggling to ever imagine Garrett in such a state, but Garrett only frowned before continuing.

"Unbearable as he was, Riddian taught me everything about the horses and started to ask me along when he would transport goods across Easthaven. I even started to make a bit of money."

Cyrus listened on, fidgeting with the mirror until he noticed a small crack in the glass, which he guessed must have happened during his fall in the storm. He remained silent, which encouraged Garrett to continue.

"One day, we were summoned to the castle, where we collected three cloaked figures to travel in our finest carriage. It wasn't lavish, but Riddian didn't name the passengers, nor did he share our destination. We simply travelled west beyond the city, just like our journey to Eriwald."

Cyrus nodded to show he was still listening. Repairs on the Dirty Dagger seemed to have quietened, and the only other sound came as waves broke gently upon the cliff face below their feet.

"I can still remember the moment," said Garrett, pausing as his head lowered. "We weren't far beyond the city when they attacked. It started with an arrow through Riddian's chest. I was sat beside him at the front of the wagon, but he dropped the reins. The horses panicked, and the weight of the carriage dragged them to the ground."

Cyrus sat up, suddenly gripped by the story. He noticed a sadness in Garrett that contrasted with his otherwise cheerful disposition.

"There were five of them, presumably Simeon's men, but we will never know. I was hidden by the horses, but Thane climbed from the carriage and started to fight back.

"Thane?" asked Cyrus.

"He was Anselm's chosen shield at the time," answered Garrett, placing a hand on the pommel of his sword. "He fought ferociously, killed three of the men with ease." He laughed, shaking his head, before the corners of his lips turned downward. "There were just too many in the end. They caught him with an arrow and ran him through before pursuing Anselm and Adaline in the overturned carriage."

"The king?" said Cyrus, shocked by the volume of his voice.

"The very same. I found out later that the queen had been with child. Adaline was very superstitious as a young woman and was travelling to seek the blessing of a revered minister, though I can't remember where. And well..." Garrett trailed off as Cyrus understood the sad conclusion to that story.

"But how did they survive?" asked Cyrus, keen to break the sombre mood.

"Ah yes, you're one for action, aren't you?" responded Garrett with a smile. "Well, Anselm was a capable warrior, but they were trapped inside the carriage. He had his sword, but he could only swing it in defence as the two men came at them. It looked like the end for both of them, but fortunately for their royal highnesses, they were saved by a surprise arrival."

"Who?" asked Cyrus, hanging on every word, his eyes trained on Garrett.

"Me," said Garrett, pulling his sword from its scabbard and holding it in the fading light. "Of course, I had no skill with a sword back then, but Thane's blade was as inviting as the exposed backs of Simeon's men. They never saw it coming."

"And that—" ventured Cyrus, his eyes wide as he stared at the blade.

"Yes, it's the same sword," finished Garrett, sheathing the blade once more. "Anselm and Adaline made it back to the castle, and though much was lost on that day, they insisted that I take up the role as chosen shield. I had to go through the very same training you've had with Thaddeus, so I know what he's like!"

The two of them laughed, and Cyrus felt his mood lifting.

Garrett continued, "I spent the first few years feeling like an imposter, but Anselm always told me that I earned my chance through my actions and that this meant more to him than all the money and titles in the world." Garrett stopped as his voice started to break, and Cyrus noticed tears tracing a path down his cheek as he finished gently, "I swore to protect his life with mine."

They sat in silence for a moment as Cyrus interpreted Garrett's words. He knew Roscoe was right and that he'd never have made it this far without his chosen shield for counsel.

"It's not who you are, but rather what you do," continued Garrett as he wiped tears from his eyes. "You care for people. You want to do good, and more than anything, you are keen to learn from your mistakes. These are all great qualities in a man, and what is a king, if not the very best among men?"

Cyrus nodded, looking down at his mirror as he tried to fight back tears of his own.

"Your parents would have been very proud of you, Cyrus," continued Garrett, the sound of his own name taking Cyrus by surprise. "I'm sure they were very fine people, and who knows, we might still find your adopted family yet."

They sat in silence for a moment as the sun seemed to sink into the ocean before them.

"This is supposed to be a magical mirror," responded Cyrus sadly, running his finger over the cracks in the glass, "to show me the way in my hour of need."

"Yes, well," said Garrett, closing Cyrus's hands around the small silver object. "I know little of magic, but I do know that we need an alliance and that Queen Mathilde is said to love travel as much as she hates men. Perhaps it would be wise to extend an invitation?"

Cyrus smiled, narrowing his eyes with a purposeful expression as the discarded fishing pole tugged towards the edge. As Garrett reached for it, Cyrus noticed the same tremble in his protector's hands that he had seen on a number of previous occasions.

"Your hands, Garrett," he said feebly, looking on with concern. "I've been meaning to ask."

"It's nothing," came Garrett's immediate response. And though it was said with a smile, there was newfound colour in Garrett's cheeks as he fumbled to steady himself.

A moment of awkward silence played out between them before Roscoe's voice finally sounded from the beach. "Sorry to interrupt your special moment, gentlemen, but some of us are ready to go home. I understand that there's a war to be won?"

A week had passed since their time in Mirramar, and Cyrus was surprisingly relieved to sit upon Isidore's Chair once more. Their return from the islands had been uneventful, and though he had been sad to part with Roscoe, Cyrus was comforted to have Thaddeus back at his side. It was little more than a week until Simeon's deadline, and while all in the castle remained positive around him, Cyrus knew an alliance with Cornesse was their final chance and far from guaranteed. General Broderick had gratefully accepted orders to begin preparations for war, while news of Cyrus's family had yet to arrive from the other direction. Cyrus knew this was his most important moment yet. His chance at salvation. He wore the same breastplate and robe as he had for the visit to Eriwald, and he was keen, above all else, to provide a more hospitable welcome than the one that he had received in Verdera.

It was a bright, warm day, a hint at the approach of summer, and Cyrus adjusted the robe around his shoulders as he prepared to address the room.

"Welcome to Highcastle," he said, straightening to project his voice. "You find yourself in the throne room of Eldred's Keep, from which the great kings of old ruled over Easthaven."

"We are grateful for your invitation," came a booming response, as the man from Cornesse knelt before him. "And I for the privilege of meeting another such king here today."

Cyrus smiled, both relieved and flattered by the man's words. "You are most kind," he ventured, leaning forward on his throne. "Please rise and introduce yourself."

Cyrus watched as the man stood to reveal the full extent of his remarkable stature. Where guests were typically lost in the enormity of the throne room, the Cornessian stood as a giant, surely seven feet tall, with a solid, muscular physique that made him look very much at home.

"I thought he'd be bigger," said Garrett, turning with a smile, but Cyrus remained straight-faced, encouraging their guest to continue.

"Thank you, great king," said the man, removing a plumed hat to reveal dark shoulder-length hair and a thick beard that left few of his features visible. "My name is Lucien, and I am chosen shield to our first queen, Mathilde."

"You are most welcome, Lucien. I trust that the queen's quarters are suitable?"

"Yes, King Augustus, and my queen begs your forgiveness for her absence. She is tired from her recent travels and hopes you will understand."

"Of course," answered Cyrus, reflecting wearily on his own recent journeys, "though I trust the queen will be well enough to join me for dinner this evening?"

"She is excited to join you, great king," answered Lucien, placing his hat back upon his head. "Queen Mathilde is most intrigued to know the purpose of your invitation."

"All in due course," said Cyrus. "You are our guests, first and foremost. Tonight is an opportunity to celebrate the friendship between our two nations and demonstrate a little of our famous hospitality."

"A fine occasion indeed," said Lucien, inclining his head. "We are of course keen to add a little flavour of our own to proceedings." He glanced at the door, where a young squire entered the room, rolling an oak cask that was almost his equal in size. "Cornessian red," Lucien continued. "An excellent vintage, favoured by your father I believe?"

"Most kind," said Garrett before Cyrus had the chance to respond. "I will personally ensure that this fine gift is handled with the appropriate care."

"You would be so rude as to leave our guest?" asked Cyrus, raising his eyebrows at Garrett. "No. I'm sure that there are others perfectly capable of handling this particular task. You never know, they might even leave some for the rest of us!"

Garrett scrunched his face at Cyrus, who simply smiled in response.

"Lucien, may I introduce Garrett, who has the misfortune of being my chosen shield? He will be happy to show you and any of your people around the castle."

"Thank you, great king."

"We are also joined by Thaddeus," added Cyrus, gesturing towards his mentor. "But you'll have plenty of time to get to know each other. For now, please enjoy the comforts of the capital, and do let us know if there is anything you need."

Lucien bowed a final time before ducking through the doors, leaving Cyrus with his most trusted aides.

"If wars were won with charm," said Thaddeus warmly. "You've really blossomed, young king."

"I've had the very best counsel," responded Cyrus, smiling as he looked at Garrett.

Music graced the banquet hall for the first time since Anselm's birthday. Lively melodies were matched by the hum of friendly conversation and laughter. Giant oak tables were configured in a horseshoe formation, and Cyrus sat at the top table while the other two were given to members of the royal guard from both nations, with the space in the middle reserved for the performers. Garrett and Thaddeus sat to Cyrus's right while the dowager queen Adaline separated him from Mathilde and the closest members of her entourage on his left side. This was the closest Cyrus had been to Adaline since his return to the castle, and though he had longed for her comfort, the threat of discovery still lingered over him whenever he was in her company. Tonight was no exception.

Queen Mathilde was of a similar age to Cyrus, with pure white skin and prominent cheekbones accentuated by dark, tightly plaited hair. He had been warned of her beauty, but it was the queen's presence that really intrigued him. She wore a hooded, floor-length gown befitting a queen, yet her shoulders were adorned with shining plate armour, and a sword rested ominously at her side. She had greeted Cyrus on arrival but had spoken no further words to him. He might have described her as cold or prickly, but she had spent much of the evening locked in conversation with Adaline, and Cyrus was relieved to see this relationship strengthening even if he was struggling to develop his own with the Cornessian queen.

"A wonderful feast as always," commented Thaddeus, reaching to clink his glass against Garrett's as food was cleared from the tables.

Cyrus felt a warm fuzz from the wine, but his brows were lowered at Marcia, who seemed to draw constant attention from their guests. As with Adaline, Cyrus had spent much of the past few days avoiding Marcia and the awkwardness that existed between them, a decision he suspected had only made things worse. There was so much to say, so many stories to tell, and it frustrated him that they had grown so distant. He had become a convincing king under Garrett's guidance but was still a way short of being the man he wanted to be. This was one challenge he would have to overcome alone, perhaps the most daunting prospect yet.

"Indeed," he muttered eventually, glaring at Marcia as she laughed with a handsome guard, "but we are here for more than simple pleasantries."

He stood hastily, bringing the music to an abrupt halt, his eyes lingering on Marcia until Garrett nudged him gently.

He cleared his throat to begin. "Ladies and gentlemen, Queen Mathilde and our most cherished guests from Cornesse, it is a pleasure to dine in your company this evening."

He paused to the sound of hands thumping on tables and cheers of agreement before the noise settled, prompting him to continue. "Indeed, it is a privilege to host our northern neighbours after so many years of peaceful union. I only hope that we will not leave it so long next time!"

His words earned him another round of applause, but Cyrus was surprised to see Mathilde unmoved, her eyes narrowing as she sat in silence. "I would like to raise our first toast this evening to those who are sadly unable to join us." His expression saddened as he raised his glass in Mathilde's direction. "We were heartbroken by the passing of King Maxim, a fine man who—"

"Do not speak of my father!" spat Mathilde unexpectedly, kicking her chair back as she stood to a collective gasp. "The man was a fool who drank himself into an early grave, leaving me with the burden of his kingdom."

Cyrus's eyes widened at the unexpected outburst, and he stood in stunned silence, allowing the queen to persist.

"My father died months ago, and this is the first we hear from Easthaven. Do not pretend you have invited me here for anything other than your own agenda!"

Desperate to calm the situation but grateful for Mathilde's forthright approach, Cyrus found himself eager to respond in kind. "You're right," he answered with a raised palm. "I didn't ask you here to discuss Maxim or my father or any others we've already lost. I invited you to try and ensure the future of my people so that perhaps I will have achieved something with the power that I've been given....so that we can yet make a difference."

"We?" scoffed Mathilde, her frustration seeming to grow. "There is no 'we.' As for power, Simeon will crush you and swallow your lands. You'd do well to negotiate with him while you still can."

"So, you think I should surrender to pressure?" asked Cyrus as the room watched on, captivated by their exchange. "I should accept my role as a young novelty of a king and smile nicely as Simeon ravages my lands?"

She glared at him. "You should think with your head, not your sword, or are you just the same as the rest of them?"

"I have tried talking!" said Cyrus, slamming his hand against the table, causing wine to jump from his glass. "I didn't want any of this, but there comes a time when you can no longer stand by and watch as terrible things happen around you."

"And you think an alliance will deliver the outcome you seek?" challenged Mathilde, her voice lowered as if taken back by Cyrus's outburst.

"Maybe," said Cyrus, breathing heavily as he worked to quell his rising temper. "At least we would be able to say we tried." He fleetingly remembered his plans to have a nice feast and then talk to Mathilde and her advisors privately. When would he stop being surprised when things didn't go to plan?

Mathilde stood for a moment, her lips pursed as she considered his words. It was clear to Cyrus that she was deep in thought, but recent actions made her next move hard to predict.

"You believe yourself capable of beating Simeon?" she asked finally, her voice restored to conversational level.

"I believe that, together, we can," came Cyrus's confident response.

"Then show me," said Mathilde, summoning Lucien to his feet. "I trust Lucien will determine the strength of your convictions. At the very least, it will provide us with the distraction of sport. The evening has grown somewhat…tiresome."

Cyrus watched as the giant Cornessian made his way to the middle of the room, the musicians clearing a path. He felt Garrett rising from his seat but placed a hand on his shoulder to prevent him from meeting the challenge. It seemed to him that this was a defining moment, a task he had to face alone, one that he had to win. This was the chance to prove to himself, if no one else, what kind of man he really was. Perhaps it would even give him the confidence to face Marcia, assuming he survived anyway. The decision, unlike the challenge, was a simple one.

"As you wish," he said after a brief pause. "I only hope I am not found wanting."

"My king!" cried Thaddeus, reaching at his sleeve as another gasp sounded around the room.

"Don't worry yourself, Thaddeus," continued Cyrus. "I need our guest to see that some things really are worth fighting for."

He gestured to Garrett for his sword before walking slowly to join Lucien in the centre of the makeshift arena, his every footstep echoing about the room. The Cornessian seemed uneasy with the contest but tightened the grip on his longsword with a nod of reassurance from his queen.

At closer inspection, Cyrus found himself level with the tip of Lucien's cascading beard, arching his neck to meet the man's stare. Despite the hulking mass and deadly intent of his opponent, Cyrus saw a kindness in Lucien's eyes that he had noticed earlier in the day. Their courteous exchange already seemed distant and offered little comfort as Cyrus steeled his resolve against unlikely odds. He took a deep breath and looked to the light of the setting sun as it spilled through the windows in what felt like a call for divine intervention.

"I'm sorry to have to do this," Lucien said ominously.

Then the giant was upon him.

Cyrus moved swiftly, with Thaddeus's instructions ringing in his ears. Lucien was bigger, stronger, he had a longer reach, and perhaps most importantly, he was a trained killer. Cyrus's only hope was to evade the onslaught and tire his opponent, but Lucien was surprisingly quick, and Cyrus felt the enormous longsword cut through the air as he rolled for cover.

"Use your head," called Thaddeus, forgetting himself. But this was not the training circle, and Cyrus knew that he alone would have to defeat the Cornessian.

Another heavy blow fell upon him as Cyrus deflected the blade and retreated, his hands shaking with the impact. Garrett's sword was a fine weapon, but it was dwarfed by Lucien's, and panic set in as Cyrus stumbled backward, attack after attack crashing down before a nimble feint left the Cornessian's blade lodged in a table, splintered wood showering the guards of Easthaven as they recoiled instinctively.

Cyrus was off-balance but snatched at the opportunity, slashing as Lucien tore his blade from the table to meet him. He attacked with all that he had, twisting and turning to find an angle, but there was no gap in his opponent's defence, nor any hint of the giant's next move. It was his most graceful and technical showing to date, but Cyrus soon realised that he was utterly out of his depth and that his attempted heroism would likely cost him his life. Lucien raised the longsword above his head, striking with enough power to force Cyrus to the ground, his blade sent skidding across the stone floor.

He had expected to see his life flash before him, a reminder of happier times perhaps: a small boy learning stories with his parents in Coldwynne, or a slightly older boy sharing those same stories with Fran in Corhollow years later. He took some comfort in knowing he would see them all again soon, that Lucien's blade could free him from his suffering. Had he been foolish enough to think he could beat the man before him, or was this always just a cowardly way out?

Shafts of light fell upon him as Lucien circled, and Cyrus let his hands fall in defeat, wondering how he would compare to the great kings of old. An object of ridicule, surely? A boy king killed in his own castle, while Zacharias had beaten the Verderans on the open seas and Isidore had harnessed the sun to achieve victory against impossible odds. He fumbled for his sword, the fear of certain death causing his hands to shake. But at that moment, a glint of light caught the blade, and an idea gave him a glimmer of hope.

"You would kill a king?" he asked as he scrambled backwards across the floor.

"I do only as my queen commands," answered Lucien, stalking Cyrus as the room watched on.

"Then perhaps you follow her blindly!"

Cyrus smiled as he pulled the Mirror of Amabel from his pocket, angling the glass to send sunlight into his opponent's eyes. Lucien turned immediately to shield his face, crying out as Cyrus shouldered him to the ground, the back of his head thudding loudly as it bounced from the stone floor. Finally, the momentum was with

Cyrus, who pinned the giant's arms with the extent of his bodyweight before throwing an onslaught of punches to the man's face. The fight soon faded from Lucien's eyes, and with victory in sight, Cyrus reached to reclaim Garrett's blade, holding it inches above the Cornessian's neck with a menacing scowl.

"How do you judge me?" Cyrus called out, meeting Mathilde's emotionless expression with the blade still trained upon Lucien's throat. "A warrior is most dangerous when they fight with purpose, don't you think?"

"It would seem so," came Mathilde's response, and Cyrus noticed the hint of a smile upon her face. "Perhaps I owe Lucien an apology for underestimating you? Your mother told me what a remarkable man you are, but I had to see for myself."

"You flatter me," answered Cyrus as he dropped the sword to help Lucien to his feet. "Every man has his day, but I know better than to test my luck against such long odds again." He patted Lucien on the back to show he meant no offense in his onslaught.

"Modest as well?" asked the queen light-heartedly. "Simeon will not be defeated with steel alone. We will need all the resourcefulness, cunning, and imagination we can muster." She smiled at Cyrus as she stood, extending her hand towards him graciously. "What a relief it is, then, to find Easthaven with a king so very well suited to the task."

The room erupted with applause as Cyrus took Mathilde's hand and the alliance was made.

"We will march with you, King Augustus," yelled Mathilde, raising her voice above the commotion. "Your ranks will swell with the finest archers this world has ever known!"

A wave of relief washed over Cyrus as Garrett and Thaddeus embraced each other in celebration. He noticed Marcia watching on, but even so, it was the face of another that stood out in the crowd. Eyes twinkling and with an expression Cyrus thought he had forgotten, Adaline smiled back at him with the look of a proud mother.

"Who are these people?" asked Mathilde, peering from the ramparts as the morning sun rose above the courtyard of Eldred's Keep.

"They are the exiled peoples of Eriwald," answered Cyrus, joining the queen at the crenelated wall. "Simeon took their homes and their city."

"But they still have their lives," finished Mathilde, smiling back at him. "A king who actually cares for his people. You really are different, King Augustus."

Cyrus gave a half-smile, his eyes shifting to activity in the tents below, the smell of food hanging in the morning air. "It's a start. I won't rest until these people return to Eriwald and Simeon is back in his own lands."

"Can you imagine what the stories will say of us?" asked Mathilde, laughing as she spoke. "A boy king and a girl queen challenging the fiercest leader of our age. We'll guarantee our legacy if nothing else!"

Cyrus nodded in agreement with a brief chuckle of his own before silence fell between them. "You know what? I've spent enough time worrying about what people think and say about me.

We fight Simeon because it is the right thing to do. History will take care of the rest."

"And my armies will join you, four days from now on the plains of Freyburn," answered Mathilde. "Let us hope that Simeon brings his very best."

Cyrus smiled at the sentiment, but his expression was short-lived as Mathilde stepped forward and kissed him wholeheartedly on the lips, her eyes closed and hands tight around his face as he stood rigid with shock.

"Sorry to interrupt, my king," came a hesitant voice, and Mathilde withdrew with pink cheeks, wiping quickly at her mouth as Garrett appeared from behind her. "Lucien informs me that preparations have been made and the queen's horse is readied for departure."

"Thank you, Garrett," answered Mathilde, her voice even as she quickly regained her composure, turning from Cyrus as though nothing had happened. "You have been most courteous during our visit. My faith in men might yet be restored!"

"You're too kind, Queen Mathilde," said Garrett, bowing his head and stepping aside, and it was then that Cyrus saw her.

"If you'd like to come with us," said Marcia, and though her words were warm and welcoming, she left him with an expression that told him all he needed to know.

Cyrus slammed the door to his chambers and hurled himself onto the bed, the solid wood frame creaking as he sprawled out, gazing aimlessly at the canopy above. He had done everything right, and yet, with every step forward, he seemed to take twice as many in the other direction. The kiss had meant nothing; he didn't even ask for it! What was Mathilde thinking, and why did his sorry luck dictate that Marcia was there to see it?

The same old thoughts resurfaced. Maybe he was cursed and destined to fail. Perhaps he was leading Easthaven to an inevitable defeat. But, even as these thoughts threatened to overwhelm him, he recalled Garrett's words in Mirramar and knew that he was ultimately responsible for making his own luck.

Besides, he thought despite himself, he had just been kissed by a queen, and a beautiful one too. That seemed like a strange thing to complain about. He wondered what Edgar would have said about it, or what Fran would think about such a powerful woman, and he realised how much he missed having someone with whom to share his experiences. He had been so focused on achieving the alliance that war was now only days away, and he had scarcely taken the time to enjoy this extraordinary opportunity. Mathilde's armies had given them every chance of victory, but he would likely ride into battle not knowing the fate of his family, and if he didn't return, would anyone mourn his passing? Yes, they would mourn Augustus, but who would mourn Cyrus?

As if by fate, a knock sounded at the door, and Cyrus sat up on the bed as Queen Adaline swept into the room, smiling warmly. "I see that Queen Mathilde has left us," she began. "It seems you made quite the impression!"

Cyrus's cheeks coloured slightly. He knew Adaline didn't know about the kiss, but her words held an unintentional double meaning. "All for the good of the people," he said, with Adaline now perched on the bed beside him. "I couldn't have done it alone. I meant to thank you for your help last night."

"Oh, I sense that she was plenty fond of you without my intervention, though we all have our part to play."

Cyrus mirrored Adaline's smile. She had a habit of arriving when he needed her most, and he was pleased to have this time together before his departure.

"I feel very fortunate for my life in the castle," Adaline continued, stepping away from the bed in the direction of the window, "but I do wish that the world would just slow down from time to time. There was always a conflict, a treaty, or an important journey with your father, and now here you are, riding for war so soon after returning to the castle. You are more like Anselm with every day." She smiled sadly.

Cyrus felt a pang of guilt. Adaline's affections were comforting, but he hated to mislead her. "I do as I must," he said finally, his eyes lowered at the dreadful prospect of war.

"Then I will ride with you," responded Adaline, turning to face him. "I will not be parted from you so soon."

"No, you can't!" he protested.

"Excuse me, but I can. You may be a king, but you are still my son, and I will join you in camp if it pleases me. Besides, you'll need someone to keep an eye on Wendell and Broderick!"

They laughed together briefly before Cyrus nodded to signify his reluctant approval, and Adaline returned to the bed, where she placed her hand on his. "You've come a long way, my boy, but I will not see you leave the castle like this."

"Like what?" asked Cyrus, with eyebrows raised.

"You know very well," answered Adaline, with a wry smile. "The girl, Marcia."

"Oh, that," conceded Cyrus, grimacing as he brought his hands up to cover his face. "I think that ship has sailed. It would never have worked anyway."

"Why?" asked Adaline, with a frown. "You like her, she likes you."

"But I'm a king, and she's just…"

"She's just what?" Adaline asked, a small fire behind her eyes. "Whatever she is, it is no less than anyone else. People love you because you relate to them. Don't distance yourself now. Anyway, you are king. The rules are yours to make."

Cyrus hung his head as a wave of guilt overcame him. Life had changed so quickly around him, but Adaline was right: he was no better than Marcia. She didn't owe him anything, and he was certain that he would have to fight for her.

"What do I do?" he asked, scratching at his stubble. "Everything I try seems to fail."

"Have you tried just talking to her? It's hard around the castle, but when your father and I were young, we used to ride out to Dalhart Forest. It's beautiful this time of the year."

"I don't even know if she can ride," answered Cyrus.

"Well," said Adaline, smiling, "there's only one way to find out."

"I don't like this," said Garrett, stroking Allegro at the neck, his beautiful white coat shimmering with a hint of silver in the midday sun. "I told you the story about Anselm and Thane."

"Yes, but you also taught me not to miss an opportunity," answered Cyrus with a smile. "I just need a little time with her, and this might be my only chance."

"Don't speak like that," Garrett said seriously, pulling Cyrus close. "It's not that I don't understand. It's just…leaving the city alone at a time of war?"

"That's why you made me wear the hood," said Cyrus, pulling the garment to cover his face. "Look, Garrett," he continued, gazing back at the city gates, "if it makes you feel any better, you can ride with us, but I would like a bit of space. There are…. things I need to say."

"Of course, my king," responded Garrett, dropping to one knee to help Cyrus onto his horse. "You know me, the very essence of subtlety."

"The very essence of something," said Cyrus with eyebrows raised, but their exchange was cut short by Marcia's arrival, the maid joined by a young stable hand and a bay horse which trotted elegantly between them.

"You summoned me, my king?" said Marcia, her voice decidedly cold and monotone as they arrived at a halt.

"Yes," came Cyrus's instinctive reply, one that might have been a great deal more assertive but for a break in his voice. "I thought it might be nice to spend some time together, but I wasn't sure if you were able to ride?"

A momentary silence played out before Marcia forced a half-smile. "Very kind of you my king," she began as the stable hand helped her onto the horse. "And how could you possibly know of my skill with a horse," she steadied herself in the saddle and took hold of the reins. "You never asked."

And with that, she was away.

It seemed Garrett could hardly contain his amusement as Cyrus ushered Allegro to follow in pursuit. He was more than a little embarrassed but saw the truth in what she had said. There was so much he didn't know about her. His physical attraction to her was undeniable, and she made him feel things he'd never felt before. Above all else though, he realised it was the idea of getting to know her that really excited him. He wondered if this was what love felt like and was saddened to think that he might never know, if the worst were to happen in battle.

He rode hard to make ground on Marcia, her auburn hair plaited tightly against the breeze as they raced with green fields to their left and the fast flow of the River Aramere on the right. Despite her previously stony expression, she laughed once they gathered speed, the sound like music in the air behind her. Her flowing gown had been replaced by a green doublet, breeches, and long, dark boots such that Cyrus barely recognised her. She was not as feminine or delicate as usual, but she was no less beautiful and had a purposeful look about her that made Cyrus more nervous still.

"Slow down," he called out, as the treeline of Dalhart emerged before them. "We can tie the horses and leave them with Garrett. He'll be here soon enough."

Cyrus looked back with a smile at seeing Garrett as no more than a speck in the distance. Marcia was already slowing by the time he looked ahead, and he arrived to watch her dismount with graceful precision.

"As requested, my king," she ventured coldly, the laughter gone, her face emotionless as she avoided eye contact. "Now, was there something you wanted to show me? Only, we are very busy at present what with the war and our guests from Eriwald."

Cyrus stepped down from Allegro, Garrett's approach sounding ever closer as Cyrus walked over to Marcia before taking her by the hand.

"Let's get the horses tied, and then we can talk. We have enough trouble at the best of times without Garrett standing over us."

He smiled, but Marcia rolled her eyes in response and took her hand back. He had delivered some important speeches since arriving at the castle, but Cyrus knew that his words now would need to be perfect. He stroked Allegro's mane one last time before joining Marcia to tie the horses, and together they entered the forest.

Sunlight streamed through the trees, the scent of bark and flowers in the air as Cyrus walked at Marcia's side. They had not spoken properly since his departure for Eriwald, and despite all the words swimming in his head, the right ones still seemed to evade him. He gazed at Marcia for a moment and caught a look of disinterest that made Prince Rafael seem comparatively welcoming. Likely, she had already given up on any thought of them being together, or maybe it was never there in the first place, but there was only one way to find out.

"Seems you made quite an impression on Queen Mathilde," said Marcia unexpectedly, her jaw set hard. These were the same words Adaline had used, but Marcia's voice took on an entirely different tone. "She is very beautiful, and a queen after all. A fairy-tale story!"

Cyrus had been so busy collecting his own thoughts that he had not expected Marcia to speak first. It occurred to him that this was probably part of the problem, but he was taken back by the accusation and keen to set things straight.

His heart thumping, he said, "It's not like that. I just did what I needed to do." He winced immediately, fists clenched in frustration as Marcia's sneer told him this wasn't the best of starts. "Anyway," he continued. "I'm surprised you even noticed, given how busy you were with Mathilde's guards. All the girls in the castle, but only one that they couldn't stay away from. Perhaps they could tell how much you were enjoying it."

"I was working!" yelled Marcia, stopping in her tracks. "My job was to make our guests feel welcome, remember?" She stepped forward and pushed him in the chest. "Like a great king once said, 'I just did what I needed to do.'"

"I'm sorry," said Cyrus desperately as he replayed the previous evening in his mind. "I'm just under a lot of pressure at the moment." He felt frustrated with himself for even bringing up the guards. What did that have to do with anything?

"Aren't we all?" answered Marcia heatedly. "Except that some people get to make decisions and others just have to follow."

"What does that mean?"

"You know exactly what I mean."

Marcia walked over to a flat, moss-covered boulder, water flowing down the rock face behind her. She perched on the boulder and began to loosen the braid in her hair before continuing. "People follow you because you're their king, but do you know why I think you will win this war?"

Cyrus shook his head in silence.

"Because they love you and they believe in what they're fighting for. I suppose it's the same thing that helped you defeat Lucien." She kept her eyes on her unravelling braid and off of Cyrus.

Cyrus nodded at the sentiment and found himself thinking what a perfect moment it could have been under different circumstances, silent but for the gentle sound of trickling water.

"I've been working in the castle for almost four years now," Marcia continued, rising to her feet, "and I was in awe of you from the first moment that we met. You were the handsome prince after all, and I was just…" She trailed off and turned away from him, fidgeting to jerk the interlaced strands from her hair with both hands. "I knew it was crazy and that it couldn't work. I was so nervous around you I could barely even make eye contact. Then, I started to notice you looking at me, or at least I thought you were, and it gave me hope. What a fool I was. You treated me like I was nothing to you, less than nothing. You must hate me, and this is just some kind of game. Is that what this is?"

"No!" shouted Cyrus without thinking. "I'm sorry, I've changed."

"What has changed? You are king now. If anything, that makes it even more ridiculous. What would you want with a lowborn girl like me?"

"Everything," Cyrus exclaimed desperately. "You're right— I'm king, and I won't have anyone tell me what to do anymore!"

Marcia breathed deeply as tears glistened in her eyes. "I tried, Gus. But unlike your council, your warriors, and everyone else, you never really gave me anything to believe in…anything to fight for." She wiped the tears away as a subtle smile appeared on her face once more. "I know you've changed since your injury, Gus, and it means a lot. I see the man that you can be: a man the people will love. A man that this lowborn housemaid could love." Cyrus returned a sad smile as Marcia took him gently by the hand, "But you should be with a queen or a princess. I can't go through this all again because you've decided that it is right for you this week. It won't last."

Cyrus felt his heart sink and his skin prickle as he felt his options running out. "I'm not the same man, Marcia," he said eventually, taking a deep, steadying breath. "There is something I need to tell you."

"There's nothing you can say to change this."

"It wasn't me before, the thing is, I'm not—"

"Gus!" came a voice, and Cyrus let his head drop as Garrett emerged through the trees. "It's getting late, and we still have a lot to prepare before our departure. I really must insist that we return to the castle."

"It's okay, Garrett," called Marcia. "We've said all that needs to be said."

"But—"

"We're done here, Gus," said Marcia assertively, one side of her mouth raised in a wistful half-smile. "Just be safe, all right? Try not to get yourself killed."

"I'll look after him, don't you worry," said Garrett, gesturing back towards the way they had arrived. "Go ahead, Marcia. I'd like a moment with the king before we head back."

"Of course," said Marcia, offering a brief curtsy before turning to leave. It seemed like an age before her horse could be heard echoing in the distance, and Cyrus realised he'd been holding his breath as he waited.

"Ugh" he exhaled finally, moving to rest against a nearby rock face. "Does life never get any—"

"Wait!" exclaimed Garrett, and Cyrus nearly jumped out of his skin. He'd known Garrett to be vigilant but could hardly see the threat in a smooth rock spattered with moss.

"What now?" he asked. "Has the old man finally lost his mind? Come on, Garrett, I'm not having the best of days, you know that."

Garrett's blank expression suggested that it was no joke, and Cyrus simply shrugged his shoulders as if to reinforce his question.

"It's a door," said Garrett finally, his voice firm, a grimace of reluctance upon his face.

"Well great, at least I have my answer then," said Cyrus. "You have lost it!"

"It's a secret door," added the older man, lowering his voice as if to heighten the sense of mystery. "It's prudent for a king to have a means of entering or exiting the castle in times of need."

"The castle?" asked Cyrus. "This story just gets better and better! You're telling me that this door of yours leads all the way into Eldred's Keep?"

"All the way," answered Garrett his face developing into a smile. "There's a ladder behind the rock face that leads to an underground tunnel. It opens into one of Thaddeus's offices in the bowels of the castle, a small room fool of old tomes. There's a hatch built into the stone floor, but it's hidden by a rug, so it's virtually invisible unless you know where to look."

"And Thaddeus knows about this?" This was exactly the kind of excitement Cyrus had expected from castle life, and he struggled to contain the tone of childlike wonder in his voice.

"Just you, me, and Thaddeus among the living. It was forged many years ago during the days of King Leopold and passed as a secret from one king to the next. It was meant as an escape in times of war, but we've had little cause for such measures in recent times." Fear of discovery seemed to have faded, and Cyrus noted a nostalgic glint in Garrett's eyes. "Anselm used to enjoy drink and cards in the villages nearby, you know, an opportunity to be normal, one of the people." He moved to join Cyrus and placed a hand upon the rock face. "Oh, we had some adventures! We used to wear hoods to protect our identities. Brilliant, really. All those times we managed to sneak out, and Adaline never had a clue."

"But it's there, right there in front of us," exclaimed Cyrus.

"It's hidden in plain view," Garrett answered with a hint of sadness in his voice. "Things aren't always as they seem. You of all people should know that!"

Cyrus nodded as Garrett lowered his palm and stepped away.

"My own escape tunnel," Cyrus uttered eventually.

'Your own *secret* escape tunnel," added Garrett. "And let's keep it that way because if your mother finds out, she's likely to kill me before Simeon has the chance!"

"Fine," said Cyrus, snickering as he shook his head at Garrett in disbelief. He placed a hand of his own against the rock face and noticed that the stone was not only smooth but speckled with translucent white stones so that it shone in the light. On closer inspection, he traced a fine crack in the rock that framed a raised surface, and he wondered how he had failed to notice it previously. The protruding rock was his equal in both height and width, and Cyrus was desperate to see it opened. If nothing else, it was the perfect distraction from his recent failings, and Cyrus wondered if it was all a ruse, one of Garrett's ploys to keep his spirits high or another joke at his expense.

"So, can we use it?" he asked, more in hope than expectation.

"You and your sense of adventure!" answered Garrett, his tone serving to quash Cyrus's curiosity. "It's a fine tunnel, but I wouldn't describe it as spacious. It was difficult enough for Anselm. I can't imagine we would have a great deal of luck with the horses!" Garrett moved to rest a hand on Cyrus's shoulder. "No, save it for a day when you really need it. That or when you learn to play cards!"

Laughter echoed between them as Garrett tightened a playful grip around Cyrus's shoulders, and for a moment, Cyrus was back with his father in Coldwynne. With Osbert in Corhollow. A fairytale ending with Marcia seemed unlikely, but Cyrus knew the task that stood before him. It was like Thaddeus had said: "No man is bigger than a country."

He'd lost the battle to win Marcia's heart, but it was time to win a war.

Garrett's grip finally relented, and Cyrus wriggled free so that they could walk side-by-side to meet the horses. The sun had already started to set when Garrett helped him back onto his mount, and they rode silently with Cyrus at the front until they arrived back into the city. It was a beautiful evening, pink sky with hints of purple, the kind of evening to comment upon, but the time for talk was over.

A full moon shimmered in the night sky, the flames of a thousand torches flickering amid the hustle and bustle of the camp. Their army stretched as far as Cyrus could see, warriors from both nations singing and laughing or exchanging stories around fires with no hint of the terror the new day would surely bring. Cyrus couldn't help but think that it was only a matter of weeks ago that he was drunkenly telling stories by a fire in Corhollow.

"Have you ever seen anything like it?" asked Garrett, joining Cyrus at the crest of a hill. "Eight thousand men—"

"And women," said Cyrus reactively, raising a single eyebrow.

"Eight thousand men and women," continued Garrett, correcting himself. "The largest force any king of Easthaven has ever commanded."

Cyrus laughed to himself, shaking his head at the very thought of it. The long list of legendary kings, and here he was, about to lead the largest army of all. "It's quite something, but will it be enough?"

"Can't say for sure," answered Garrett, scratching at his bearded cheek. "Our scouts estimate Simeon's forces at nearer ten or twelve thousand. Our warriors are skilled, though, and many of them fight for their homes, their livelihood. That makes them dangerous."

"And General Broderick?"

"Yes, he's in fine form. He commands five thousand of our troops, a mixture of spearmen, infantry, and cavalry. We also had some two hundred skilled archers, but they have been posted to Mathilde's company. I must say, the general didn't respond so well to the prospect of fighting alongside women, but I think this will be good for him!"

"They all came then?" asked Cyrus, squinting at an array of banners and flags shifting in the evening breeze.

"All twelve of the noble families, and their troops are well-armed and disciplined. There is still a great deal of anger about Anselm's death. I believe they will provide an excellent foil for Mathilde's archers."

"Let's hope so," said Cyrus solemnly, "for the sake of us all." They shared a silent moment as the enormity of the situation caught up with Cyrus. "All of those people out there, Garrett. Husbands, wives, sons, and daughters—all willing to risk their lives. Could I have done more to avoid this?"

"It's a mad world we live in, I'll give you that," came Garrett's response. "You did everything you could for your people, and now here they are, doing the same." Garrett turned to rest a hand on Cyrus's shoulder, his distinctive grin illuminated by the moonlight. "What has it been, six weeks? We've had some adventures already, haven't we?" Cyrus couldn't help but smile, nodding as Garrett continued, "We didn't know what to think when you first arrived at the castle. I guess we didn't really have a choice."

"Thanks!" exclaimed Cyrus dramatically, rolling his eyes.

"No!" said Garrett, scratching at his head. "I only meant…you were just hope at that point. You looked right, but we didn't know if you had any of the characteristics to actually lead the country. Come to think of it, I'm not sure if Gus did!"

Cyrus laughed. Though the memory of Augustus's death still haunted him, it was comforting to hear that he was not alone in struggling with the demands of kingship.

"I cannot forgive myself for what happened to Anselm or Augustus," continued Garrett, lowering his head, "but we are fortunate that it is you who will lead us into this war."

Cyrus felt tears form in his eyes as Garrett dropped to one knee, both humbled and embarrassed to stand over a man who had taught him so much, a man who had saved his life and guided him through every challenge since.

"Get up, you fool," he said eventually, lifting Garrett from beneath the arms, "before you get stuck down there. You aren't getting any younger!"

Garrett laughed briefly, but then his voice turned serious again. "I mean it, Cyrus," he said, returning to his feet. "I have never been prouder. Now let's go and eat since it might be our last. I know Broderick is desperate to share his strategy!"

Cyrus smiled as he followed Garrett back down the hill, the smell of cooked meat and the sound of familiar voices guiding their way.

"We will overwhelm them!" yelled Broderick, pausing to tear the last few gristly scraps of chicken from the bone. Queen Mathilde's face was a picture of revulsion as the general wiped grease from his mouth with the back of his hand.

"And this is the extent of your plan?" asked Thaddeus, drawing the attention of the room. Adaline sat beside him, wine glass halfway to her mouth. "It's just that it's rather…vague."

"No, of course not," answered Broderick, the vein on his forehead pulsing with every word.

"Our archers will rain death upon Simeon's troops," added Mathilde.

"Yes, thank you, young lady," interrupted Broderick, eyes widening as he realised his misstep. He cleared his throat. "I mean to say, your Majesty, that we will send cavalry to ride at the flanks and force their troops to bunch together. This will allow the queen's archers to pick them off while our infantry strikes at the very heart of Simeon's line."

"We will cut them to pieces," added Lucien viciously as captains from both nations voiced their support.

"A fine plan," said Thaddeus raising a glass to the room. "What could possibly go wrong?"

"What indeed?" came a voice as Wendell ducked into the tent. "It seems you have everything worked out."

"Wendell!" called Garrett, standing up with open arms to greet their new arrival. "So good to see you. We were wondering when you would join us. Please take a seat."

"Most kind, Garrett," responded Wendell. "I would, only I've rather lost my appetite."

Garrett's smile fell slightly.

"Sit anyway," added Adaline, gesturing to an empty chair, "while we are all together."

Wendell paused for a moment, his lips pursed in a thoughtful expression, before strolling theatrically towards the centre of the tent. The tables were configured in the same horseshoe shape as during the banquet at the castle, and Wendell continued towards the top table, adopting the space in the middle as his stage.

"A very fine assembly," he said finally, gesturing around the room with no effort to conceal his disfigured right hand as he had on previous occasions. His confident swagger was unsettling, and he had a mischievous smile that made Cyrus shift nervously in his seat. "It is lovely to see you, young queen," he said, inclining his head towards Mathilde. "So many of our beloved friends from Cornesse, and of course my good friend, Broderick. No doubt itching to get at Simeon's troops already!"

"Just waiting for you to finish your damn performance!" joked Broderick to the amusement of his captains.

"Adaline," continued Wendell, gazing longingly at the dowager queen. "I see that the hardships of war have not made you any less beautiful." Cyrus stared at Wendell in puzzlement. Why was he acting as though it had been years, and not a few short weeks since he last saw everyone?

"Yes, thank you, Wendell," answered Adaline abruptly, her eyebrow quirked. "Now, please sit. You're really being rather strange."

"Strange, me?" exclaimed Wendell, placing a palm on his chest as though greatly offended. "Oh, I don't think so. Though there is certainly something strange about our gathering here this evening." He looked around the room conspiratorially.

"Wendell!" growled Garrett, glaring as he rose to his feet to face the Master of Coin.

"That's me," said Wendell, his smile broadening further. "Which leaves kindly old Thaddeus and you, Garrett, shield to the king and most trusted servant of Easthaven. But if you don't mind me asking, who is this man?"

Confused expressions appeared on faces around the room as Wendell aimed a stubby finger in Cyrus's direction. Cyrus's stomach dropped.

"What's wrong with you, Wendell? It's the king!" shouted Broderick. "I think you've been spending too much time out in the sun!" He chuckled at his own joke but continued to look at Wendell as though he had lost his mind.

"It certainly looks like the king, Broderick, I'll grant you," Wendell continued, "but things aren't always as they seem, are they, Garrett?"

Cyrus felt his heart racing as he watched Garrett fall back into his seat, eyes narrowed in anticipation of Wendell's next words, mouth slightly open.

"I hate to put you on the spot, Garrett, old friend, only I wonder if you care to explain this?" The bald man turned to a squire who opened the tent, allowing a figure in a dark brown hood to join them.

"What is the meaning of this?" shouted Broderick, standing as his captains drew swords in the direction of the hooded figure.

"I suggest that you lower your blades," said Wendell with an air of confidence.

"On whose authority?" yelled Broderick, morsels of food flying from his mouth as his face turned a deeper shade of red.

"Mine," said the mysterious man, drawing the hood from his face to plunge the assembly into a stunned silence.

Cyrus sat rigid, his heart beating furiously as his eyes widened at the ghostly figure. The hair was longer, his eyes somehow darker than before with a mess of scars and a patchy beard. He stood in the clothes of a common man, yet there was no mistaking King Augustus before them.

"My boy!" cried Adaline, rushing to embrace her son.

"Yes, your boy," said Wendell, with his most pompous tone. "I am as loyal to your family as ever, my queen, and I will help you to see this treachery removed!" He moved towards Cyrus menacingly.

"How dare you!" shouted Garrett, slamming his hands down on the table as all others sat shocked and confused by what was unfolding.

"I don't know what sorcery this is," continued Wendell, "but that boy is an imposter, a liar, and he is certainly not Augustus!"

The room went silent for a moment as Adaline pulled herself away from Augustus, her hands still resting on his shoulders as she smiled at the returning king. "Yes, we know, Wendell," she said finally with a smile. "Please calm yourself."

Cyrus felt his stomach sink even further and his brows lower as he found himself trapped between fear and confusion. Had Adaline known about him all along? While the king's appearance had seemed to surprise everyone, he sensed this was not the end of the evening's revelations, and a wave of mistrust struck him as his eyes twitched around the room.

"Perhaps we can discuss this privately, Wendell?" Adaline continued with an assertive tone. "It's a rather delicate matter and not something that I care to bore our Cornessian guests with."

"I'd be happier if we all stayed just as we are, thank you," said Mathilde curtly, and Cyrus noticed Lucien reaching for the handle of his sword. "At least until you help me to understand the meaning of all of this. Was I wrong to place my trust in your family?"

"You knew of this, my queen?" added Wendell with a look of bewilderment that gave Cyrus a brief flutter of pleasure before it was once again replaced with the anxiety that Augustus's arrival had brought. "What is this madness?"

"Enough!" shouted Thaddeus, silencing the commotion. "Adaline, my dear, I think it is time."

All eyes turned to the queen, who kissed Augustus's forehead gently before turning to address the room. He had no idea what to expect, but Cyrus held sympathy for Adaline in that moment. Though beautiful as ever, there was fear in the wide shape of her eyes and the deep sigh she let out, and she appeared frail under the questioning gaze of those around her.

"It was almost eighteen years ago," she began softly, her eyes falling on Cyrus. "We were expecting our first child. We had started to think that it would never happen, but we were blessed with a boy," Adaline turned back to Augustus, smiling as she wiped tears from her eyes before continuing. "Anselm was delighted. He finally had his heir, but I knew that something wasn't right. The pain wouldn't pass, and I prepared myself to give my life for yours in that birthing bed. But then a miracle happened." She turned back to Cyrus. "You happened."

Cyrus felt his breath stop and his hands shake as everything finally fell into place.

"I was so happy. You were more than I could have ever dreamed of, but the dream soon turned to a nightmare."

"The terms of independence state that any second-born prince of Easthaven is to be bestowed upon the king of Auldhaven," said Thaddeus, rising to aid the dowager queen. "In an official sense, the prince would be an emissary, a living expression of peace, but with a king like Simeon upon the throne, it would have been tantamount to imprisonment."

"You have to understand, Cyrus," said Adaline desperately, his name surprising but sweet in her voice, "they would only have used you against us!"

"You are the only second-born prince since the time of our independence," continued Thaddeus steadily. "Add the fact that you were unexpected, and we had to find a solution fast, before Simeon became aware of you."

"There was a couple in the Low Country," said Garrett, his head dropped, and his gaze fixed on the table where he sat. "Ned and Ida, but you'd know them as—"

"Mum and Dad," said Cyrus sadly, all of his realities crashing together.

"My brother and his wife," added Garrett, and Cyrus felt a strange pang for Garrett in the midst of it all because he had lost his brother and sister-in-law, just as Cyrus had lost his parents. Garrett continued, "They had always wanted a son, and we thought you would be safe."

"We visited you when you were little," said Adaline, her voice catching in her throat. "We never forgot you, but when Simeon burned Coldwynne, we thought…"

"You were all in on this?" asked Cyrus as he glared at Adaline, Thaddeus, and Garrett.

"A despicable plot to usurp the throne!" yelled Wendell.

"Oh, shut up, Wendell!" boomed Augustus. "This is as much a surprise to me as it is to you, but what I do know is that the man over there," he paused for a moment, "my brother, is no usurper!"

Cyrus looked at Augustus in surprise.

"I will need time to consider this," said Mathilde. "My people trust me with their wellbeing. I will not mislead them."

"Take your time," replied Augustus. "But know this. The alliance you made was with a man who fought at my side when I stood alone against desperate odds, a man who was willing to surrender his life for that of another. One whom the king of Easthaven will gladly follow into battle." The king let his words hang in the air for a moment before continuing. "Our position in this conflict remains unchanged. I trust that we can expect the same of our brothers and sisters from the north."

"Fine words," said Mathilde, nodding respectfully as her eyes shifted between the two identical boys. "We will leave you to…catch up, but expect our answer within the hour."

"Thank you, great queen," added Augustus as the Cornessians made their exit. "Cyrus, Mother, Garrett, Thaddeus, we need to talk."

Cyrus pushed open the entrance to his tent and saw the hooded man immediately.

"Hello, young man," came his voice as Garrett stepped forward, drawing his sword in the stranger's direction.

"Now, is that any way to treat a man who saved your life?" said the man, removing his hood to reveal a golden smile.

"Seth!" said Cyrus, voicing the name to be certain that his eyes were not deceived.

"The very same," answered Seth, "But what am I to call you these days?"

"Cyrus will do just fine. It's okay, Garrett, this man poses no threat." Garrett sheathed his sword slowly as Cyrus rushed across to clench Seth in a warm embrace. "But how?" asked Cyrus. "There were so many of Brogan's men."

"Aye, well, I told you what a fantastic swordsman your old father was, but you didn't hang around long enough to see the very best in action." He winked.

"My father," muttered Cyrus with a sullen tone, his eyes lowered to the ground, still trying to process everything he had learned that evening. "Do you bring any news from the Low Country?"

"I searched," answered Seth. "As soon as I realised you were gone, I looked everywhere, but Corhollow was in ruins, and there was no news of your father and brother. No doubt they fought bravely to save your village. A heroic way to go!"

"Yes, heroic," Cyrus uttered. "Except that it leaves me all alone."

"Well, not exactly," added Augustus, stepping into the middle of the tent. "We have our mother, of course we have each other, and it seems we have a sister now." He gestured to the mouth of the tent, and Cyrus nearly fell over with shock as Francine emerged through the entrance behind his brother.

"Oh, Cyrus!" she called, as Cyrus lifted her from the ground. "I thought I would never see you again!"

"I never stopped believing," answered Cyrus, drawing her close, his face in her hair. "But how?"

"Ah, well," began Seth once more, "you mentioned you had left your sister in Mistcliff, so I went back. The villagers abandoned their homes after the battle, but I found young Francine hiding in one of the damaged houses. Quite the little survivor!" He nudged her with an elbow.

"Uncle Seth has been looking after me ever since," added Fran, smiling up at Cyrus.

"We've been looking out for each other," Seth corrected her. "We heard that the town of Ironwell had secured food from our generous king, and that's where we met Gus."

"But I saw you fall from the cliff edge," said Cyrus shaking his head at his brother.

"I wish you hadn't," answered Gus, scratching at the side of his head where angry scars protruded through his hairline, "but I was lucky. I only fell ten or fifteen feet before a ledge broke my fall."

"How did you survive?" asked Adaline, stepping forward to take the king by his arm.

"Well, I couldn't have done it alone, that's for sure," said Augustus smiling. "The fall broke my jaw and did a fair bit of damage to the rest of me. Not that I'm any less handsome for it!"

They all laughed in unison, Adaline stifling her tears as Augustus continued, "I spent the next few days chipping away at the cliff face with a small knife to create footholds, and I was eventually able to climb out, but the village was deserted, or at least I thought it was."

He smiled at Francine, who poked her tongue out in response.

"It's a long story, but I've had a lot of time to think, and I'm not proud of the man I used to be. I thought our country was about royalty, nobility, and common people, but under it all, we're all just the same."

It was Adaline's turn to smile as Francine took the king by his spare hand.

"I walked for days, unable to talk because of my jaw," said Augustus. "Town after town ravaged by Simeon, our people left with only what they could salvage, yet I was never refused food and water. Generosity without compare."

"But how did you wind up with Wendell?" asked Garrett.

"Good question," came Augustus's answer. "I heard that Eriwald was under Simeon's influence and tried to make it to a town, but my injuries worsened, and I fell unconscious. The next I knew, I was in Ironwell, where a kind family had taken to caring for me. They reset my jaw, and I was just getting back to my best when Seth and Francine found me. Seth told me about his daring escape and informed me that the capital had sent Wendell to administer food. The rest, as they say, is history."

"Well, I for one am glad to have both of my boys back," said Adaline, gesturing Cyrus over to where she stood with Augustus and putting her arms around them.

"Me too," said Augustus, "but my arrival is timely. I was briefly captured during my travels before a group of locals set me free. My wounds were so bad that Simeon's men were unable to recognise me, but I overheard them discussing Simeon's strategy before I escaped."

"What did they say?" asked Cyrus urgently.

"There's a wooded area," answered Augustus, "to the west of the battlefield."

"Yarlford," added Thaddeus, nodding. "It was the largest forest in Easthaven until many of the trees were cleared to provide wood for the development of Eriwald."

"Yarlford, that's it," Augustus continued. "Simeon plans to conceal his elite cavalry in the forest and invite your attack before sending them behind our lines. He means to draw us in. It's an ambush."

"Garrett," said Cyrus forcefully, "fetch Broderick. He needs to hear this."

"They'll have us surrounded" said Cyrus, as he finished explaining Simeon's plan. "We cannot fall into their trap."

"Nothing but silly games," scoffed Broderick. "Let them come, their tricks will be no match for our swordsmanship."

"No, he's right," said Mathilde. "If we are going to win this, we have to stay one step ahead of them. We are no match for their numbers."

"Thank you, Queen Mathilde," said Augustus, flashing a smile of relief at Cyrus. "I think I have an idea."

"What is your plan?" asked Thaddeus.

"It's a long shot," answered Augustus, "but I believe there's only one thing greater than Simeon's cunning, and that's his ego. I think he created this plan so he could be there when we fall, so he can claim victory with his own hands. I believe he will be there in those woods, and if we can get to him first, we can cut off the head of the snake, so to speak!"

"I think Augustus is onto something," added Cyrus, turning to Thaddeus. "When we met Simeon, you described him as smart and ruthless, but I don't think that reputation alone is enough for someone like him. I think he met us that day partly out of curiosity, but mainly because he wanted to show what he is capable of. I doubt this plan will be any different."

"It's not going to be easy," Augustus continued, but we finally have the initiative. If I can take a small force to intercept Simeon, we might be able to end this before too much blood is shed."

"I'll come with you," said Cyrus with clenched fists. "I've a few things left to say to him yet."

"Nonsense!" cried Garrett. "There is no way I can allow either of you to enter that camp. You are Easthaven's future!"

"Allow?" asked Augustus, his eyebrows raised at Garrett. "I understand your concern and know I have been somewhat absent of late, but I am still your king, Garrett."

Garrett inclined his head, taking a step back in defeat. "Of course, my king."

"Perfect," answered Augustus, exchanging a smile with Cyrus. "Broderick, if the worst should happen, we'll need you to lead the main force alongside Mathilde's units. Seth will join your forces. From what I hear, he should be a rather useful addition."

"Of course," said Broderick, exchanging a silent nod with Seth, who stood beaming with pride, "but this is crazy, my king. Why not send me into Simeon's camp instead?"

"As unusual as it is for me to say this, I agree with Broderick," said Thaddeus.

"I understand your concerns, both of you," continued Augustus, "but this is our best chance at victory. If Broderick is caught, they'll kill him for sure. I might be able to negotiate my way out of there."

Cyrus's head was spinning as the room fell momentarily silent. Broderick's bloodlust seemed to fade with Augustus's words, and Thaddeus stepped forward to assume his position as the voice of caution.

"My king," he began softly, "you are as brave and steadfast as your father. No doubt you are destined to forge your own great path, your own great legacy. I know this seems like the right choice, but courage is so often the folly of youth. There is too much at stake here. I implore you to send soldiers in your stead."

"I can't," said Augustus without hesitation. "You've always said that no man is bigger than a country, Thaddeus, and you were right. I am a soldier, and it is my duty to win this war."

"This is madness!" yelled Garrett, tearing at his hair. "I will accompany you, my king but there is no sense in sending the prince as well, it's too dangerous."

"Dangerous?" called Cyrus, incensed at Garrett's lack of faith. "Did I not defeat Lucien in front of all of you?" He moved to look Garrett in the eyes. "I did everything you asked of me, and yet you speak on my behalf like I'm not even in the room?"

"But Cyrus—"

"No, Garrett, you can't protect me forever. I'm tired of people making decisions for me. Where I should live, who I should be, what path I should take!"

"Take some of my men at least," pleaded Broderick, his voice softer than usual in an uncharacteristic attempt to calm the mood of the room.

"It's a kind gesture," said Augustus, "but this will only work if we can move quickly and undetected." He paused for a moment, eyes narrowed at Cyrus. "Garrett is right, though. It is dangerous. I appreciate everything you have done, Cyrus, but I will not put you at risk. Garrett, you will join me in place of the prince."

"You can't do this!" shouted Cyrus as Garrett nodded in acceptance.

"It's already done," said Augustus, moving to place a hand on Cyrus's shoulder. "Rest, brother. Your time will come." He turned to Garrett with a purposeful expression. "Make ready to leave. This ends tonight."

CHAPTER

XVII

*T*oo dangerous? thought Cyrus, pacing about his tent. Perhaps they had forgotten the battle at Mistcliff in which he had saved both of their lives? He thought back to the skirmish on the cliff edge, Augustus swinging his sword wildly as Simeon's men came at them. His brother was the king, but he was no warrior. As for Garrett, the man had spent most of the past month using words for a weapon. He rode into Mistcliff as a killer, but maybe the instinct was knocked out of him when he fell from his horse in battle. He'd grown soft. Sure, he had plenty of great stories and advice, but did he still have it in him to get the job done. To end Simeon?

"Argh!" Cyrus snarled, swiping a wine glass off of a nearby table, delicate crystal cushioned by the tent's fabric framework to land undamaged only inches from his feet. His head ached. He was angry, insulted, frustrated, and everything in between, but most of all, he was scared. His entire life had been a lie, but the fates had seen him reunited with his brother and his family. He finally felt as though he belonged somewhere and that Fran would have the future that she deserved. He wasn't ready to lose his brother for a second time, and he certainly wasn't ready to reclaim the crown. Two men walking alone into Simeon's camp—it wasn't just dangerous; it was reckless, and he couldn't let them go alone.

Cyrus placed the wine glass back on the table and snatched his sword before exiting the tent. There were fewer torches burning than before, and darkness had descended upon the camp with pockets of conversation being held in hushed tones to create an air of nervous energy.

Keeping to the shadows, Cyrus crept quickly but quietly beyond the guards and out into the open grassland, where his pace increased until forest appeared before him, orange light dancing among the trees to cast fearsome shadows all around. He knew that one mistake would see him killed, and it suddenly occurred to him that he had no idea of Augustus's plans or whereabouts. He froze, adrenaline coursing through his body as he stood on the cusp of Simeon's camp. What had he been thinking? Same old Cyrus, rushing to the rescue with little more than heroic intentions to offer anyone. For all of Garrett's kind words, Cyrus was still the same boy that had stood and watched the slaughter of Fran's parents, paralyzed by fear. He knew then that it had all been a mistake and he should never have left his tent, but his regrets were cut short when a strong hand clamped over his mouth and pulled him down into the thicket.

"What are you doing here?" spat Garrett through gritted teeth, and though Cyrus's heart seemed set to burst from his chest, a wave of relief washed over him.

"I knew you'd come," whispered Augustus, smiling as he knelt beside them. "You share our father's bravery, and together we will see him avenged."

"You cannot stay," continued Garrett, a look of increasing desperation on his face. "Get out of here, and—"

"Is someone out there?" One of Simeon's guards appeared through the trees, and Garrett signalled for silence, pulling Cyrus deeper into the shadows. Moving ever closer, the man's boots crunched through the undergrowth. He was just one man, but as sounds of sleep rose from a few dozen tents beyond him, Cyrus was under no illusion as to the danger they were facing.

"Stay here," mouthed Garrett noiselessly, his teeth glinting in the moonlight. And with that, he pounced to cover the guard's mouth, restraining his target with the same efficiency he had applied to Cyrus only moments before. This time, however, his technique was deadly, and Cyrus felt foolish for ever doubting those instincts. This was the Garrett he had seen in Mistcliff, and it was ridiculous that Cyrus had ever thought to rescue such a practiced killer.

A few moments later, Garrett emerged from the darkness wearing the dark green, hooded tunic of the Auldhaven guard. "Stay where you are," he said, glaring at Cyrus before wandering confidently into the camp. "And keep quiet."

Cyrus nodded silently, but his body went cold as Garrett walked into the mouth of the beast. He could see the silhouette of Garrett's hand shaking as he raised a sword at his side, yet Cyrus held greater concern for those who might stand in his path.

"I'm glad you came," whispered Augustus. "Don't worry about Garrett. He knows what he's doing. Watch, he'll be back any moment."

"I know," Cyrus answered. "It's just—"

"Didn't I tell you two to keep it down?" Garrett reappeared before returning to their position in the trees. "It's a good job they aren't expecting us because I can hear you both as plain as day. If you must come, at least be quiet!"

Cyrus and Augustus followed Garrett into the camp, snaking their way between the tents until Garret knelt to halt their advance.

"Can you stop that?" he asked through gritted teeth.

"Breathing?" responded Cyrus in a whisper, suddenly aware how loud his breaths had become.

"Well, tone it down a little," said Garrett with a sneer. "If Simeon is here, he will be in that tent up ahead." Cyrus followed Garrett's view to where a large red tent stood away from the rest of the camp. "Two guards," Garrett continued, "so maybe you can make yourself useful."

"What can we do?" asked Augustus, chewing the inside of his cheek.

"You stay here, and stay alert," said Garrett, looking at Augustus. "Cyrus, since you wanted this so much, you come with me."

Cyrus nodded, crouching as he trailed Garrett behind a line of tents and back into the trees. He'd come this far and doubted that he had any choice.

"Okay," said Garrett with his voice lowered. "Keep yourself covered. I'll distract them, and when the moment is right, I'll need you to take care of one of them."

"Take care of...?" Cyrus asked, his breath catching in his chest.

"Don't tell me you came without a weapon?"

"No, of course not." He put his hand on the pommel of his sword.

"Well good, no better time than war to use it," said Garrett with a grim smile.

"But what if you get caught?" asked Cyrus. "They'll kill you."

"Well, I guess I'll die trying to save your life," answered Garrett with a smile. "I suppose there's no greater honour than that."

Cyrus watched as Garrett walked back through the trees and into the camp. He couldn't hear what was said, but when Garrett turned away from the guards, they seemed to be following him back towards the treeline.

"Over here," urged Garrett quietly when they had passed the last row of tents. "I definitely heard something."

"It had better be something," said one of the guards impatiently. "You know what Simeon is like. He'll kill us for leaving our post."

"No, he won't," answered Garrett, "but I will."

Cyrus leapt to restrain the guard nearest him as Garrett punched the other. "Quick!" he called to Garrett as his grip loosened around the man's neck, but the guard stopped struggling when Garrett plunged a knife into his torso, his body turning heavy as Cyrus let him fall to the ground like a rock.

It all happened in an instant, and as Cyrus looked down at the corpses, he found that his own hands were shaking with shock. They were just another two men; he knew nothing of them, and they would gain little from his sympathy, but they had died following the whim of their king. Once again, he had let his own prideful nature obscure the truth. War is not heroic or romantic but truly dangerous, and he knew now, better than ever before, that he was not a killer.

"Good," said Garrett, wiping blood from his hands. "You did good. Now, let's finish this."

Cyrus stood in a daze as Garrett dragged both bodies to conceal them in the trees, following mindlessly as Garrett summoned him back towards the camp, where a cacophony of snoring and wheezing reminded him that they were not alone.

"This is it," said Garrett, as they re-joined Augustus only steps from Simeon's tent "Remember, though, this is Simeon we're dealing with. Stay alert."

Cyrus nodded, falling in behind the other two as they made their advance on Simeon's position. Those few moments felt like hours as it dawned on Cyrus that this really was the end, one way or the other. After everything he had been through, all the sacrifice and loss, it would take just one more life to end it all. He thought back to the lifeless faces of the two guards, the final rasping breath of the man in black and everyone else who had died for a stretch of land. Was this *really* what he wanted? Would another wrong make everything right? It was too late to back out, but perhaps there was another way. He steadied himself and took a deep breath as Garrett pushed through the entrance.

"Gentlemen," came an immediate voice which Cyrus recognised as Simeon's. The inside of the tent was scattered with candles, and it was a moment before Cyrus's eyes adjusted to the light. "So lovely to see you," Simeon continued. "A little later than expected, but a pleasure nonetheless." Cyrus furrowed his brow at Simeon's words.

"Enough of your games, Simeon," snarled Garrett. "We're giving you one last chance to return home, or—"

"Or what?" asked Simeon as he reclined in an ornate golden chair with deep-red fabric from behind a dark wooden desk. "You sneak into my camp in the middle of the night and accuse *me* of playing games?"

"We have your life in our hands," said Garrett, drawing his sword. "The time for talk is over."

"Oh, I don't think so," Simeon replied. "There's still so much to discuss, wouldn't you say, Gus?"

Cyrus turned to find his brother shaking as he glared at Simeon.

"Stop," said Augustus firmly. "I did what you asked. I brought the prince. Queen Mathilde is back at our camp. I can take you to her."

"How could you?" called Garrett, but he was barely able to finish his question before Simeon lifted a crossbow from beneath the desk and put an arrow through his chest, his last indignation reverberating around the tent as he fell to the ground.

Cyrus was paralyzed by shock. He wanted to try to save his friend, but Simeon had the crossbow levelled at him, while Garrett was perfectly still, a pool of red developing around him.

"I think we had heard more than enough from him, don't you?" continued Simeon. "Now, where were we?"

"You have my brother," said Augustus. "I can give you Mathilde, but I need you to stand your army down, as we discussed."

"What are you saying?" exclaimed Cyrus. "You can't do this!" He felt sick with himself for trusting Augustus so quickly and sicker still as he glanced again at Garrett's body.

227

"Easthaven needs a king, Cyrus, and not just a pretender. It needs strength and direction," answered Augustus. "It's better for everyone this way."

"You see, boy, there's really no loyalty or honour these days," said Simeon, rising to his feet with the crossbow still trained on Cyrus.

"I've delivered him to you like I said I would," continued Augustus. "The Low Country is yours, and I will take you to Mathilde, but we need to go now."

"We?" said Simeon with a mocking tone. "I spared your life when we captured you before, but surely you aren't stupid enough to think I was going to let you walk away from me a second time?"

"But you said!" said Augustus with all the composure of a small child. Cyrus thought bitterly that Augustus seemed like no king at all.

"Yes, I know what I said, boy," answered Simeon, turning a sinister smile at Augustus, "but it's important for a king to be changeable, I think, flexible. One minute you're up, the next you're down. One minute you're alive, the next you're—"

Cyrus flinched as Simeon fired another arrow from his crossbow, and Augustus crumpled to the floor.

"Dead," Simeon finished, looking extremely pleased with himself. "Cyrus, isn't it?" he asked, reloading his crossbow methodically, looking down at the weapon and not at Cyrus. "You thought to trick me in Eriwald, and here you are again. I'm sure you've noticed a recurring theme this evening, so the next arrow shouldn't come as much of a surprise." His finger lingered over the trigger.

"Wait," said Cyrus, sweat pouring from his brow as he fought desperately to buy time. "What is it that you want? You killed Augustus. That makes me king—we can find a compromise!"

"I think you've answered your own question," said Simeon as the bowstring creaked. "Dead kings don't wear crowns. Even your brother could see that."

Cyrus closed his eyes as the crossbow trigger snapped and an arrow whistled through the air before landing with a sickening thud.

He'd heard that death was painless, but if that was the case, then why were his hands so sore? He made to reach for the arrow wound but realised that his fists were clenched tight and that his fingernails were cutting into the skin. He could feel blood upon his hands, but he was still breathing. The sounds of the room were distant but growing ever closer. He was still alive, but how? He tried again to reach for the wound, but there was no wound. No arrow. Simeon couldn't possibly have missed from that distance…he wouldn't have. But if he didn't miss, then…

"Now, Cyrus!" came Garrett's voice, and as Cyrus opened his eyes, he saw the older man sprawled at his feet with a second arrow protruding from his shoulder, the arrow that Simeon had intended for Cyrus.

Without hesitation, he sprinted across the tent as Simeon rushed to reload. "You bastard!" Cyrus yelled, jumping across the desk just in time to knock Simeon backwards and send a wayward shaft into the roof of the tent. Simeon was startled but still much the stronger of the two, and a desperate scuffle ended with Cyrus pinned to the floor.

"You die here tonight," taunted Simeon, retrieving a knife from his belt. "Our two countries will finally be united under one true king." Simeon put all his bodyweight behind the blade, and the knifepoint lowered towards Cyrus's chest. He could see the veins straining in Simeon's neck, sweat dripping from his forehead as strands of grey hair fell over his eyes.

"No!" Cyrus snarled desperately, mustering all his strength, and suddenly the downward pressure subsided. Cyrus's eyes refocused, and he noticed arms around Simeon's neck, pulling him away. It was all a blur, but Cyrus sprang to his feet, and though he couldn't believe his eyes, he rushed to where Augustus was wrestling with Simeon, an arrow-sized tear in his padded jacket, exposing the chainmail beneath.

"Kill him!" cried Augustus, his face contorted as he fought to restrain his enemy. Simeon's knife was on the floor in front of him, and in one slick movement, Cyrus swooped down before driving the blade into Simeon's thigh. Simeon howled in pain, but Augustus quickly covered his mouth, silencing the old king as he lowered him to the ground.

"Do I have your attention now?" asked Cyrus, pressing his boot against the stab wound on Simeon's leg. "Augustus is going to let you go, but make one stupid move, and I will do as he asked and kill you."

Simeon nodded, propping himself against a small bed frame in the corner of the tent.

"Good," continued Cyrus. "Now I am going to make this simple. I want you to take your armies and return to Auldhaven."

"How do you expect me to do that?" snapped Simeon. "What do I tell my generals? They hunger for war."

"I think it's important for a king to be changeable, don't you? Flexible," said Cyrus with a wry smile. "One minute you're up.... that's right, isn't it?"

"Yes, yes," answered Simeon, eyes narrowed in frustration as he considered his options. "But there is one condition."

"Name it."

"You will be coming with me."

Cyrus considered his words. "Fine," he said, "but I need to try to save Garrett first. Let me take him back to our camp, and I'll return as soon as he is safe."

"And why would I trust you?" asked Simeon, wincing as blood poured from the wound on his thigh.

"Because you'll die if you don't get someone to look at that leg soon," answered Cyrus. "Besides, I am trusting you to follow through on your side of the bargain. We are both men of honour, aren't we? Augustus," he continued turning to his brother, "If you want to make this right, find a horse and take Garrett back to camp. I'll catch up with you as soon as we are done here."

"Honour?" scoffed Simeon, as Augustus nodded before pulling Garrett over his shoulder. "Your entire life has been a lie."

"Maybe so," said Cyrus sadly, "but today is a new day, and I'm ready to be who I was always meant to be."

"Fine," came Simeon's response. "Get your boot from my leg and get out of here. I expect you to return before sunrise, or Easthaven will fall."

Cyrus agreed and turned to leave, but his exit was halted as Simeon began to speak unexpectedly.

"You're nothing like your brother," he continued, "but just like Anselm: a good man in his own way, but he also believed any

231

problem could be solved with clever words, and look where that got him." Simeon winced as he dragged himself to his feet. "Now would be a good time to run, boy. Guards!"

Cyrus burst through the tent as voices began to sound around the camp.

"Over here," called Augustus, and Cyrus noticed he was supporting Garrett on the first of two horses. A second stood impatiently, readied for their escape. The next he knew, he was on the horse, adjusting in the saddle as they left the camp behind. The beast would have been no match for Allegro, but they moved quickly enough through the forest as voices called out behind them and arrows flew past, thudding into the trees.

"We aren't going to make it," called Augustus, grimacing as the cool night air tore at his face. "We're too heavy for the horse. He's already starting to slow!"

"Keep going!" called Cyrus, with less concern for his brother than for Garrett, who was slouched lifelessly to one side of the horse with only Augustus's grip keeping him astride. Cyrus ducked as an arrow narrowly missed his head, and the horse broke out onto the vastness of the open plains. He could hear Simeon's riders approaching, but it was a straight race from this point, and he wasn't ready to give up on Garrett.

"Not far now. We can make it," he called, but his words trailed off as the silhouette of a line of warriors began to appear through the darkness in front of them.

"We're trapped!" cried Augustus, yanking his horse's reins to come to a stop and looking desperately back at Cyrus. "Simeon must have planned this all along."

Cyrus was speechless. He'd been outmanoeuvred again, and this time it was going to cost lives. A volley of arrows launched into the air, and Cyrus's heart stopped, but his expression quickly turned from fear to confusion as the shafts passed overhead and agonizing screams sounded from their pursuers.

"Over here, Cyrus!" called a female voice. "I told you we'd rain death upon them!"

A wave of relief washed over Cyrus as the faces of the warriors became visible: rows of Mathilde's archers, bowstrings now drawn with flaming arrows. Broderick's spearmen braced for attack. Seth, sword in hand, calling orders to those around him.

"Fire," called Mathilde, and Cyrus slowed to turn as the forest went up in flames.

"Garrett doesn't look so good," called Augustus, drawing him back into the moment.

"Get him beyond our line," said Cyrus forcefully. "I hope for your sake that we can save him." His mouth was a hard line, and he thought he saw Augustus flinch at his words.

Broderick's men rushed forward to meet Simeon's troops, parting to let the riders pass through their ranks before lowering Garrett to rest against a small ridge.

"What do we do with the arrows?" asked Augustus, looking fearful.

"Leave them, you fool," croaked Garrett, choking as blood trickled through his beard.

"We are going to save you," insisted Cyrus. "Just hang in there."

Garrett's lips trembled as he forced them into a smile, the sound of laughter bubbling in his throat as he reached to place a hand on Cyrus's arm. "I've taught you well, young king," he said gently, "but you'd better be ready to go on without me because I'm not making it out of this one."

"Don't speak like that," answered Cyrus. "You taught me never to give up."

"No, I didn't," said Garrett, raising his voice against the sounds of battle. "I taught you to embrace your fate and be the best that you can be. I don't care what happened here tonight. The two of you are going to need to work together." He paused for a moment, and the three of them watched as swords clashed and arrows were loosed in both directions. Lucien hacking away with his enormous longsword, while Seth and Broderick called infantry to push Simeon's troops back towards the burning treeline. "Never forget what is truly important," Garrett continued, "and together, you can finish all that your father started."

"I'm sorry, Garrett. I didn't know what to do," said Augustus, his face a picture of shock.

"I know," came Garrett's response as his breathing became slow and heavy, "but you have a lifetime to make things right. Now if you don't mind, I would like a moment with Cyrus."

Augustus nodded and walked a few yards away as the battle continued behind them. Even in poor light, Cyrus could tell how pale Garrett had become, his breath seeming to stop and start at irregular intervals as his body lay limp on the cold ground.

"I wasn't joking, you know…" said Garrett, straining to form his words. "I might have let Anselm down, but it has been an honour to give my life in serving you, my king." Cyrus felt tears welling in his eyes as he steadied Garrett's shaking hand with his own. "Look after your mother," Garrett continued, "and above all else, always believe in yourself."

A roar of victory echoed in the night sky, and Cyrus turned to see Mathilde, sword raised, while Simeon's forces lay decimated before her. Seth smiled as he embraced those around him, and Broderick crashed the handle of his sword against his plate armour in wild celebration.

"We did it, Garrett," said Cyrus. "We won."

And though he didn't receive a response, he knew that his friend had heard him. A restful expression had appeared on Garrett's face, his lips upturned in a characteristic grin. He finally seemed to have found some peace, and his hand wasn't shaking anymore.

The morning sun rose as they buried the dead. Cyrus's swollen hands throbbed with each new grave as he ignored Thaddeus's insistence to rest. He was beyond the point of exhaustion but compelled by a painful sense of responsibility, and besides, to sleep was to accept that Garrett was gone.

When the work was done, Cyrus returned to his tent and fell into a fitful sleep, tormented by the faces of those they had lost. Garrett. Men and women, fighting for a cause that he had commanded. Garrett. Good people who had died helping him escape from Simeon's warriors, from Augustus's betrayal. His own pride had delivered him to Simeon, and Garrett had died for it. He knew his brother's actions had been driven by desperation and a lack of options, but Cyrus wondered what solace this would provide to the families of the dead. Garrett had offered his life in service, but what had given Cyrus the right to accept?

It was mid-morning by now, and Cyrus stared aimlessly at the ceiling from his bed, sweat beading on his forehead as he picked at the sores on his hands. The bright sun shone orange through the tent, and he refused to move from the stifling heat, trapped in his own purgatory. A hum of activity sounded about the camp, but the cacophony of songs and laughter gave no hint of the events of the previous evening. Though the voices were mostly distant, Cyrus noted two growing ever closer until they dropped to a whisper and footsteps halted outside his tent.

"Cyrus," called a voice that he recognised as Adaline. "It's me, your...it's Adaline. I've got Fran with me. Can we come in?" Her voice was familiar and reassuring, and while he couldn't think of anyone he would rather see in that moment, his dry mouth could form no words.

"We just want to make sure you're okay," added Fran. "We're coming in." The tent opened, and though Cyrus continued to stare up at the ceiling, he heard a pair of despairing sighs that gave him a good indication of their expressions.

"Simeon's men have gone," ventured Adaline. "The General, Lambert, led them away at dawn. No sign of Simeon, but he has a way of surviving."

"You did it," said Fran when no response came. "You won."

"Did we?" spat Cyrus, sitting up in his bed to face the new arrivals. "Tell that to the warriors who are sleeping off last night's battle in the ground."

"Cyrus!" exclaimed Adaline. "Don't take things out on your sister. Besides, their sacrifice has saved us all. It was for the greater good."

"Seth told me how you snuck up on Simeon. Can you imagine what the storytellers will say about you and Augustus, the two kings of Easthaven?" said Fran.

"I'm no king," sneered Cyrus, shaking his head. "We were lucky. Well, some of us anyway…"

Adaline wandered over to perch on the bed, and Cyrus felt his anger fade to sadness as she took him by the hand. "Garrett thought that Simeon would be up to his old tricks," she said softly. "That's why he asked Mathilde and the others to come as back up."

"He never stopped saving my life, right up to the very end," Cyrus responded, his eyes pink and swollen as he wiped tears away with the back of his hand.

"He wouldn't have had it any other way," said Adaline, her face turned to a smile. "He served this family long enough. I think he has earned his peace."

"But what happens next?" asked Cyrus. "How do we go on? I can't do this without him."

"We go on like we always have," said Fran. "We've lost people before, haven't we? Do you think I don't know what happened in Corhollow or in Coldwynne all those years ago when you found me in the woods?"

Cyrus opened his mouth to speak but Fran interrupted before he had the chance.

"I loved the stories you told me because you took something bad, and you made it good. You gave me hope."

She paused, and Cyrus realised he had underestimated her all along. She wasn't a helpless girl, but a young woman, and one who he needed every bit as much as she needed him.

"I know it's tough," said Adaline. "The weight of responsibility is a heavy burden for any king, but you and your brother have saved many lives. There's still a lot of work to do, but now is the time to reflect and remember what you have achieved. This is the best way to honour those we have lost."

"My brother…" muttered Cyrus, jaw clenched as he replayed the previous evening in his mind.

"He is preparing for a return to the capital," came Adaline's response. "There will be celebrations, I'm sure."

"And Mathilde?" asked Cyrus.

"Ah yes, the young queen," answered Adaline, eyebrows raised. "It seems she has a very particular type in men. She was due to travel back to Nivelle today, at least until she met with your brother, that is." She smiled knowingly.

"We might get a royal wedding!" yelled Fran excitedly.

"It seems like it has all worked out for Augustus," said Cyrus in a bitter tone, unable to meet his mother's gaze as he forced his anger down.

"He is a changed man, Cyrus," said Adaline. "He will go on to be a great king, but he will need you at his side. I couldn't be happier to have my boys back together."

"It certainly is a blessing," said Cyrus solemnly, and he found he didn't have the heart to puncture her happiness with so sharp a needle as the truth.

The sound of horns echoed around the capital as Augustus rode triumphantly astride Allegro with Queen Mathilde and Lucien beside him. Sun shone in the clear blue sky as people from all over Easthaven came for the chance to glimpse their victorious king and the exotic young queen.

"Hail the great king, Augustus," called a voice as Cyrus followed his brother upon the back of a tall, brown mare, his appearance concealed by the hooded tunic that had become all too familiar.

"King Augustus, saviour of the Low Country!" came another voice, and Cyrus turned to Thaddeus, but the old man's look of disapproval served to halt his rising frustration.

He wanted justice for Garrett. He wanted people to know what had happened. He had shared the story with Thaddeus, but in the end, it felt like nothing more than an attempt to relieve his own guilt. Life goes on—that was Thaddeus's message—not for Garrett of course, but no man is bigger than a country, after all.

"I thought I'd never know happiness like this again," said Adaline, drawing level with Cyrus and his mentor. Her long golden hair was arranged in loose curls that bobbed gracefully with her horse's every step. "But the people love him, and to have my two boys in the castle...it's beyond a dream."

"It's an exciting new beginning," agreed Thaddeus, shielding his eyes from the sun. "Anselm's passing was a sad day for all of us, but between them, Cyrus and Gus have given the people hope again."

"They don't even know I exist," said Cyrus sullenly, tightening his grip around the reins of his horse.

"Not yet," came Adaline's immediate response, "but your brother is about to give his victory address. Have faith in him."

Cyrus reflected that Adaline had no idea what she was asking of him, but he nodded as he followed on in silence, his brother waving jubilantly as his adoring public showered him with flowers and compliments. It was as if no lives had been lost, but Cyrus knew he would never, could never, forget.

"Cyrus," called a girl's voice, and his sour expression broke into a smile as he turned to see Fran amongst the crowd, waving from Seth's shoulders.

Their procession continued towards the grand staircase of the basilica, where Wendell stood with the Master of Prayer, his pale face already turning pink under the hot sun. Broderick's men rode at either flank to quell the rising fervour, and several squires rushed to meet them as Augustus and Mathilde were helped from their horses to rapturous applause.

"It seems he can do no wrong!" said Thaddeus, as he and Cyrus dismounted to join Adaline at the bottom of the staircase.

"Yes, but things aren't always as they seem, are they?" answered Cyrus, his voice dropping away quickly as the crowd silenced in anticipation of Augustus's speech. A palpable air of expectancy could be felt around the city. Faces young and old looked proudly upon their king, and in that moment, Cyrus felt decidedly relieved to have the weight of responsibility removed from his shoulders.

"People of Easthaven!" boomed Augustus as though he was born to do so, and even Cyrus had to admit that his brother looked spectacular with his gleaming breastplate and silken red robe. "Not two months ago, I stood before you and promised victory. Victory against those who had so cruelly taken my father, your king, from this world!"

Cyrus surveyed the crowd as they swelled with Augustus's words. "He's good," he uttered to no one in particular, though Thaddeus nodded in agreement.

"As I stand before you today," Augustus continued, "I am proud to say that justice has been served, and Simeon's troops are retreating as we speak, all the way back to Auldhaven with tails between their legs!"

Another round of fevered applause broke out, and Cyrus was surprised to find himself stirred by Augustus's words. His stomach turned at the thought of any kind of celebration without those he had lost, but perhaps Fran was right: true power lies in the ability to make people feel good, even in the worst of situations.

"Our troops, your loved ones," began Augustus once more, "stood beside our brothers and sisters from Cornesse in the face of Simeon's forces when we needed them most." He paused to flash a sickly smile at Mathilde, who eyed him as a starving man might look at a hot meal. "Without their support, I would not have been able to infiltrate our enemy's encampment and rid the world of their murderous king."

"What did he just say?" asked Cyrus, but the crowd was so loud that his voice was lost. "He tried to sell us out," he said through his teeth, turning to Thaddeus so that Adaline was out of earshot. "He as good as killed Garrett, and we don't know that Simeon is even dead."

Thaddeus did not respond but looked disturbed.

"While you were sleeping safely in your beds," Augustus persisted, with a closed fist pressed to his chest, "your king entered Simeon's camp and secured victory with less than a handful of men. The greatest tactical manoeuvre of our age!"

Cyrus scowled as guards all around him struggled to keep the people under control. "This is madness," he said to Thaddeus. "We'd all be dead if it wasn't for Garrett."

"That may be so," Thaddeus finally answered, leaning towards him for discretion, "but remember that history is written by the winners."

"But Isidore, Zacharias, the great kings of Easthaven—they'd turn in their graves!" pleaded Cyrus, his expression turning sour when Thaddeus laughed in response.

"Ah yes, the great King Isidore, who harnessed the power of a setting sun to surprise his enemies," he said. "A king who was famously poor at reading maps. I heard that they simply arrived late and happened upon King Edmund's complacent armies at an extraordinarily opportune time."

"Nonsense," cried Cyrus as Augustus continued to thrill his audience with tall tales of his achievements, while Adaline looked proudly on. "What about Zacharias? He defeated the Verderans in their own waters, putting their ships to ruin on the Islands of Mirramar."

"His adversary, King Adalberto, was renowned for heavy drinking and inflated self-belief," answered Thaddeus once more. "Another case of poor navigation, only this time it left half of their fleet decimated on the rocks before Zacharias arrived to finish them off. Or so the story goes…"

"But—"

"Cyrus," interrupted Thaddeus, placing a hand on his shoulder, "life is so often a case of what people want to hear rather than what they need to hear. You know better than anyone that great stories are told by great storytellers. Are you going to tell me you've never twisted the truth?"

"Well, no, but—"

"Exactly," said Thaddeus. "And what about all the people whose names are forgotten? Families and friends, small acts of love and kindness that are lost but no less important?"

"Garrett," Cyrus said, breathing deep to control his emotion. "Aunt Aggie, Osbert, Edgar, Mum and Dad…"

"Do what you believe to be right," Thaddeus finished, turning to face Augustus once more, "because when you finally leave this world, it's how you measure your own achievements that is truly important."

Cyrus took a moment to consider Thaddeus's words before Adaline appeared in front of him, beaming with pride as she ushered him up the steps to where Augustus stood waiting.

"But if victory is defined by our continued freedom and independence," bellowed Augustus as Cyrus took his place at his brother's side, "then there is surely no greater symbol of liberty than my brother, Prince Cyrus, returned to us after many long years in the wilderness!"

A moment of confused silence fell upon the crowd as Augustus pulled Cyrus's hood away from his face. The sun beamed down upon him, and an immediate sweat formed on his brow as the dreaded look of expectation fell upon him.

"Prince Cyrus!" yelled Augustus, raising Cyrus's hand to a new wave of celebration. The battle was won, the people were happy, and Cyrus began to enjoy his moment, until a familiar face appeared in the crowd, and Cyrus felt his heart stop as Marcia stared back at him with narrowed eyes.

"A pleasure to see my brother back in his rightful home," Augustus continued, pulling Cyrus back into the moment. "Yet his visit will be fleeting." Cyrus turned to see a ludicrously exaggerated expression of sadness appear on the king's face. "Bound by a sense of responsibility, your prince will assume the role of magistrate in Eriwald and will lead the proud people of the Low Country home at first light."

"What is this?" hissed Cyrus, turning Augustus away from the pandemonium.

"It's like I said," came Augustus's immediate response, his voice lowered so only Cyrus could hear him, "Easthaven needs strength and direction. I've waited a lifetime for this crown, and I will not have you here to complicate things."

"I have no desire towards the throne," whispered Cyrus desperately.

"Be that as it may, you will return to the Low Country and take every single flea-infested lowborn that you invited into my castle with you." A broad smile appeared on Augustus's face as he turned and waved at his people.

Adaline's was the first face that Cyrus saw, and he forced a smile of his own as she applauded with elation, a look of pride upon her face. His eyes eventually wandered as the revelry continued, and as he looked to the empty space at Thaddeus's side, he regretted above all else that Simeon's third arrow had not reached its intended target.

The banquet hall of Eldred's Keep was a place for celebration once more, the soft pink glow of an early summer sunset complemented by tall, flickering candelabras to create an air of warmth and light. The surface of every table was covered with fragrant meats and breads, and Cornessian wine flowed freely to heighten the mood.

"To victory!" called Augustus, raising his glass without warning to their entertainment, the discordant twang of a broken lute string drawing laughter from those around him. "And to the beautiful Queen Mathilde, who will always be welcome in my castle, and indeed at my table."

A roar of approval broke out around the room, punctuated by the sound of glasses clinking together as representatives of Easthaven and Cornesse celebrated in unison. Cyrus noticed that Augustus had remained seated for his toast and had spotted his brother's hand close around Mathilde's beneath the table as he spoke.

"Thank you, great king," said Mathilde in response, turning a smile upon Augustus. "I have learned a great deal from the kindness and bravery of your people, but let us not forget that without your brother, we would not be celebrating together today."

Cyrus coughed, nearly choking on a mouthful of overcooked mutton as the entire room turned their attention towards him. The room was full of familiar faces, but Cyrus fixed on Fran, who sat beside Seth with more poise and confidence than he had managed since his arrival to the castle.

"You exceeded my expectations from the very moment we met, Prince Cyrus," Mathilde continued. "You earned the victory that you desired, a triumph that has seen you returned to your family after many long years, and yet you are so quick to leave the castle for your next adventure. You continue to surprise me!"

"I must say that I was surprised at the news myself," said Cyrus, and it was less of a surprise to find Augustus glaring at him from across the room. He took a moment to steady himself before continuing, "While I am flattered by my brother's most generous offer, I will see the people of Eriwald home before appointing a local representative to stand in my stead."

"But where will you go?" asked Thaddeus, standing to beat Broderick to the question.

"I go where I must," said Cyrus, forcing a smile as his eyes met with Fran. "To Auldhaven, and to Simeon's castle in Ravensward."

"No!" cried Adaline, but all eyes soon turned to the corner of the room, where a silver serving plate crashed to the floor and Marcia rushed to tidy the mess she had created.

"It is my fate," continued Cyrus above the rising hubbub, "and perhaps the only way that I can deliver the peace we all desire. I made Simeon a promise on my honour, and I intend to keep it."

If there was any relief in voicing his plans, it was short-lived. The space beside Seth was now empty, Adaline sobbed quietly as Thaddeus consoled her, and Broderick sat silent in shock, his generals following suit. It was a melting pot of emotion, and while Cyrus found himself lost for words, Augustus was not so afflicted.

"A very noble gesture," said the king, his smile gracious and wide as he attempted to reclaim the room. "You go with the king's blessing. I only hope that they treat you with the respect you deserve!" His words rang sincere, but the steely glint behind Augustus's eyes told Cyrus all he needed to know.

Sombre applause was lost to the din of returning musicians, and Cyrus met his brother's glare with a smile, tipping his glass to show an appreciation for Augustus's carefully selected words.

"I hope you know what you're doing," said Thaddeus, setting an empty wine glass down on the table.

"Time will tell," answered Cyrus, finishing his own glass with a deep gulp. "I just know that it feels right."

Cyrus stood with his hand hovering over the handle to a heavy oak door. He'd been standing there for several moments already, but his heart was still beating audibly in his chest, and he realised that of all the difficult conversations he'd had since arriving in the castle, this was the one he'd been dreading most. He didn't know if she would still be awake, but time was running out, and he had to make her understand. He hesitated as he knocked on the door, the resulting sound so quiet that he could hardly hear it himself.

"Can I come in?" he asked, cringing, but as he turned to walk away, her voice welcomed him, and he steadied himself before entering the room. "You're still awake then?" he ventured, stepping forward to close the door behind him.

"I am now," Fran answered, her face pressed into the bed covers to muffle her words. "Nice of you to come and see me. Your conscience must be bothering you?"

Cyrus had been expecting her scorn, and he knew that it wasn't about to get any better.

"Can I sit?" he asked, gesturing towards the bed.

He had known this room to be guest quarters, but Cyrus noted the delicate pink tones of the newly decorated canopy bed as well as a trunk full of expensive-looking dresses and gilded mirrors adorning the walls. Fran had always known how to get her own way, and Cyrus smiled at her willingness to make a home of the castle.

"I like what you've done with the place," he added, perching on the edge of the bed when no answer was forthcoming. "From Corhollow to the capital, eh?"

Fran sat up on the bed, wiping at pink, puffy eyes. "And yet you're ready to leave already!"

Cyrus was taken back by his sister's directness. He grimaced, squinting as he pinched the bridge of his nose in thought. "I don't think I have a choice," he said finally. "I wish there was another way."

"There is," Fran answered desperately, shaking him by the arm. "Just stay here with me, and Gus and Adaline. Why are you always looking for another adventure? You have everything you've ever wanted, and it still isn't enough for you."

"It's not that, it's—"

"What, Cyrus?" Fran interrupted. "We're alive, and we're safe. Please don't do this."

"I'm sorry, Francine," began Cyrus, "but I am done running. I know why Adaline and…." He paused for a moment, to correct himself. "I know why my mum and dad did what they did all those years ago, but I have to face my destiny. Too many lives have already been lost."

Fran slammed her hands down on the bed before standing to walk away. "What can you possibly do, Cyrus?" she called in frustration. "You're just one man, and none of this is your fault. What about the people who care for you? What about me?"

"Fran," said Cyrus sadly, his eyes fixed on the floor. "When I found you in the woods all those years ago, I promised I wouldn't stop until you were safe. You're here now, in the castle. You are protected, and you can have anything you want, but whether it's Simeon or whoever replaces him, they will come for me. This is the only solution. This is how I keep you safe."

"I'll come with you!" She looked wildly at her trunk as though considering packing it up that moment and calling for a carriage.

"No, Fran," answered Cyrus, reaching for his sister's hand. "This is just something I have to do alone. Besides, I need you to look after Adaline. I know she's excited to have another girl around the place. You're going to have plenty of time to wear all of those dresses."

Fran laughed, sniffing as she wiped her nose and eyes. "I don't even like any of those dresses," she said with a mischievous grin. "Is

249

it always like this here, people just giving you everything you ask for?"

"Takes some getting used to, doesn't it?" said Cyrus, lifting an elegant blue gown from the trunk. "Just remember who you are, Fran. In the end, none of these objects really mean anything."

"That's easy for you to say," Fran ventured. "You'll be spending the rest of your life in a dungeon somewhere in Auldhaven, and that's only if they don't kill you first."

It was a funny thing to laugh at, but Cyrus was relieved to feel the mood lifting, and the two of them shared an untroubled moment before Fran's expression turned serious once more. "Thaddeus has agreed to teach me how to use a sword," she continued, "and Uncle Seth said he will practice with me."

"That's great," said Cyrus. "It's good to have a hobby."

"It's not a hobby. I'm serious," Fran responded. "I want to be powerful like Mathilde." She cut through the air with an imaginary blade. "Mathilde said I could be her chosen shield one day, but only if something really terrible happens to Lucien!"

Cyrus laughed again, and the two of them sat back on the bed. He curled his arm around Fran, and she yawned with the same tired look that she'd had as a small girl.

"Get some rest, Fran, and try not to worry. We've survived this far, haven't we?" Cyrus kissed his sister on the forehead and began to rise from the bed when his hand brushed against his pocket.

"Wait," he exclaimed, falling back onto the bed. "I almost forgot; I have something for you." He reached into his pocket and withdrew a small object wrapped in deep-red velvet cloth. "I bought this for you while I was travelling," he said, unfolding the piece of fabric. "The merchant called it the Mirror of Amabel. He said it was magical and that if you use it in a time of need, the reflection will show you the way."

Fran cooed as she looked down at the mirror, and Cyrus's smile widened to see the elaborate silver frame shine as it had in the market of Casarossa.

"You'll have to excuse the crack," he said finally. "It's a long story."

"Tell me," Fran exclaimed, snatching the mirror as she climbed under the bedcovers.

"Well, if you insist," began Cyrus, beaming as he rose to stride flamboyantly around the room. "Our story begins on the most spectacular pirate galleon you have ever seen. Its name was the Dirty Dagger!"

First light rose over Eldred's Keep, and Cyrus yawned deeply as he sat upon the brown mare, who he had chosen to rename Adagio. His breath hung in the cool morning air like a haze, one hand on the reins while the other reached to shield his eyes from the bright orange glow. Adagio would be a change of pace after his time with Allegro, but she was nevertheless sturdy and dependable, and it occurred to Cyrus that there was little need for magnificence where he was going.

Pensive with his thoughts, the sound of five hundred voices echoed about the walls of the castle as the people of Easthaven waited eagerly to return home.

"You have enough food and water for your journey?" asked Adaline, approaching with Thaddeus at her side. "A change of clothes and anything else you need?"

"Yes, Mother," said Cyrus, smiling as he rolled his eyes. The word still felt foreign on his tongue, especially when applied to Adaline. "And you're sure you will be okay to look after Francine?"

"Of course," came his mother's response, stepping forward to smooth Adagio's hindquarters. "I'll treat her as though she were my own."

"Well, as though she were Augustus, ideally!" said Cyrus dryly, causing the three of them to laugh.

"So, my name is a punchline these days?" came Augustus's voice, and Cyrus noted that he was dressed in his finest tight-fitting breeches and waistcoat, the shirt beneath enhanced by shoulder pads, presumably to impress Mathilde, who stood at his side. "I'm glad you are all able to have a good laugh at my expense."

"It's not like that," said Adaline in a calming voice, taking Cyrus's hand. "We're just sad to see your brother leave so soon."

"You're still going through with this then?" asked Mathilde.

"I am," answered Cyrus. "No more tricks or games." He looked at Augustus, who narrowed his eyes at the hidden meaning behind Cyrus's words.

"Well, I think it is very brave and noble," Mathilde answered, turning to find a broad smile on Augustus's face, where a scowl had been only moments before, "traits that seem to run in the family."

Mathilde gestured for Cyrus to lean from his horse so she could whisper in his ear. "Obviously, I'm aware that your brother is as vain as he is stupid," she began, and it was all Cyrus could do to keep himself from smiling or possibly falling off of his horse in shock, "but a queen is meant to have pretty things, and I do tend to get what I want."

She pulled away, her voice returning to conversational volume. "Do let me know if you are ever north of the border. You will always be welcome at my castle, Prince Cyrus."

Cyrus nodded and suspected that his cheeks must have turned red with embarrassment, though his expression soon straightened under his brother's glare, which was directed at Mathilde this time.

"You will return to Cornesse then?" Gus asked, clearing his throat. "Back to the city of Nivelle?"

"Oh, I think I might remain here a while yet," said Mathilde, with a demure tone that had Augustus smiling once more, the rest of the group left silent, eyes twitching awkwardly until a girl's voice broke the tension.

"Cyrus!" called Fran, running across the courtyard with Seth in tow. "I thought I'd missed you."

"No, still here," Cyrus answered with mock impatience, "and at this rate, I'll have more grey hair than Simeon by the time I make it to Ravensward." He turned to where the people of Eriwald were already beginning to grumble anxiously behind him.

"Just be safe, all right?" she said as Cyrus leant down to embrace her. "And take this to remember me."

"Fran—"

"No, I want you to take it."

Cyrus reached and took a small bracelet of woven leather from his sister's outstretched hand, squeezing her hand briefly before looking at the bracelet more closely. "I'll treasure it."

"It's not made from flowers like the ones I made when we first met, but it should last longer," said Fran with a smile.

"Be safe, boy," added Seth, with a golden grin that took him back to their very first meeting. "Make your father proud." And though Cyrus didn't know which father Seth was referring to, it didn't seem to matter.

"To the gates," Cyrus called, marshalling the people of Eriwald to the portcullis, which stood invitingly open, but they made it only a couple of steps before another voice called his name.

"Wait!" she cried, and though Cyrus reared Adagio in frustration, the sight of Marcia gave him the biggest surprise of his morning so far. "You were going to leave without saying goodbye?" she asked breathlessly, arriving at his side to lower the hem of her gown after a sprint across the courtyard.

"No," said Cyrus awkwardly, scratching at his scalp. "I mean, yes, I thought…"

"I know," she said, eyes full of sadness as she took him by the hand, "and we were just getting to know each other."

"I tried to tell you," he ventured, and though Marcia opened her mouth, no words escaped her. "I'll write to you," he finished after a momentary pause.

"I'd like that," she said finally, and her hand fell away as Adagio began trotting towards the gates. People lined the streets to bid them farewell, but Cyrus never looked back as he passed through the city. His time in the castle had come to an end, but his adventure was only just beginning.

EPILOGUE

The carriage rattled as it swung through the bumpy backstreets of the capital. It had a simple yet elegant wooden frame with four large wheels, a "must-have" for the wealthy and noble of Highcastle. The driver sat at the front upon a raised platform, the light of a torch flickering beside him as he guided two horses through narrow passageways towards the city limits. It was late, and the capital was covered in darkness, but the sound of their progress seemed to draw attention like moths to a flame. Captivated expressions appeared at candlelit windows, while more unsightly residents emerged from shadowed alleyways and who knew where else. Toothless grins beamed at the body of the carriage as they wondered who, or what, might lie within.

Their destination was beyond the reaches of Highcastle, but passage was halted when two officious members of the city watch stepped out in front of the carriage, palms raised and swords at their side as they made to inspect the vehicle.

"Good evening, gentlemen," said the driver. "How can I be of assistance?"

"A little late to be travelling, isn't it?" asked one of the guards. "The war may be over, but these are still dangerous times. Perhaps you might prefer to travel by daylight?"

"I'm afraid we can't do that," answered the driver assertively, though his tone only served to fuel the guard's curiosity.

"Excuse me for asking," came the guard's response, the only other sound that of his colleague shuffling up the side of the carriage, "but do you mind telling me the purpose of your travel?"

"Let's call it official business."

"Official business?" asked the guard. "Perhaps I could press you for detail?"

His enquiries were interrupted when his partner called out through the darkness, "It's okay, Cedric, let them pass." There was more than a hint of fear in his voice, and Cedric drew his sword as he proceeded carefully around the carriage.

The horses whinnied, either through impatience or exhaustion, and the only other sound was a hushed muttering of conversation from where the other guard, Lawson, stood at the carriage window.

"We really are very sorry," he heard Lawson say in a most deferent tone, but this only made Cedric more cautious still, and he primed his blade as he closed in on their conversation.

"What's going on?" he asked forcefully, drawing level with the window, but his face dropped, and his sword hand fell limp at his side as torchlight identified the passenger within.

"Please excuse us, Wendell, sir," continued Lawson. "You know how things have been of late. Our only aim is to keep you and the other good people of Highcastle safe."

"Of course," answered Wendell with a forgiving smile. "Your vigilance is as valuable as your discretion." He reached into a small velvet pouch before flicking a gold coin out the window, which Cedric snatched from the air. "You never saw me, understood?"

"Never saw who?" asked Lawson with a smile of his own.

"Who indeed?" answered Wendell, pulling a dark hood to cover his pale, bald pate. "Now, I'll be leaving if it's all the same to you. I am a rather busy man, after all."

Cedric bowed graciously before patting the nearest horse's hindquarters to send them on their way. He remained on the path as the carriage rolled away from the city, little more than a speck in the distance by the time Wendell reached through the window to arch his neck and look back.

The river Aramere now ran at their side, and the horses broke into a canter over uneven ground, loose rocks causing the carriage to jump and jolt as Wendell held onto the window frame for comfort. The evening was unusually dark, with only a sliver of moon in the sky, and he squinted to follow their progress as hooves landed rhythmically, encouraged by the incoherent rambling of the driver.

Finally, his destination came into view: the developing thicket of Dalhart Forest with shadows dancing amongst the trees as the carriage drew ever closer.

"Leave me at the entrance," Wendell called to the driver, wincing as the cold night air slapped him in the face. "I'll complete my journey on foot."

The horses began to slow before arriving at a complete stop. The sound of the driver's boots echoed as he jumped from his perch, shuffling to open the carriage door.

"Most kind," said Wendell, placing a coin in the driver's hand. "I shouldn't be too long. Just stay out of trouble and be ready to leave when I return."

He took the torch from the front of the carriage and followed the dirt path into the wood, where trees seemed to close in around him. Owls hooted from branches above, and other unseen creatures scuttered through the undergrowth as he pressed on into the darkness.

"You're late," came a man's voice, causing wings to flutter in the canopy, startling Wendell such that he nearly dropped his flame. It was only a matter of steps before he broke through the brush and found two hooded figures in a torchlit clearing with water trickling among the rocks behind them.

"How nice of you to join us," came another voice, and the veiled man rose from a moss-covered boulder to remove his hood and reveal long, dark hair, his jaw lined with neat stubble.

"What do you expect, Rafael?" said the first speaker, revealing a near identical appearance. "These people have no manners, no sense of occasion."

"Prince Rafael, Prince Alonso, I didn't expect to see you in person," Wendell exclaimed. "As you can imagine, things are rather…complicated in the castle at the moment."

"So we hear," said Rafael, pursing his lips thoughtfully. "We asked you to kill one king, and it seems that we now have two?"

"Events have been somewhat unforeseen of late, I'll admit," Wendell continued, "but Augustus is little more than a foolish boy, and his brother has already left the castle to spend a lifetime in Simeon's dungeons."

"You are testing my patience," scowled Rafael, his hand looming ominously over the handle of his cutlass. "Was I wrong to place my trust in you?"

"No, no!" cried Wendell, before lowering his voice. "I had Anselm killed, didn't I?"

"You did," said Alonso, and he turned from Wendell, reaching to touch a smooth rock face that was glinting in the moonlight. "But the idea was to reduce Easthaven's armies in battle with Simeon. As it is, Augustus lives, and with a new ally in the bitch queen of Cornesse." He turned back with eyebrows raised. "All of this and barely a drop of blood spilled!"

"We have waited long enough," Rafael added. "Ten thousand of our people have already sailed for these shores, and we will fight with weapons the likes of which this world has never known."

"But—" cried Wendell desperately.

"Your task remains the same," Rafael continued. "You will be our eyes and ears inside the castle when the time comes. I make no promise of your safety, so do take care."

"Understood, my liege," said Wendell, bowing as he backed away. "And what of the dowager Queen Adaline?"

"Our warriors will be under order to take her alive," came Rafael's response. "Once the city is secured, she will be yours to do with what you please."

"My most gracious thanks," said Wendell as he bowed again before turning to leave.

"Oh, Wendell?" called Alonso, halting the bald man's exit. "If you are going to sell your country out, you might as well collect payment." The young prince dangled a coin pouch in the air before throwing it to land at Wendell's feet, where coins burst onto the ground.

"Stay safe, Wendell," he said finally, and by the time Wendell rose to his feet once more, both of the princes were gone.

Acknowledgements

This book is the achievement of a lifelong dream, and though the writing process is a somewhat solitary journey, *The Look of a King* would not exist without the following people:

Linda and Greg Dumbrell – for always encouraging me to read and pushing me to pursue my ambitions.

Steve Cooling-Smith at Chilligraphics – for bringing my creation to life visually and ensuring that there is at least one thing to like about the book. You can find Steve at www.chilligraphics.com.

Breana Dumbrell at Bee, Your Editor – for helping me turn an idea into a story and then turn a story into a legible book. Breana is the most talented writer and editor I know, and she has reignited a passion for reading and writing that had long laid dormant in me. You can find Breana at www.beeyoureditor.wordpress.com.

Finally, thank you to everyone who read early versions of the book and shared their feedback. There are too many to mention here, but particular thanks go to Fran Hayden, Jess Foye, Marietta Maidman, and Tina Dumbrell.

About the Author

Tom was born in 1987 in Chelmsford, Essex. As a boy, he fell in love with the fantasy worlds of video games and those written by the likes of J.R.R Tolkien and Philip Pullman.

Despite an early passion for storytelling, Tom obtained a BA in Tourism Management before a varied career in the travel industry, bringing to life another of his passions. When he is not working, Tom is an avid fan of his beloved Ipswich Town. He also writes and performs music and enjoys long walks with his wife and dogs.

Tom currently lives in Colchester, Essex, and *The Look of a King* is his first novel, written during the 2020 pandemic with huge influence and editing support from his wife, Breana.

Contact Tom: tomdumbrell@aol.com

Suggested Reading

Joe Abercrombie – *Shattered Sea* & *First Law* Trilogies
Chris Wooding – *Tales of the Ketty Jay*
Scott Lynch – *The Gentleman Bastard Sequence*
V.E. Schwab – *The Invisible Life of Addie LaRue*